Lethal in Old Lace

Also available by Duffy Brown

Consignment Shop Mysteries

Demise in Denim

Pearl and Poison

Killer in Crinolines

Iced Chiffon

Cycle Path Mysteries

Braking for Bodies

Geared for the Grave

Lethal in Old Lace

A CONSIGNMENT SHOP MYSTERY

Duffy Brown

NEW YORK

Published in the United States by Crooked Lane Books, an imprint of The Quick Brown Fox & Company LLC.

Crooked Lane Books and its logo are trademarks of The Quick Brown Fox & Company LLC.

Library of Congress Catalog-in-Publication data available upon request.

ISBN (hardcover): 978-1-68331-535-3
ISBN (ePub): 978-1-68331-536-0
ISBN (ePDF): 978-1-68331-537-7

Cover design by Matthew Kalamidas
Book design by Jennifer Canzone.

Printed in the United States.

www.crookedlanebooks.com

Crooked Lane Books
34 West 27th St., 10th Floor
New York, NY 10001

First Edition: March 2018

10 9 8 7 6 5 4 3 2 1

For Spooky and Dr. Watson…my two feline writing companions who make my house a home.

Chapter One

"You want to marry *me*?" I asked Walker Boone, who just happened to be the hunkiest guy in all Savannah. "Why in the world would you want to do such a thing?"

Walker Boone wanted to marry me, Reagan Summerside, owner of the Prissy Fox Consignment Shop, Bruce Willis (the black-and-white canine version who'd rescued me more than I'd rescued him), and a dilapidated Victorian that I loved, peeling paint and all. How had I gotten lucky enough to have this delicious man want to marry me?

Good question. I'm not exactly a lucky kind of girl. I'm more of a my-hair-turned-orange-because-I-dyed-it-myself kind of girl, or a will-you-go-to-the-prom-with-me-because-there's-no-one-else-to-ask kind of girl. Why wasn't I seizing my moment in the sun? Why didn't I tackle Boone to the ground and have my way with him, all the while yelling, "Yes, yes, yes, I'll marry you!"? What was my problem?

Reality!

"I have bad man karma," I blurted, determined to spill my guts and tell all. "I signed a prenup with Hollis

1

Beaumont the Third, for crying out loud, was left high and dry in our divorce with a run-down house, and then had to save Hollis's whoreson cheating hide from the gallows to keep my run-down house. It wasn't pretty, Boone. There was a dead body in a trunk wearing my favorite pink chiffon dress, I accidently shot up a really nice wood-paneled office, and Hollis still drives me nuts to this very day. Does any of this sound familiar?"

Boone's dark eyes danced, a hint of fire lurking in them and a devil smile at his lips. That he'd been on the run from the cops for the last two weeks for a murder he hadn't committed and looked more bum than attorney didn't detract from his hunkiness one little bit. "I represented Hollis in your divorce, and that office with the bullet hole is mine. Trust me, I remember."

"See, doesn't that worry you that I'd get mixed up with such a guy in the first place?" I paced the brick walkway, which was dappled in golden lamplight slicing through old oak trees and wisps of Spanish moss. "And I sort of had this *thing* for you even though you were my soon-to-be-ex-husband's lawyer and totally cleaning my clock in the divorce. How dumb is that?"

I spun around, arms spread wide. "And what about me stumbling across all these dead bodies lately? I don't go around looking for them; they just sort of show up on their own. *Poof,* and there's trouble right in front of me. I think I've acquired some kind of dead body syndrome. Why would anyone want to marry me with all this going on? Heck, I scare myself half the time."

Boone slid his arms around my waist, bringing me close and warm as the cool evening breeze ruffled his too long black hair. "You had a thing for me? Does that mean you still do?"

My arms slipped around his waist. "There is that."

His smile got bigger. "I'll take that as a yes?"

"You're a strong, professional, know-how-to-get-the-job-done kind of guy. I'm more a let's-try-this-and-see-what-happens kind of girl. I love junk food, and you hate it."

"I'll trade you two carrots for a Snickers."

I closed my eyes and thanked the gods of love and good fortune for this amazing man. "Yes, Walker Boone, I'll marry you."

He kissed me right there under a full moon in that lovely old Southern park, taking my breath away, curling my toes, turning my brain to oatmeal, and melting every bone in my body.

"Lord have mercy and time's a wastin'," came a voice I knew all too well. My dearest Auntie KiKi was here, now! I'd recognize my one and only auntie a mile away; problem was, she wasn't a mile away. She was close and getting closer. My eyes snapped open to see KiKi's best funeral hat flapping and her black dress flowing behind her as if it couldn't keep up.

"You two need to finish up your smooching later. There's work to be done right quick."

"But . . . but we found the real killer, and Boone's free as a bird and not on the lam, and we're getting married," I gushed to KiKi, the best auntie in all the world except at this moment. "Can you give us a minute here?"

Auntie KiKi and Uncle Putter lived next door to me in a perfectly restored Victorian done up in blues and greens. He was a cardio doc extraordinaire who carried a putter at all times in case a golf ball dropped to earth and he had to sink a birdie to save mankind. KiKi taught the belles of Savannah how to waltz so they wouldn't embarrass their mammas and daddies at the cotillion. Lately—due in large part to my recent dead body syndrome—Auntie KiKi had solved murders with me and BW (Bruce Willis) on my front porch over a silver shaker of chilled martinis and frosted glasses. The complexity of the case determined whether it was a two-olive situation or, in desperate times, a three-olive one.

Auntie KiKi wagged her head, sending her auburn curls into a tizzy. "Honey, I got the free-as-a-bird news from the kudzu vine gossips five minutes ago. That's how I knew where to find you. Every one of us in this fine city knew you and Walker would be getting together sooner or later. You two just took your old sweet old time is all." KiKi stood on her tiptoes and kissed Boone on his scruffy cheek. "Hope you know what you're getting yourself into, honey. Mark my words, life as you know it will never be the same." KiKi made the sign of the cross and added, "The man has a right to know, and now that this engagement thing is taken care of, we got other things to be fretting over, important things that just can't wait."

Knowing there'd be no peace till I gave in, I gritted my teeth. "Okay, okay, as long as it doesn't involve another dead body. I really can't take another body right now. Is it a nice bank robbery for a change? I wouldn't mind poking around a bank or maybe a jewelry store heist. It's been a tough two weeks getting Walker off the hook, and I'm all dead-bodied out."

"Well, that's just too bad because, in a manner of speaking, a body it is." Auntie KiKi straightened her hat. "Elsie and Annie Fritz are needing our support over at the House of Eternal Slumber, and I promised to drag your sorry self along with me."

"You're taking me to a funeral?"

"Willie Fishbine's wake, but the sisters' weeping and wailing doesn't seem to be packing 'em in like usual, and that's bad for business. Their big old house is in desperate need of a new roof and we all know what those cost these days. I got an SOS tweet—that's code for 'save old sisters'—saying they're worried something fierce about attendance and getting future bookings. They need folks to show up right this minute, and that means us."

Elsie and Annie Fritz were retired schoolteachers who lived on the other side of my house. They'd inherited the place when their dear uncle OD'd on Southern deliciousness and joined that great fried-chicken-and-buttered-biscuits buffet in the sky. The sisters were now professional mourners to supplement their income, and no one could get a crowd blubbering better—the mark of a truly successful wake.

"But . . . but I'm supposed to go dancing," I whined to KiKi. "Run through fields of yellow daisies, drink champagne."

KiKi's brows narrowed. "And who fills in for you over

5

there at your shop at a moment's notice when you have a dead body to tend to, tell me that, huh? Elsie and Annie Fritz, that's who, so shake a leg, girl. I parked down the street, but we can walk on over to the Slumber from here."

Auntie KiKi gave Boone a critical once-over. "Since you look like something that should be right in the casket with Willie, you're excused from participating on this particular occasion. But as you'll soon be part of the family, these things will be commanding your attention now and then, and you are now officially put on alert."

Boone laughed, then kissed me. The heart-stopping thing happened all over again. He gave KiKi a hug. "The family, huh. I like the sound of that." Then Boone headed across East Congress toward his oh-so-lovely house on Madison Square, and I hooked Old Yeller, my yellow pleather purse that had seen me through thick and thin, onto my shoulder. KiKi and I headed for the Slumber.

Streetlights cast fat gray shadows across the sidewalk, and the aroma of blooming azaleas hung heavy in the evening air. Auntie KiKi gave me a sideways glance, frowned, then dug a starched hankie out of her purse and shoved it into my palm. "You need to be getting that sappy smile off your face and bring on the tears. In case you forgot, Willie's toes-up and eyes-closed and lying flat in a box. That means we're in dire need of some red eyes and snotty noses."

"But I'm happy, really happy." Fact is, I wondered if a person could actually die from so much happiness. "I'm getting married," I sang in a too-loud voice, making passersby smile and stare. "Me, Reagan Divorced-and-Left-for-Broke Summerside, is getting hitched to the best guy ever. And besides," I added in a lower voice. "Willie was older than dirt and mean as a skunk and that last part's why no one's at his wake. He chased me out of his yard with a hoe when I tried to sell him Girl Scout cookies. How am I supposed to work up a cry for that?"

"Think of Hollis, that donkey's butt you married the first time around. I tell you, that man's enough to make any woman weep a river."

We took a right on Broad, the Slumber up ahead softly bathed in lighting to die by. The place had a white frame and black shutters and an original widow's walk at the top. A maze of add-ons jutted out here and there, the place having been passed from family to family over the last hundred-plus years before finally becoming the home of funerals, flowers, and embalming solution.

"See what I mean," KiKi said in a quiet voice as we joined a few others on the walkway lined with tulips, daffodils, and fresh mulch. "It's a mighty sparse crowd showing up and, sweet mother, you're still smiling." She elbowed my side, bringing tears to my eyes.

"Ouch!"

"Quit complaining. It's for a good cause."

We signed the I-was-here book, then padded across the thick maroon carpet in the entrance hall. We maneuvered around cherry end tables polished to a high shine, gold brocade couches, and a series of ferns and palms. These were the just-in-case plants the Slumber kept around to fill in if there happened to be too few sprays of flowers sent from grieving mourners. All things considered, it looked as if old Willie was gone from Savannah and would very soon be forgotten.

We aimed for the nice bronze casket with the not-so-grieving Arnett Fishbine on one side and the Abbott sisters trying to make up for that too-obvious fact by standing on the other side bawling their eyes out. I hankied my nose because it was the right thing to do as KiKi said to Arnett, "We're very sorry for your loss, honey. And your daddy looks right . . . peaceful."

Actually, Willie's scruffy goatee was trimmed for once, but his skin tone resembled a pomegranate and there was a little black chicken pinned to his lapel. What was that all about? Usually the Slumber did better work, but with the place under new management, who knew what was going on. "If there's anything I can do," I added to Arnett to be polite, "please let me—"

"You bet there's something you can do," Arnett said as if we were standing on the corner talking about the weather. "You need to stop by Sleepy Pines Retirement Home, pick up Daddy's things, and sell them at your consignment shop."

"We're talking business? Now?" I stuttered.

"Send me a check when you get everything sold." Arnett waved her hand at Willie. "It'll help with the cost of all this."

Arnett waved her hand dismissing me then turned to Auntie KiKi. I stumbled off to take a final view of Willie.

"I don't know what you did to piss off your daughter," I whispered, "But it must have been a doozy."

I had started to leave when a teenage boy shuffled up beside me. He sniffed, wiped away real tears, then slid a Snickers into Willie's breast pocket and hurried off. Love of Snickers—apparently the one and only thing Willie Fishbine and I had in common.

"Don't even think about it," I whispered to Auntie KiKi when she drew up next to me, both of us staring into the casket—or, more precisely, staring at the candy bar.

"These are dreadful times in my life," KiKi said with a hitch in her voice. "Your Uncle Putter has our house on sugar lockdown. He read me a three-page article on Satan Sugar and made me promise to buy healthy. I tell you, if it was up to the medical profession, we'd eat nothing but fruits and vegetables and die of complete and total boredom."

"That's no excuse."

"It's kind of an excuse." KiKi opened her purse to display two Clif bars. "Will you take a look at these things? They taste like sawdust with raisins." KiKi snapped her purse closed, her gaze drifting back to the Snickers. She licked her lips, her pupils dilating. "Putter didn't say boo about stealing unhealthy."

I felt my own pupils dilate. "You cannot rob a dead man," I hissed through gritted teeth. "People will notice."

"For crying in a bucket, Reagan, it's candy, not the Hope Diamond." She let out a sigh. "All right, all right, no swapping."

"Promise?"

"What am I, ten?"

"Right now, eight would be a stretch." I gave KiKi one last "Mind your manners" glare; then she headed off for Lila Witherspoon. I aimed for the tea table and the latest in Savannah gossip. Tonight Walker and I would be the topic of choice, and that was fantastic. For once I was connected with something really good instead of "What dead body did that Reagan Summerside person trip over this time?" The problem was the puny crowd. The kudzu vine regulars were MIA, and I had the teapots, windmill cookies, piped-in organ music, and bragging rights of getting engaged all to myself.

I poured out a splash of Earl Grey and glanced back at Auntie KiKi and Lila, who were no doubt speculating about Willie's will, the best part of any funeral, and . . . and, holy cow, what was that on KiKi's lips? It was chocolate! And was that a Clif bar in Willie's pocket? My one and only auntie was heading straight to hell in a handbasket.

Annie Fritz gave me a little nod, the super-sprayed gray curls framing her face not daring to move as she scurried my way. "Mercy me, what a night. I don't know how much more of this Sister and I can take."

"I'm so sorry about the Clif thing."

"Cliff? His name's Willie, honey, and I'm not sorry one little bit he went and kicked the oxygen habit. He's nothing but the south end of a northbound mule, no doubt about it. Sister and I might be crying up a storm on the outside, but inside our little old hearts are singing 'Highway to Hell,' 'cause that's where Willie's headed for swindling us like he did."

Annie Fritz cut her eyes side to side, then hiked up her long black dress, revealing pink flats with rhinestone bows. "We wore our party shoes for the occasion." Her mouth dropped into a sad frown. "This is all my fault. I should have known better than to get mixed up with Willie Fishbine and his get-rich-quick scheme, but that's what happens under the influence of bourbon balls and limoncello."

"Did you go to the police?"

"The scam is getting gullible people like me and Sister to invest in a company that sells junk, and Willie made his money before the vitamins he peddled got proved to be junk. Then he just walked away and we had worthless stock certificates. Spring Chicken Miracle Capsules are perfectly legal, since who can say what constitutes a miracle? They just happened to be dried dandelion leaves, wheat, dried carrots, and aspirin, and that 'spring in your step' it claims to give you is from the terrible gas. Pricilla Day said it grew hair on her toes, but if you ask me, that woman's always had hair on her toes and everywhere else if she bothered to look around. Can we say tweezers?" Annie Fritz snagged my teacup and, using her big floppy funeral hat like a shield, plucked a tiny silver flask nestled in her ample cleavage and filled the cup to the brim. She tossed back the tea in one big gulp, the aroma of fine bourbon drifting my way.

"But you can recoup, right? Your mourning business is doing well ever since you partnered up with Sleepy Pines in offering the Premium Woeful Weeping Package to residents." I waved my hand at Willie. "Nice casket, nice flowers, lots of howling and sniveling—makes for one terrific funeral. What a deal."

"Except for the fact that lately folks at the Pines are now dropping like flies, and it's looking like Sister and I have a pox upon us. I'm right nervous the Pines is going to dissolve our agreement. No one's going to a place that's a short stopover on the way to Bonaventure Cemetery."

"It's just a glitch," I soothed. "I bet there won't be another termination at the Pines for months and months. No one else is looking poorly . . . right?"

"And if they are here's praying no one finds 'em," Annie Fritz mumbled, then hurried on. "I need to be getting back and help Sister before she's all warbled out. Good thing I baked a nice red velvet cake with double-chocolate icing to revive us when we get home. Nothing revives like cake, especially if there's a hot toddy to go along with it."

Annie Fritz replaced the flask, trotted off, then stopped dead and turned back. "You're not aiming to move, are you?"

"Not as long as the windmill cookies hold out."

"With your getting engaged to Walker, it only makes sense that you'd live in his fine place over there on Madison Square. I suppose you could always find a storefront for the Prissy Fox and sell Cherry House, but I'd hate it if you did such a thing."

Annie Fritz swiped her eyes, and this time there were tears for real. "Sister and I would be sorely depressed to lose you and Bruce Willis as neighbors. He is a mighty fine pup, even if he does go burying his bones in my garden and do his business right there in the lilacs. I don't know what your auntie and Sister and I would do without you two around to liven up the place."

"Me? Move?" I finally managed to croak out around the big lump sitting in my throat.

"There's another person in your life now. Fine man that Walker is, he's got his own take on things, and now you got to consider what kind of ham the man wants to be serving up with the red-eye gravy on Christmas and what toothpaste you two are going to use. When my niece over there in Garden City got married, her husband liked that bubblegum-flavored stuff, and she had to put up with it for twenty years thinking she'd hurt his little ole feelings by switching."

Annie Fritz gave me a hug, then joined Elsie in a renewed belt of crying, and I felt like joining right in. Not because of Willie or using bubblegum toothpaste, but the thought of leaving Cherry House, named after the old gnarled cherry tree in the front yard, was a knife to the heart. I loved that tree. I loved my house. Okay, the windows should be updated and the front door didn't close tight and the chimney was ready to slide right off the roof, but I'd done a lot of the repairs myself. With the help of YouTube, I'd put in a new bathroom and fixed holes in the walls and reinforced the joists. Before Cherry House, I'd thought a joist was another name for smoking weed. Cherry House was the only good thing to come out of my seven-year marriage to Hollis-the-Horrible, who had wanted to sell the place when we got divorced. I'd opened the Prissy Fox Consignment Shop on the first floor to keep my adorable money pit standing, and things had been going okay until lately. But sell? Move?

"Cripes almighty, my feet are killing me," Auntie KiKi grumped as she hobbled up to the table and poured tea. "My toes are squashed up in these new shoes like pickles jammed in a jar. That's what I get for buying cute instead of going for sensible. I asked Elsie to give us a ride back to my Beemer, but she said her Caddy's in the shop and they took a cab and . . . and, honey, you're the saddest-looking person in the whole place. When I told you to look down in the mouth, I didn't mean it had to last all night."

"I have to talk to Boone right now."

"That's better." KiKi gave me a sly wink. "I'm assuming that's code for something a lot more fun than talking?"

But it wasn't code for anything. I was freaking out. With one failed marriage under my belt, the freaking came pretty easily.

"Give Mamma a call to come get you," I said to KiKi. "She's filling in at night court for a judge friend, but she's probably finished by now. You can talk about the wedding."

"Honey, this is your wedding, your day. You can have it any way you want, and we'll be thrilled just to be in attendance."

"Really?"

"Of course."

"I mean it's not exactly the Summerside way to just sit on the sidelines. I want something simple. Just family will be prefect." I kissed KiKi's cheek and headed for the side door of the Slumber. The sisters' faux sobbing drifted out the open windows as I circled around to the back. The alley wasn't the most scenic route to Boone's house, but it was more of a shortcut and, considering my present level of premarital angst over living arrangements and toothpaste, every minute counted.

Grimy bulbs dangled from phone poles and over rear doors of businesses closed for the night. Loose gravel crunched underfoot and bits of broken glass sparkled in the dingy light. Heart pounding, I ran full out, then stopped dead, staring down the empty alley. What the heck was wrong with me? What was I thinking? Sure, I loved Cherry House, but I loved Boone so much more. I could sell my house and move into Boone's big fancy house. It was pretty much unfurnished except for the ugliest dining room set on planet earth, left by the previous owners, who wouldn't pay to move it. But the house was lovely and faced an amazing Savannah square, and Boone really liked his house.

Here's the thing. Boone had grown up dirt poor, had gone from member of the gang to member of the bar, and having a really nice house had probably been a dream. Boone deserved the dream. He deserved to live in his house. Could I do that for him? Sure! But the dining room set had to go.

I hopped a puddle of something green and slimy, dodged a stack of wooden pallets, and spotted a white Caddy nearly as old as me. It was parked in the shadows, but I could still make out the pink tulips taped to the antenna and a WWJD sticker on the front bumper. There was only one Caddy in all Savannah like this, the sisters', and this was the rear entrance to Soap Box Cleaners. Last time I'd checked, they didn't repair cars, and who was that sitting in the back seat?

I cupped my hand to the window. It was a woman in a blue hat. Sleeping? Maybe a street person catching a few Zs—except she looked kind of hunched over, and who could sleep like that . . . and . . . her eyes were open. No one slept sitting up with their eyes open, and what the heck was that running across my foot? I dropped Old Yeller and jumped.

"Yikes!"

Chapter Two

Something gray with a skinny tail and beady eyes scurried right between my legs. Dead people and now rodents too! The syndrome was getting worse. My shoulder smacked against a green scummy dumpster, and the hugest roach in all of Christendom landed on my arm.

Dead body *and* rat *and* ginormous bug. At times I could be kind of badass, but at this particular moment, huddled in a back alley, alone, I was totally wimpyass. I grabbed Yeller, swiped at my blouse, screamed like a two-year-old with an earache, and tore down the alley.

Stepping in God-knows-what, I didn't stop till I got to the streetlights on Abercorn. Panting and sweating and swearing like a sailor under my breath, I yanked off my blouse. When it came to bra versus bug, bug won out every time. I shook my blouse in the air and snapped it hard to dislodge anything with antennae and wiggly legs determined to hang on. If wiggly flew out and landed back on me again, I'd die right where I stood and they could just bury me under the stop sign.

I held my blouse up to the light to check it out and got a round of applause from three guys across the street coming out of Wall's Barbecue. I took a bow . . . what else is a girl to do, and, besides, I did just happen to have on my new pink lace push-up bra, though truth be told there wasn't all that much to push up. With a little luck, no one had recognized me. Without luck, Mamma would be getting a phone call tonight saying her one and only was doing a striptease right out there in the open air.

Promising God I'd get my behind to church on Sunday if he saved me from roaches, rodents, and dead people tonight, I shrugged back into my blouse. I gulped some air to calm myself down, then turned for Madison Square. I knew I should suck it up and go back into the alley and take another look at the Caddy, but I just didn't have it in me to face her alone. Boone would go with me, but did I want to dump a dead body on him the very night we got engaged? How could I put this? *I love being the future Mrs. Boone, and by the way, I found another body . . .*

Trying to figure out what to do, I headed for Boone's stately gray Federalist that overlooked the park with William Jasper, resident Revolutionary War hero, standing guard in the middle. One light glowed from Boone's upstairs window and one in the living room. For the first time in two weeks, Walker Boone was home legally. Illegally we'd run into each other in his pantry when we were hiding from the cops.

The moon silhouetted hanging fern baskets that neighbors had obviously kept watered in Boone's absence. Neighbor helping neighbor was the Savannah way. Blue-and-yellow pansies overflowed the two stone urns by the black front door complete with pineapple knocker, and Boone sat on the top wrought iron step. He held a beer in one hand and shared cookies with BW with the other.

"You're a dognapper," I said, sitting down on the other side of Bruce Willis and giving his ears a scratch. "And you're going to give BW jelly belly with this junk food, and his teeth are going to rot and fall out of his head."

Boone held up a cookie. "Doggy treats, the only thing left in my house to eat, and right now I'm too tired to be picky." He picked up the bag and read, " 'Organic, low-fat, and contain no animal byproducts.' That makes them the healthiest things I've eaten for a while." He popped a cookie in his mouth and added, "And the way I see it, there's no dognapping. I own BW's snout and tail after paying that vet bill, and the rest of him just followed along when I got him from your house. I figured you'd be at the wake a while. We came out to meet you."

I gave Boone a sideways glance and swallowed a groan. Not because he was eating dog food, but because he smelled really good and looked great. Droplets of shower clung to his dark hair so long it curled at the ends, and even though he had probably shaved fifteen minutes before, a forever scruff darkened his jawline. If he'd had on a fur coat and a Valyrian steel sword, he could've passed for Jon Snow. *Game of Thrones* fans, eat your heart out.

"Friends at Wall's give you a call?" I asked to distract myself from his jumpability.

He held up his beer. "The boys say thanks."

I took a deep breath. "After we're married, what do you think of me moving in here? I can sell Cherry House. But who's going to cook dinner? That's got to be you or we'll have SpaghettiO surprise every night and we'll get pasta butt and I really like your butt the way it is and what toothpaste are we going to use? That whitening stuff tastes like battery acid but brown teeth are gross and as for my blouse coming off tonight there was a bug on it and I saw a rat and I sort of found a dead body in a Caddy."

Boone threw back the beer and gulped. That he didn't raise so much as one eyebrow when I threw in the Caddy comment was a clue as to how crazy my life was. "You like my butt?"

"Every female east of the Mississippi likes your butt. There's talk of putting it on a coin."

Boone gulped again. "Well, you can't sell Cherry House because KiKi is next door, and if you move away she'll beat me up. I'll cook, and SpaghettiO surprise once in a while is okay by me. I'll relocate my law office here to this place and you can pick the toothpaste." He kissed me on the forehead. "I have no intention of waiting till we're married to move in together—we've been apart long enough—and where exactly is this body?"

"The Abbott sisters' Caddy is parked in an alley, and there's a lady, old best I could tell, in the back seat sleeping with her eyes open, so that kind of means she's . . . dead. What if somebody else finds the car and the body and calls the cops? Isn't there a law about hauling around dead people? Annie Fritz and Elsie can't go to jail; they taught my catechism classes and got me ready for my First Communion, and now they're my friends and they're going to be your friends."

Boone dropped his arms around me, pulling me close, the heat from his body making me feel warm and safe and all mushy inside. "We got the house and toothpaste thing covered. The body thing might take some doing, but we'll figure it out."

My gaze met Boone's. "You said you'd do the cooking, so how do you feel about us planting a nice big six-feet-deep garden this year?"

* * *

"It's . . . it's gone," I said to Boone as the three of us— Boone, me, and BW—pulled up behind Soap Box Cleaners in the alley. I jabbed my finger at the shadowy spot where the Caddy-plus-dead-person had been parked. "It was right there."

I noticed that Boone's eyes didn't sparkle quite as much as usual and he looked worn and tired to the bone. Running from cops, killers, and estranged relatives takes it out of a guy no matter how tough he is. And now that I thought about it, there was the fact that Boone had just gotten out of one mess and didn't need to get mixed up in another if he intended to keep his law practice in good standing. "You know, maybe it was the sisters' laundry in the back seat. This is the Soap Box Cleaners after all." I smacked my palm against my forehead. "What was I thinking?"

"You're thinking you saw a body."

"Well, maybe not." Before Boone could press the issue, I slipped my arm through his and steered him back down the alley, adding quickly, "Look, we caught a killer today, nearly got killed ourselves, and last but not least and the best part of my life ever, we got engaged. Maybe we should just leave it at that."

"Sweet thing, laundry doesn't look like a dead person."

I snuggled close. "Or maybe it was a . . ." *Think, Reagan, think.* ". . . a reflection in the window. The lighting back here sucks, and even though it's late, I bet Zunzi's will deliver a Conquistador sandwich right to your doorstep if you talk sweet to Angie Mae. And"—I needed to up the ante—"if you mention there's no food in your house and you're eating canine kibble, I just bet Angie Mae will throw in extra fries and slaw. How does that sound? Pretty good, huh? Better than a Caddy in an alley for sure, but just be sure Angie Mae and her short-shorts don't throw anything else your way, got it?" I held Boone's hand tight. "You're almost a married man now."

Boone stopped next to a telephone pole, moths and bugs swarming around the light over our heads. "You're not coming back to the house with me? Who's going to defend me against Angie Mae?"

I handed him the leash. "You need sleep."

"I was thinking we'd do that together." Boone wagged his brows.

I was beyond excited about being engaged to Boone, and my feet hadn't touched the ground since he'd asked me to marry him, but Elsie and Annie Fritz needed help. A body in a car wasn't something I could put off a day or two. I needed to find the Caddy and figure out what the heck was going on before the cops got involved.

"I need to stop by Mamma's and tell her we're engaged."

"It's Savannah, the land of dishing-the-dirt and all things fried. She knows."

"Yeah, but she should hear it from me or she'll have hurt feelings and for the next twenty years I'll hear about how I didn't tell her myself. Do you know how long twenty years of guilt from Mamma can be? And she'll want to talk about wedding dresses, venues, flowers, churches, brides-maids, wedding colors. I was thinking sage green and cream, by the way. What do you think?"

Boone's look of splendor-in-the-sack gave way to deer-in-the-headlights. Nothing turned a guy off more than wedding colors and flowers. "Big wedding?"

"Maybe." A very distant maybe, so it wasn't a lie, and I really did need to tell Mamma. Not that I hadn't lied to Boone before. Heck, I did it all the time to keep him out of my hair, but now that we were permanently and forever in each other's hair, lying was a big no-no.

"Think I'll get that sandwich." Boone gave me a kiss, a really good kiss that I didn't want to end.

"And for the record," I said, our hands together holding the leash. "I really, really like being your fiancée."

Hating every minute of it, I watched the two guys in my life walk away, then took a deep breath and headed for York Street and Mamma's house. I'd give her the good news on the engagement and then somehow make a quick getaway. I had to find that Caddy and have a little come-to-Jesus meeting with the sisters about their part in all this.

I passed Columbia Square and the Davenport House, the first house to be saved by the Historic Savannah Preservation. These were a group of steel magnolias hell-bent on keeping the best of Savannah from the wrecking ball, thank you very much. The mansion was a museum now, the only permanent residents being a hundred-year-old tabby cat and a little girl who refused to leave, much to the delight of the operators of the local ghost tours.

I cut across Oglethorpe Square, the fountain gurgling merrily in the center, then Wright Square with a canine watering fountain—how cute is that! Mamma's cottage was just ahead, surrounded by a white picket fence I'd painted more times than I wanted to remember. The house had been built for General William Hardee and still had three musket balls embedded in the living room ceiling. Talk about a great conversation piece.

"Hi, Mamma," I said when she opened the front door, the light from the entrance hallway spilling out onto the porch. "Boone and I are engaged; isn't that great? I'm really tired and I need to get home, and I'll stop by tomorrow and we can chat over coffee, and—"

Mamma yanked me inside and, without a word, led me into the kitchen done up in yellow and white with pink lilacs fresh from the garden sitting on the counter. She shoved a glass in my hand and held up her own. "And here's to keeping you two engaged and staying married for a long, long time." Mamma downed her glass in one gulp. She smacked her lips and added another splash. "KiKi and I stopped by the church and lit three candles to enhance your chances. We'll start a novena in the morning."

"This is apple juice, and why don't you think Boone and I are going to last? I thought you liked Boone. You even paid his way through law school."

"The juice is to keep a clear head, and of course I love Walker. He's the son I never had, and I love you." Mamma finished her splash and took the glass from my hand, downed the contents, and thumped the glass on the round oak table where the two of us had shared meals and talked my whole life.

"But the thing is, dear," Mamma went on, "you and Walker are not exactly the dental-hygienist-and-accountant sort of couple. You're more mayhem super-sized than marital bliss."

"Hey, we're the lawyer and the shop girl. That's pretty close to hygienist and accountant."

"What about all the bodies you come across and killers on the loose and one or both of you right in the thick of things? 'Till death do us part' takes on a whole new meaning with you and Walker. Who's dead isn't specified. I can't bear the thought of you two breaking up."

"We just got together!"

Mamma let out a resigned sigh. "In case you didn't get the memo, Walker doesn't cotton to you chasing after the bad guys, and you don't take kindly to being told what to do and . . . and . . ." Mamma took a step back, looking me over, her eyes widening. "Oh, sweet mother," she said in a strangled voice. "You're flipping your hair and your eye's twitching. You're nervous as a pea on a drum. I know this look, Reagan. You got something going on right now. Is it a live something or a dead one?"

Mamma pinched the bridge of her nose and closed her eyes. "You've only been engaged three hours. How in the world does this keep happening to you? Normal people don't have bodies popping up in their lives like this except for that Jessica Fletcher woman in Cabot Cove. I can't understand why anyone in their right mind would want to be her friend. They all wind up dead, and now you're getting to be the same way."

"It's not my fault," I said as Mamma blinked her eyes open. "I've thought about this body thing too, and the way I see it, it's all Hollis's fault. When he divorced me, that took one lifeless piece of crud out of my life, and now the fates feel they have to fill the void by sending in a bunch more. You've got to admit I only find the bodies of nasty people who've got it coming. These dead guys are taking Hollis's place, and you know as well as I do this body situation started with Hollis and Cupcake and my favorite pink chiffon dress that she got her mitts on."

"Not the best excuse I've ever heard, but it'll have to do for now till we figure out something else to tell people." Mamma tramped to the back door, snagged her really nice pocketbook off the counter, and fluffed her hair in the little mirror with a gilt edge. "We got work to do and it can't wait."

"Window shopping for wedding dresses?"

"I finally get you on the verge of being married off to a fine man while you're still of breeding age and I'm aiming to protect my grandbabies like any decent grandmother would. That means we're finding the body that has you in a tizzy, putting an end to this particular event right quick, and concentrating on the important things of life."

"Breeding?"

"And your time's fading fast in that department, so don't just stand there." Mamma gave me the "I have spoken" look that no lawyer or daughter would dare argue with. She shouldered her purse and opened the door. "Forward march!"

And I did. Not that I thought the *b* word was a bad idea; I just hadn't thought about it, period, having been engaged only a few hours. Obviously Mamma had thought about the *b* word a lot and nothing was getting in the way.

A woman on a mission, Mamma followed me across the moonlit path lined with big white gardenias, jasmine, pink lilacs, and roses. A budding magnolia flanked the white clapboard garage to one side, a huge crimson crepe myrtle on the other. Next month they would be ablaze with flowers, the whole garden like something out of a Van Gogh painting except for the right side of the yard where Mamma had run off the drive and into the grass a few times. And then there was the daffodil bed she'd taken out last fall along with the birdbath. The rock wall was streaked with various colors from various cars, the whole thing listing precariously to the right.

Mamma was a great judge of everything but distance. The bad news was that her insurance was through the roof and people dove for cover when they spotted her coming. The good news was that she always had a new car to sport around, even if it did have a few dings here and there.

"So where are we headed to locate this dead person?" Mamma asked as she propelled her black Buick (which looked a little too much like a hearse to suit my taste) down Whittaker.

Getting Mamma involved in a body hunt was just like getting Boone involved. They were officers of the court, upholders of the law. They'd taken oaths and given their word to do the right thing, and if something was wrong, they pretty much had to call the cops. I, on the other hand, could snoop around, and it didn't matter as long as I didn't get caught. What I needed now was to keep Mamma uninvolved. I had to come up with a dead-body story quick to explain away my twitchy eye and hair flipping to Mamma; then I could go hunt for the Caddy on my own.

"Actually," I said as we tooled along. "I was at Willie Fishbine's wake, and I wanted to visit the Abbott sisters this evening to tell them what a great job they did with his big farewell sendoff. They were fretting because Willie's turnout was so light."

Mamma scrunched her forehead. "This dead body you're fretting over is Willie Fishbine? The same Willie Fishbine who chased you out of his yard with a shotgun when you cut across his grass? And you were dropping in on the Abbott sisters at this hour to tell them what a great job they did in sending him off to that great NRA meeting in the sky? Why in the world did you even go to his wake in the first place?"

"The sisters were feeling insecure about their low attendance." Counting on the Summerside addiction for all things sweet and delicious, I added, "And Annie Fritz baked a cake, red velvet with chocolate icing, and it probably has a big red cherry right there in the middle. I thought I could stop in for a slice, and now you can come with me. Great idea, huh?"

"Cake?"

"With cream cheese icing."

Mamma gripped the steering wheel, a glint in her eyes. She took a hard right onto Gwinnett, squealed into the sisters' drive, and was out of the car and ringing the bell before I even unbuckled my seat belt. Never underestimate the power of a Conquistador sandwich or the Summerside sweet tooth.

"Well, now, this is sure an unexpected . . . uh . . . pleasure," Annie Fritz stammered to Mamma while I climbed the wooden steps.

"Sister," Annie Fritz yelled over her shoulder. "Judge Summerside and Reagan are right here on our porch, of all places. What do you think of that? Best get yourself presentable, if you know what I mean."

"I do apologize for calling at this ungodly hour," Mamma gushed to Annie Fritz, who was ready for bed in her blue terry cloth robe and bunny slippers with little pink eyes. "But everyone's talking about what a lovely performance you and Elsie gave at Willie Fishbine's wake, and

Reagan and I thought you should know just how much it's appreciated."

"It's after nine."

"These things are important to the community. Give us all a sense of peace and security that we'll be sent off to meet our maker with dignity and respect." Mamma reached in her purse and plucked out a half-full container of orange Tic Tacs. She handed them over to Annie Fritz. No Southern lady worth her pearls would ever come a-calling without a hostess gift, and some were clearly better than others.

"I'm sure you'll enjoy these, and, my goodness, is that cake I smell?" Mamma jutted her head into the doorway. "I sure could do with a nice slice of cake."

Just as no Southern lady would ever come calling empty-handed, neither would she turn away a visitor at the door, no matter what the hour. That might suggest her house wasn't completely up to snuff twenty-four/seven, and God forbid a Southern gal would have that hanging over her head. Annie Fritz forced a grin. "Cake?"

"And everyone knows yours is so special; best in Savannah." Was that a drop of drool in the corner of Mamma's mouth?

Annie Fritz shifted her weight from one foot to the other then stood aside, letting us into the hallway with daisy-flowered wallpaper and a brass umbrella stand in the corner. She shuffled across the original pine floor and into the parlor awash in blues, reds, and pinks from the glass lamp in the front window that was lit every night like clockwork.

Mamma followed and I trailed behind, then veered off

toward the kitchen. I was sure Mamma would never miss me with red velvet on the brain, and if Elsie found me lurking about, I'd say I was going for a glass of water. This was all part of my great two-for-one plan to satisfy Mamma and see if, since the Caddy was not in the alley, it just might be in the sisters' driveway.

I knew Annie and Elsie Fritz's kitchen as well as my own, and theirs was a whole lot better. They had food. I made my way past the white vintage fridge with the coils on top humming away and rounded the oak table sporting a vase of daffodils sitting on a white crochet doily. A collection of wooden spoons, rolling pins, and bowls sat on a shelf over the white enamel stove with six gas burners, two warmers, and huge ovens. Oatmeal raisin cookies cooled on a wire rack. Oatmeal raisin were not as good as the cake sitting on the counter but a darn good second choice, and swiping cookies was a heck of a lot easier to get away with. I snagged two and rearranged the pile so there wasn't a gaping telltale hole, took a bite, and spotted a stack of bills on the end of the counter with "OVERDUE" stamped in big red letters.

It wasn't like the sisters to have overdue bills. They were responsible and thrifty and probably had an okay pension from teaching besides the Woeful Weeping business. Then again, Annie Fritz had worn party shoes to Willie's funeral and had mentioned bourbon balls, limoncello, and getting swindled. Swindled out of how much?

I held the screen door so it wouldn't slam, clamped the second cookie between my teeth, then rooted my flashlight from Old Yeller. Flipping it on, I slunk across the yard, leaving a trail of crumbs in my wake. A stone bench sat under a flowering purple lilac that smelled like heaven on earth, and the tips of newly planted veggies already peeked through the soil. A hose, shovel, and overturned wheelbarrow sat off to the side. A wire fence surrounded the whole patch to keep out rabbits, opossums, and—

"Reagan," came that all-too-familiar voice. "What in blazes are you doing out here this time of night?"

Chapter Three

"**M**e? What are *you* doing here?" I stage-whispered to Auntie KiKi, who was dolled up in a pink robe with matching rollers and face cream. She looked like a strawberry smoothie with eyes. "This is the second time tonight you've snuck up on me."

"I'm not sneaking; you're just not paying attention, and I saw Gloria's hearse parked in front," KiKi whispered back. "Then a flashlight started darting around down here, and I figured it had to be you. What are you up to now? You should be in your house cuddled up all romantic-like with your honey."

I jabbed my finger at the white Caddy sitting in the drive. "I thought you said it was in the repair shop. When I went to see Boone, I found it parked in an alley, and I saw a body in the back. I didn't get a good look because a rat and a roach ganged up on me. When I went back to the alley with Boone, the Caddy was gone. Go take a look inside."

"For?"

"The body!"

"Me?"

"Think of it as my engagement present."

"How about I give you a deviled egg plate instead?"

I handed off the flashlight and KiKi bunched up her robe, muttering something about family being a total pain in the backside. She pranced across the damp grass, the triangle of light showing the way. I held my breath as she cupped her hand to the window. "Nothing in here except a box of tissues, a pink pillow with tassels so Elsie can see over the steering wheel, and the plastic Jesus on the dash. Well, my goodness, will you look at that, he glows in the dark. Do you think that means something?"

I joined KiKi by the car. "Maybe they stashed the body out here somewhere."

I picked up a stick and started pushing back the greenery surrounding the house. KiKi commandeered my stick and tossed it into my yard. "There's no one out here except us, and we should take it as a sign that this is none of our business and forget about this whole thing."

I parked my hands on my hips. "You don't believe I saw a body?"

"Oh, honey, that's the problem, I do believe it with my whole heart, but it's gone now, and I say for once we go with 'out of sight, out of mind.' If there's no body, we don't have to think about who and why and how and get into trouble. We can concentrate on your wedding and be normal. Remember what normal feels like?" She pointed a stiff finger toward my house. "You need sleep, and I need to be getting home before your Uncle Putter finishes up that

DVD he's been watching on *18 Ways to Throw Your Golf Club* and starts wondering where I am. I tell you, men and golf are like a religion around here. Just put *golf* in the title and they believe. See, that's what I mean by normal—least in Savannah it is. Let's give it a try."

"You want to take up golf?"

"I want to take up anything that doesn't reference the word *croaked*." KiKi headed off into the night, cutting through my backyard and then on to hers so as not to be seen out front in her robe and face cream. For the moment, I had no comeback for the "out of sight, out of mind" philosophy, so I headed for Mamma's car to leave a note saying I was tucked safely in bed and I'd see her tomorrow. A text message would have been easier except for the little fact that my present state of financial distress didn't allow for such things as a cell phone.

I headed up my sidewalk past the adorable white Prissy Fox sign surrounded by daffodils I'd planted the previous fall. Mamma had had the sign made when I opened the Fox, and I thought of her every time I walked past it. Frogs sang their spring song of "come and get it, big boy," crickets chirped, and an owl hooted in the distance. It would have been a perfect night if there hadn't been a dead body out there somewhere. Deep in my bones, I just knew it was waiting to scare the crap out of me again.

The light was on in the bay window I used for displays. I really needed to get rid of that denim skirt on Gwendolyn, my beloved mannequin, and get her spiffed up in a floral garden party dress. I could add the straw purse and pink floral scarf that had just come in, and—who the heck was that sitting next to Gwendolyn? Another mannequin? But there was only one that I'd fished out of the trash over on Broughton. This other mannequin was a lady in a blue cotton dress with a matching hat perched on a tangle of gray curls. She was propped against the wall with a red purse in her lap. I unlocked the door, the scent of cinnamon and maybe cloves hitting me as I crept inside the house, the place quiet as a tomb. Did I have to think the word *tomb*, and why did it smell like baking in here? "Hello?" I called from behind the two figures, hoping one would answer.

Normally I had BW with me to make things like this less scary. Not that he was much of a watchdog; BW was more of a comfort dog. He was someone I got into trouble with and things didn't seem so bad because there were two of us freaking out. I nudged the sitting mannequin with the tip of my shoe and she slumped forward, hat toppling off, landing on her bony knees. I smacked my hand over my mouth to squelch a scream, because no matter what the occasion— even dead people in the front window—Summersides did not scream. A ladylike Southern belle gasp might escape now and then if the Atlanta Falcons were winning, but that was it.

Taking two steps back, I flattened myself against the windowpane like a squashed spider. Why would the sisters put a dead person in my window—and it had to have been them because the place smelled like fresh-baked cookies and the little old lady had been in their car. I mean, how many dead little old ladies were on the loose in Savannah tonight?

With my luck, it was probably best not to think too hard on that particular question.

I couldn't knock on the sisters' door to find out what was going on, not with Mamma inside visiting. It was that upholder-of-the-law thing again, and questions like "Hey, why was there a corpse in your car?" and "How'd it get in my display window?" and "Thanks for the spices because decaying bodies really stink" would get Mamma involved and she'd have to call the cops. I didn't want the sisters to get mixed up with the cops until I got this straightened out. They weren't killers, but the law enforcement officers might not be in a mood to take my word for it.

In a time of crisis and need for moral support, there was only one person to call. Batman was my first choice, but the second choice lived closer and did a mean cha-cha. I closed the door behind me and sprinted across my yard to Auntie KiKi's. I let myself through the wrought iron gate with a rose woven into the pattern, the one that gave the house the name Rose Gate. I got the key from under the mat. With Mamma having been a single parent since I was two thanks to Daddy boar hunting with friends and a bottle of Johnny Walker Red, I'd spent as much time with KiKi and Uncle Putter as I had at my own house.

Not needing a light, I meandered through the kitchen till I spotted two green eyes peering at me from the kitchen table. Either the bananas had taken on a life of their own or Princess the cat—who morphed into Princess the Hellion when I was around—had me in her sights. I was bigger, had opposable thumbs, and should be in charge. On the other hand, Hellion possessed claws and the attitude of Darth Vader.

"Eat dirt and die, you mean ornery hairball," I soothed as I inched my way to the fridge. I pulled it open, found leftover fried chicken, and snapped up a drumstick. I took a bite because no one did chicken better than Auntie KiKi, and I hoped Hellion felt the same way. I tossed the leg onto the table, Hellion dove for it, and I scampered off to the living room and headed for the steps. I stopped on the fourth one as it creaked under my foot. There was no need to go any farther because in about three seconds . . . two . . . one . . .

"Who's down there?" KiKi called from the landing, Uncle Putter's golf club clutched firmly in her left hand. It looked like the four iron.

"It's the boogeyman," I stage-whispered. "The dead body's back. What should we do now?"

"We?"

I grabbed KiKi's hand and hustled her down the steps and out the front door. "It's a woman and she's old."

"Something you're not going to be if you keep dragging me around like this."

"And she has a blue dress and her hat fell off, but what was she doing in the sisters' Caddy and now in my house?" I babbled as we crossed our front yards, me not caring who saw KiKi in her pink robe. I stopped on my sidewalk and jabbed my finger at the window. "See?"

"See what?"

"On the floor next to . . ." I blinked, then blinked two more times. "She was there. I swear it."

"Yeah, but she's not there now, so the 'out of mind' theory is still in effect, and about that sleep I mentioned before—for crying in a bucket, Reagan, do us all a great big favor and get some!"

St. John's Church chimed out eight AM as I pounded on the back door of the sisters' house. In spite of Auntie KiKi's "out of sight and mind" philosophy, I had to get some info on the resident dead-lady situation. For sure she'd reappear, the police would get involved, and with a little bad luck the Abbott sisters could be decked out in jailhouse orange before the Fourth of July.

I pounded again but the blinds stayed shut, curtains drawn, and no footsteps scurried around inside to let me in. My guess was that the sisters were still sleeping with their hearing aids parked on their bedside tables. I tried the door but it was locked. Running out of time, I put the dead-body situation on the back burner and went with Plan B: getting Willie Fishbine's stuff from Sleepy Pines. I had to get there and back by ten to open the Fox on time, not that there'd been much to open to lately with business being in the toilet.

Being a public-transportation kind of girl, I could sense deep familiar motor rumblings a few streets over. I'd never make it to the official bus stop in time to catch the hydrocarbon express, so I took off in a dead run for Abercorn to head it off. Chancing life and limb, I stood in the middle of the street and waved my arms like a castaway on a deserted island. Cars honked, swerved, and gave me a good-morning salute that didn't mean anything good at all. A car would certainly have made this retrieval of salable items a lot easier—except a car, like a cell phone, was not in the current budget. Electricity and running water were barely in the budget.

I waved harder, the bus getting closer and closer still. This kind of thing didn't happen when I had BW with me. Earlene would never run down a woman with a dog, but a woman alone trying to ride the bus and not at an official stop was obviously target practice. I started to jump to the curb when Earlene slammed on the brakes. She glared down from her perch on high and gave me the "You are one crazy white girl" look.

"Were you aiming for me?" I griped as I hopped on.

"Maybe a little."

I dug the bus fare out of Old Yeller and Earlene hit the gas. "But I thought we were friends," I said as I staggered to the seat across from the driver. "I'm the one who fixed you up with Big Joey, remember? That means you're in a relationship with the most kickass dude in Savannah, and you have me to thank for it."

"We done broke up," Earlene grumbled as the bus growled forward. "And it's all your fault, yours and Walker's. Now that I think about it, I should have run you down when I had the chance. You had it coming."

"You and Big Joey were doing great."

"Is this here the face of a woman doing great?" Her lower lip stuck out in a pout and her brows knit together in one long ticked-off line. "It's you and Walker and that *c* word that's done me in."

"*C* as in cute couple?" That's two words, of course, but I couldn't resist.

"The word's *committed*, as in going to the next step in your relationship and getting yourself engaged." Earlene pulled to the curb for two passengers and said to me, "Now my man's feeling the pressure and I'm being demoted to his friend zone. Someplace no girlfriend wants to be, I can tell you that." Earlene adjusted her blue uniform cap and started up. "Not that I've said one word to him about that commitment thing you and Boone have going on. Nuh-uh, not me. Fact is, now that I think about it, I'm happy as a bug in a rug being a single woman right here in the fine city of Savannah."

"Is that a *Brides* magazine tucked under your seat?" I looked a little closer. "And do I see a white veil tucked up under your hat?"

"How'd you like to walk the rest of the way to where you're going?" Earlene turned onto Liberty. "And where exactly is that anyway?"

"Sleepy Pines. I need to pick up some resale items."

"You mean old Sexy Pines?" Earlene laughed deep in her throat. "I guess they haven't retired from everything over there, have they?" The bottom-lip pout was back. "Mighty sad state of affairs when a bunch of seniors are getting more action than me here in my prime at twenty-nine." Earlene hadn't seen twenty-nine for about six years now, but since I didn't feel like walking I thought it best to keep my mouth shut.

"My auntie was all set to move into that Pines place," Earlene said to me. "Then she heard they're having a run on funerals lately and she's not wanting to be next on that particular list, if you know what I mean. All the sexy in the world doesn't count for much if they're putting you in a box and dropping you six feet down."

Earlene stopped next to the Barnard Street sign. "This is as close as I get with old Sexy being just around the corner. And you best watch your step, missy, or they'll be signing you up for real with all those wrinkles you got going on this morning."

"That bad?"

"Sure ain't good, not that it'll matter much to the old coots you're visiting. From what I hear, they may have snow on the roof, but they still got some fire in the furnace, and right now you're what they call fresh meat."

Earlene laughed as I stepped onto the sidewalk, but she didn't start up in her usual pedal-to-the-metal fashion. "I'm waiting for my little oldster lady." Earlene tapped her fingers impatiently on the steering wheel. "Every Tuesday she takes the 8:32 to town, and her not being here worries me a bit. She's so cute with her little red pocketbook and dress and hats that match. She meets up with a man friend who gets on at the next stop and she always brings me two toffee candies 'cause I help her on and off."

"The woman have short gray curly hair?"

"You see her?"

"Not at the moment."

"Maybe I should tell the police so they can keep an eye out for her."

"Or not," I added in a hurry. "Maybe she's taken a trip . . . a really long, long trip."

Earlene closed the doors and motored off in a lung-clogging cloud. It wasn't even ten and the day had gone from bad to wrinkles. I was on the lighter side of thirty-five, so how'd that happened? A sleepless night preceded by dead-body bingo, that's how. And was that the beginnings of a muffin top overlapping my denim skirt? With helping Boone get off the most-wanted list, I hadn't had time for exercise, not that I'd been dedicated to the idea before. *I could get shin splints if I jog*, my brain argued. Then my gut bellowed, *You've already got flab, and think how that will look in a wedding dress.* Taking a deep breath, I jogged off toward Sexy Pines.

Huffing and puffing like a three-pack-a-day habit, I turned onto Tattnall Street, focusing on the Pines at the next corner. The place had been built right after the unfortunate Northern occurrence and had been in the Tattnall family ever since. It had been a fine estate until someone invented real estate taxes; then a lot of the grounds had been sold off. About five years back, Mr. Jim Tattnall had turned the two-story Georgian plus carriage house and gardens into a retirement home.

"Howdy there, Reagan," Mr. Jim said, opening the door as a good deal of yelling and screaming inside floated my way. "Saw you running here like a bat out of Hades. Where's the fire?"

"Trying to lose some weight. What's going on inside? Is this a bad time?"

"You always look mighty fine to me, sugar, but if you do get the answer to that weight problem, be sure and let me know—though, truth be told, I bet it might have something to do with those double-chocolate brownies I keep hidden away in the kitchen." Mr. Jim patted his rounded middle, the buttons of his bright white dress shirt straining to stay closed. He nodded to the interior, the racket intensifying. "A few of our guests are a mite rambunctious this morning is all."

"Somebody get up on the wrong side of the bed?"

"Best I can tell, somebody's in the wrong bed and there's hell to pay."

Chapter Four

M r. Jim arched his brow, let out a deep sigh, then massaged his forehead. " 'Open a retirement home,' my accountant said. 'It'll be fun,' he said. 'You'll make money.' He left out the part about playing referee for fifteen residents at Peyton Place Dixie-style. I tell you, they all need a hobby."

"If you ask me, they got one."

Mr. Jim's eyes brightened with laughter as he opened the door to let me in. "Willie's sourpuss daughter said you'd be stopping on over. The apple sure doesn't fall far from the tree with that one. I do believe pain-in-the-butt is a genetic condition in the Fishbine family."

"Willie won't be missed?"

"Party's at seven, fireworks at nine. I thought that pasty-faced old crank would die of orneriness instead of something like asthma. Fact is, I didn't know you could die of asthma, but then at his age you can die of a hangnail if it hits you wrong."

I stepped inside to the smells of the South—strong

coffee and things baking and frying. None of those sissy granola live-forever breakfasts around here. Guess they figured if bacon, eggs, and butter had gotten them this far, why mess with success?

I followed Mr. Jim down the hall with brass chandeliers twinkling overhead and group pictures decorating the walls. There were the winners of the great canasta tournament, the horseshoe contest, the ballroom dance competition, the flower-arranging championship, the walkathon, and the happy hoedown. Considering the nickname of this place, I didn't want to even think about what that last one was all about.

"Willie's bloodsucking relatives done took anything of value," Mr. Jim yelled over the escalating din as we got closer to the parlor. "What's left of his belongings are parked in the closet in the back." Mr. Jim hitched his head toward the two men in the parlor who were all blue in the face from having a conniption about whatever, though they did coordinate nicely with the greens and yellows of the room. "I need to take care of this," Mr. Jim yelled, louder so I could hear him.

"They're old; they have walkers," I shouted. "How much damage can they really do?"

Mr. Jim strode into the parlor, stepping between the two men. "Foley, Emmitt, you need to be calming down now, ya hear? It's not good for either of you to be carrying on like this. You know how it ups your blood pressure. We'll talk over a nice cup of tea."

"Tea?" the man in the red Atlanta Braves cap roared to

his opponent. "Bring out the Wild Turkey and get the duel-ing pistols from over the fireplace." He took two blasts from his inhaler, snarled, then flung the thing at the other guy. "I'm teaching Foley here a lesson if it's the last thing I do. Twenty paces at dawn in Washington Square, or can't you make it that far, you knock-kneed woman stealer? Just because you had that big fancy house over there on Oglethorpe, you think you can have anything or anyone you want."

"You bet I can." The guy in the jogging suit and a blue Chicago Cubs cap picked up his walker and shook it in the air. "Bonnie Sue is looking for a real man, someone who owned land and lots of it, not some piddly, stoop-shouldered twerp who wouldn't know how to pour water out of a boot with a hole in the toe. That woman's mine, and I can take you any day of the week and I'll prove it right now."

"You're all talk and a spit's worth of glitter. Bring on the pistols."

Mr. Jim turned back to me, a line of perspiration dot-ting his forehead. "Honey, can you have Eugenia bring in some chamomile tea? And tell her to step on it."

Personally, I thought Prozac tea would work better. I rushed past the dining room, where a few guests oblivious to the bedlam were eating breakfast at adorable little round tables with starched tablecloths and fresh flowers. I turned into the kitchen and nearly collided with the chef, who was expertly flipping pancakes with one hand and scrambling egg whites with the other. Guess there were more healthy things going on here than I'd realized.

"Lamar?" I stopped dead, taking in his smudged white

apron and the pots and pans simmering on the stove, little curls of steam escaping into the air. "Thought you were doing the valet thing over at the Old Harbor Inn."

"I help Mr. Jim out in the mornings. It's a stressful time of day, with making things taste right and not upping cholesterol and blood sugar and all. I'm getting right good at buckwheat flapjacks, I can tell you that."

We both looked at Mr. Jim's daughter, Eugenia, sitting at a window seat studying her manicure and not stressing one bit. It was like Auntie KiKi had once said: if God had made someone better than Eugenia Tattnall, he'd forgotten to tell her about it.

"Reagan?" Eugenia said, finally realizing she wasn't the only person on earth. "What are you doing here? Checking out the place for that busybody auntie of yours? What's her name . . . FiFi? DeDe? Or is it BeBe? She taught me how to foxtrot."

"She taught half the people in this city how to foxtrot, and her name's KiKi, and she's just fine; thank you for asking. Can you take tea into the parlor for your dad? There's a disagreement and he thinks tea might help settle things down, and—"

"I tell you, around here drama and picking up prescriptions and hauling people to the doctor are a way of life." Eugenia swept back her salon-styled strawberry blonde hair with a flourish that would have made Lady Gaga proud. "It sure does get tiresome living around all these old people and antique furniture and creaky floors and plumbing that works half the time. Downright depressing to a young, vibrant woman such as myself. Lamar can do tea; that's what he gets paid for. I'm busy waiting for my date, Mr. Dexter Thomas."

Eugenia let out a dreamy sigh. "He's new in town, from Atlanta, and the *Savannah Sun* just called him Mr. Up-and-Comer. They did a big article on his company, the Southern Way, now owning the House of Eternal Slumber with an eye on other properties and I do declare, Reagan honey, you've done put on a few pounds over the winter, bless your little plump heart."

A horn sounded and Eugenia jumped up as if she'd had a spring in her butt. "I'm coming Dex, sugar. We're off to Charleston for the day in his new Mercedes, of all things. I think we'll eat at the Charleston Grill or that 1886 place; I hear it's divine. I know we won't be eating Italian. Dex simply hates Italian, and I told him I don't like it either. We just have so much in common." Eugenia snagged her purse off the table and held up her hand, a gold bracelet with a crystal heart catching the light. "He gave me this just last night. Dex is such a dreamboat. Ta now. Try not to get too bored around here without me to liven things up for ya."

Eugenia giggled and hurried out the back door into the garden, past the cherub fountain spitting droplets into the air, past the horseshoe courts and the putting green. The wrought iron gate clanked shut, and Lamar and I exchanged looks that said "Thank heavens she's gone." Back in the day, Eugenia and I had gone to school together. She was a cheerleader and captain of the spirit club; I came in third in the sixth-grade spelling bee and was captain of the sprinkle-doughnut club. The one thing we had in common was being divorced from total jerks.

Lamar checked a red clipboard labeled "Dietary Restrictions," then slid the egg whites onto a plate along with dry toast and a dish of prunes. "Don't let Miss Eugenia get all up in your grill now; that's just the way she is. Mr. Jim raised her spoiled, and it stuck like frosting on a cake."

"More like a tick on a dog?"

"That too." Lamar took the plate in one hand, a tray with a teapot and cups in the other, and trotted down the hall, not spilling a drop. I stole a veggie sausage link from the platter on the counter, then headed for the closet. Mr. Jim had been right in that nothing of Willie's was worth selling. I folded pants and shirts into boxes and added two pairs of gym shoes and a copy of *The Badass's Guide to Making Money* to the Goodwill pile. I stacked the boxes in the corner, then headed down the hall toward the loud voices, which hadn't subsided one decibel.

"She's mine, I tell you," Emmitt bellowed as Foley backed him into the hallway, wielding his walker like a weapon. He flattened Foley and me (somehow I got in the way) against the wall between pictures of the King of Karaoke and the Mardi Gras Maiden—and I knew the maiden. Least I thought I did. It was hard to tell with a peacock perched on her head and Emmitt's walker wedged between my legs where no walker had a right to be.

"This has gone far enough," Mr. Jim yelled. "You boys were both in the Sons of Savannah Revolutionary War reenactment brigade, for crying out loud, got awards for best performers, and now you're here fighting each other like cats and dogs?" Mr. Jim hooked a strong arm around each of the Casanovas and pretty much dragged them away with, "What say we let Bonnie Sue sort this out when she gets back from visiting her kin?"

"Well, she's mine," Foley yelled at Emmitt. "And you better get used to it, you old geezer."

"You're the geezer," Emmitt yelled back. "Bonnie Sue's mine, and I intend to have her if it's the last thing I do."

I snagged Lamar coming out of the parlor and pulled him over to the pictures. "Do you know who that is?" I tapped the peacock. "Do you have any idea *where* she is?"

"That's the infamous Miss Bonnie Sue McGrath, and she must be very talented in ways of the flesh that a young impressionable man like me doesn't want to be thinking about. All I know is that she sure has got the men around here in a lather, and she's—"

"Visiting friends in Garden City," Annie Fritz said as she rushed up on my right side, balancing a try of scones, at the same time that Elsie came up on my left side with a tray of orange juice and blurted, "Beaufort."

"I thought she was in Atlanta." Lamar shrugged, then dashed off toward the kitchen and the scent of burning biscuits.

"What we mean to say," Elsie went on, a frozen smile stuck firmly in place, "is that Bonnie Sue is on a little holiday and has friends in Garden City—"

"And they're aiming to visit other friends over there in Beaufort," Annie Fritz chimed in. "And then they're on to

Atlanta, and you, missy, need to stop gossiping here with us and wasting time and be getting yourself back to the Prissy Fox right this minute. Forget all about Bonnie Sue. In fact, I think everyone needs to be forgetting about Bonnie Sue, and the sooner the better. But for you there's a line of customers waiting to get into your shop."

"Customers?" Okay, that got my attention. I hadn't had much of anyone in the shop for two weeks thanks to Anna and Bella's Boutique opening up and stealing my business. So what had brought on this sudden surge of interest in the Fox? I had no idea, but right now there was something more important than money and customers.

"Look," I said in a low voice to Annie and Elsie Fritz. "Bonnie Sue was sitting in my display window last night, and she was in your Caddy parked in the alley before that, and both times she was . . ." I checked to make sure Foley and Emmitt weren't around, as two old guys having heart attacks over the demise of the talented Bonnie Sue was not what Mr. Jim needed right now on top of everything else. ". . . dead."

"No!" Annie Fritz gasped.

I folded my arms and glared. "What the heck's going on around here?"

Annie Fritz looked innocent as the new-fallen snow, not that we got any of that stuff around here. "I believe you're overstressed with getting engaged to Walker Boone and think you saw Bonnie Sue. That must be it."

"You think I imagined Bonnie Sue?"

"Of course not." Annie Fritz's laugh was a little too

high-pitched to be real. She nodded to the picture behind me. "A picture of the woman's right there, so you think you saw her another time. It's a case of bridal brain freeze."

"Never heard of it."

"Happens all the time. Tell me this, did anyone else see Bonnie Sue in our Caddy or on your porch?"

"Well . . ."

"There you go. A case of brain freeze, pure and simple." Elsie gave me an "I win" giggle, then backed me toward the door. "I need to get these juices to the dining room, and you need to be going home now and putting your feet up and taking a deep breath so you can start planning that wedding. Sister and I will look in on you later after we finish up chatting with Mr. Jim about getting in some more business around here with Willie's room needing to get filled."

Annie Fritz balanced the tray on her arm, opened the door, gave me a little shove onto the porch, and then nudged the door with her hip, closing it in my face. I gave the door a frustrated kick, then spun around and smacked right into Hollis. "And this day just keeps getting better and better."

Hollis was in his work uniform—Brooks Brothers khakis and navy polo with "Beaumont Realtors" stitched on the pocket—and, as always, flashing his big bleached-white smile. "Kicking doors? What's the problem, Reagan, trouble in paradise already? Boone come to his senses about marrying you and run for his life like I did?"

"I'm here on business, and I'm guessing you're here to sell Sleepy Pines right out from under Mr. Jim."

Hollis glanced up at the decorative arch over the door,

the dental molding at the eaves, and salivated. "I've been trying to get him to put the place on the market for years. It's got great bones and a fine history, though a coat or two of paint sure wouldn't hurt. Robert E. himself slept in this very place, you know."

"According to you, Robert E. slept in every house in Savannah."

"Helps jack up the price, I can tell you that, but I'm here for a social call to see my dear Uncle Foley."

"Who's rich, getting up there in age, and spending way too much time with a woman who might wind up in his will instead of you? Just so you know, cousin Foley seems to be truly smitten with Miss Bonnie Sue, to the point where he's declared a duel to win her fair hand. I'd say things are getting serious between them."

"Impossible." Hollis's eyes narrowed, his lips thinning. "I'll . . . I'll get an attorney," he snorted. "I'll have Folly declared incompetent if that's what it takes. That money's mine, all mine, I'm next in line to inherit. I've sucked up to that old goat for years, and that money is not going to some woman he's taken up with!"

And there, ladies and gentlemen, is a little glimpse as to why Hollis Beaumont the Third—money-grubber extraordinaire—was my ex and not my current. I headed down the steps, turned for home, then jogged off, regretting every doughnut and cookie I'd ever eaten.

"You look like something the dog hunted down and buried," Auntie KiKi said through the open window of the

Beemer as she rolled up beside me on West Charlton. "What in all that's holy are you running from now?"

"Fat. Must . . . get . . . into . . . wedding . . . dress."

"Keep this up and you'll be getting into a coffin."

I could feel the coolness of the Beemer's AC and glanced at the exquisite comfy brown leather interior. I wanted to be part of that AC and leather more than anything. Then I imagined looking like a cream puff on my wedding day. I gave KiKi a "See you later" wave and stumbled off as she stopped for a light. Some people had great mind-clearing revelations when jogging. The only thing on my mind was trying not to pass out in the middle of the sidewalk and embarrass myself.

I cut across the grassy knoll of Forsythe Park, around the sparkling white fountain then turned onto Gwinnett, Cherry House just ahead. Holy cow, there really was a line of people on my sidewalk, and they were all looking up at something.

A bird? A plane? Actually, it really was Superman. Walker Boone stood on my porch roof, heaving boards and hammers and doing all those manly things needed to fix the gaping hole there. I didn't normally have gaping holes in Cherry House, but this one had come about the previous week when a snoopy reporter crashed through while looking for Boone in my bedroom when he was on the run. Right now, Boone had an appreciative audience, including me. I paused to catch my breath as Bruce Willis bounded my way.

"I missed you, too," I said, scratching between his ears. "You're all hot and sweaty, mister. Were you making goo-goo eyes at the cute poodle over on Calhoun again? You have to pace yourself, my friend. The heart can only take so much."

Avoiding the crowd, BW and I circled around to the back door. I needed to open the Fox on time in case any of those ogling ladies stayed around to buy something. More than likely they were there only to enjoy early-morning eye candy along with their Starbucks. Not that I blamed them. Too bad I couldn't charge for the privilege.

I got BW's daily veggie hot dog from the fridge. "Sit." BW did. "Hot dog." BW barked twice, earning his treat. BW never barked, and I wasn't big on telling him what to do; after all, he never ordered me around. This was just our little game.

I got what little cash I had from my own personal bank, which happened to be a Rocky Road ice cream container in the freezer. Keeping with the tempting treats theme, I sorted the bills into the Godiva candy box that served as my cash resister and wondered how long I could keep the Fox and Cherry House going with no customers. I hustled into the hallway and set the box on the green door laid across two chairs that I used as a checkout counter. I studied the stack of bills sitting at the end. The Abbott sisters weren't the only ones with cash flow problems, and the thought of Hollis actually getting his grimy real estate paws on my house and selling it because I couldn't afford to keep it made me sick.

I hobbled upstairs, trying to ignore my poor aching jogging muscles, then ducked into the bathroom. I peeled off my sweaty clothes, scrubbed, shampooed, then hurried into my bedroom for clean clothes, and—right there, staring in my window from his perch on the porch roof, was Walker Boone.

I stopped dead, my heart jumping into my throat. Boone was shirtless, I was clothesless, and he had . . . *the look*. Lord have mercy and saints preserve us, every woman with a pulse knew *the look*.

Chapter Five

"I have a shop to open," I said in a feeble voice that was the result of twelve years of Catholic education where hard work and responsibility had been drummed into my head and trumped everything else, including a severe hormone attack. "Later maybe?"

The smile joined *the look*, and Boone hitched his leg through the open bedroom window.

"Your fan club below will miss the view."

"But I like *this* view."

"Me?"

"Definitely you."

My heart raced, I couldn't breathe, and I felt a little dizzy as Boone slowly . . . oh so very slowly, with fire in his eyes and a devil smile on his lips . . . prowled my way. Any thought of *later* vanished. *Maybe* was not even an option. Boone took my left hand, then my right, pinning them behind my back as he kissed my lips and neck and lower, much lower. And twenty minutes later I opened the Prissy Fox with a big dopey grin on my face.

"It's about time you got here. We have plans and they don't include waiting for you," Anna said, her sister Bella right behind her as they hurried inside, their six-inch heels clacking on the hardwood floor. The women who'd watched Boone on the roof now stood on the front porch gazing into the shop, but they didn't enter. Why?

"I was . . . sort of busy," I said to Anna and Bella. I retrieved the candy box, then said to the maybe-customers huddled at the door, "The Prissy Fox is open for business. You all can come on in now. I won't bite."

"It's not *your* biting we're worried about," a lady in jeans said, still not budging from the doorway.

"We got business here with you," Bella interrupted. "And we're wanting to get it over with as fast as possible."

Anna and Bella were known far and wide as the gold digger sisters who'd married Clive and Crenshaw . . . though I could never remember who was married to whom. C and C were little old men with big houses and even bigger bank accounts. I didn't care about the sisters' trophy marriages, but I did care about the boutique they'd opened that sold designer clothes at a fraction of the cost. How could they do that? Well, they couldn't. The clothes were knockoffs bought from a sleazy company, and when the cops showed up at Anna's and Bella's Boutique one fine day, they weren't there to shop. Instead they closed them down.

The gold diggers faced the door, and Anna put two fingers in her mouth and let out a whistle that would have done any construction worker proud. "Attention, everyone out there on the porch. Listen up. Bella and I are here to say that the Prissy Fox does not have and never did have bedbugs."

My mouth opened and closed and nothing came out. "Wh . . . What?" I finally managed. "Why would anyone, any of *you*"—I waved my hand at the shoppers—"think the Prissy Fox had bedbugs?"

"Because," Bella offered in an exasperated huff, "Anna and I spread the rumor that you did, a big old infestation of the things. We wanted your customers to be our customers, and we got them, but now we have even bigger plans on the horizon and don't need your customers for that. We got our eye on a whole new demographic."

The gold diggers exchanged fist bumps as Bella raised her voice, saying to the crowd, "You can all shop at this"— she made a sour face as she glanced around—"place. So come on in, get out those little old cell phones, start tweeting and texting and messaging and spreading the word like you all do. The Prissy Fox is alive and well and open and there are no bugs and there never have been. It was just a little joke between friends, nothing more."

I wasn't laughing. The customers at the door exchanged looks again. The gal in jeans tipped her foot inside the foyer as if testing pool water.

"That's it, my little shoppers," Anna said in a singsong voice. "Come on in, all is well. See, Bella and I are in here, and you can trust that if there were a hint of a bug, any kind of bug, we'd be running for our lives and screaming our heads off."

Two older ladies in summer floral dresses slowly followed

the gal in jeans. They inched forward, other shoppers now following. Their eyes darted side to side, on high alert for anything crawling about. In unison they shuffled into what had once been my living room before I converted the first floor of Cherry House into a consignment shop.

Racks of gently worn evening and garden party dresses now hung on one side of the room; jackets, blouses, and tops adorned the other side. I'd kept the lovely crystal chandelier that came with the house along with the old Oriental rug and blue drapes pulled back to add to the prissy part of the fox. Shoes were arranged in the back, and a lovely mahogany table and chairs that once upon a time in my married life had served as a dining room table now displayed jewelry, purses, and hats.

Bella slapped two papers on the green door counter and fished a pen from her pink and totally adorable (and expensive) bag. "Okay, we apologized and set things right and even got shoppers in your place, so now we're done here. Sign these and we'll be on our way."

Still in shock, I watched the customers, real live customers, milling around, picking out clothes, trying on shoes and hats and scarves.

"Yoohoo." Anna waved her hand in front of my face, snapping her fingers to get my attention. "Eyes on me. We don't have all day, you know. Sign the blasted papers, will ya, and get this over with."

I looked at the heading on the paper with the words printed there finally registering. "Liars Anonymous? What the heck is Liars Anonymous?"

"Mostly it's a total pain in the rear," Anna huffed. "But it's better than jail, and we want to put this behind us as fast as possible so we can get on with our plans. Our lawyers are working on straightening things out, and Clive and Crenshaw pulled strings with some old fart judge they go fishing with. Now Bella and I have to do this stupid twelve-step program and attend meetings, and there's community service involved, like driving decrepit old people around who can't drive themselves. We never thought we could get into trouble for having a little fun like opening our boutique. We just opened it in the first place 'cause we're tired of everyone thinking we're nothing but dumb blonde trophy wives. We're a lot more than that, you know."

Like felons, I added to myself as Anna pushed the papers closer and handed me a pen. "Put your name at the bottom with the date."

"So your boutique is closed for good," I said as I wrote.

Bella parked her perfectly manicured hand on her perfect left hip, which was covered by a really nice cream silk skirt that cost more than I'd make all day. "You just don't get it, do you? How do you think you got your customers back? If our boutique were still open, no one would be here shopping in this hovel, that's for sure."

I parked my unmanicured hand on my not-so-perfect hip. "Meaning they'd be at your place buying knockoff junk?"

"Ancient history. We have other ideas—bigger, better ones." Anna snapped up the papers, stuck out her tongue at me, and the gold digger sisters left the building.

Lies and bedbugs? I'd nearly lost my business because of a malicious rumor and designer names glued in crappy clothes? How could those stuck-up witches do such a thing? I considered running after their shiny black Escalade and ripping up those papers and letting Anna and Bella rot in their twelve-step program. Then I heard hammering overhead. Boone! Not Clive, not Crenshaw, but my totally divine fiancé.

Forget the gold diggers. I was too much in love to think about them, and I hadn't been in love in years. Hollis had not been great at *in love*. He hadn't even been mediocre at *in love* . . . unless you were talking about how he felt about himself. But Boone . . . the man was perfection. Boone made *in love* a true art form. Mozart could compose symphonies, Shakespeare pen sonnets. How'd I get so lucky to be in love with Boone? I had no idea, but I promised myself I was not going to screw this up, no matter what.

I wrote up a sale for a really ugly green blouse I'd never thought I'd get rid of, then took in a group of nice designer clothes from a new consigner with terrific taste. Social media was the best of times and for sure the worst. Spreading rumors of bugs had kept customers away, and now tweets and messages of bargains were bringing customers back.

"What catastrophe did Thing One and Thing Two bring on this time around?" Auntie KiKi wanted to know as she swished into the Fox, her red dancing skirt floating around her ankles. "I just finished up a lesson with Aldeen Ross to get her ready for the policeman's ball and spotted the 'I M FAB' license plate on the Escalade at the curb. Gave me shivers just knowing they were in the neighborhood."

Aldeen was the local police detective KiKi and I ran into more times than any of us wanted. She was short and sometimes plump, depending on recent exercise and doughnut consumption. We'd bonded over dead bodies, trips to the Cakery Bakery, and hunting the bad guys—not necessarily in that order. Aldeen was more friend than foe, but the law was the law and she had the badge and took it seriously.

"Honey," KiKi went on as she gazed around, "what are all these people doing in here?"

"Shopping. The gold diggers came to apologize for the bedbug rumor." I looked at Auntie KiKi; she looked at me and, without missing a beat, hung up a jacket to be priced.

"You knew!"

"Everyone knew." KiKi buttoned a taupe sweater. "But we didn't have any idea how to fix the lie. The more we tweeted that the Prissy Fox was fine and the rumors were false, the more the slimy sisters insisted it was true, and of course they had just opened that boutique that had everyone talking. We didn't tell you because you had enough on your plate trying to save Walker from the gallows."

KiKi rolled her eyes up toward the hammering. "And now you have your very own handyman, and my guess is he's mighty handy in more ways than one around here, if you get my drift."

I blushed, then my right foot tripped over my left and thank heavens a high school kid in jeans and a blue plaid shirt came to the counter then, getting my mind off Boone and back on business, at least for the moment.

"Are you looking for a tux for the prom?" I said to the teen. A tux was about the only reason a boy this age would venture into the Fox unless his mother dragged him here kicking and whining. "I have a few you can try on."

The teen took a Snickers from his pocket, dropped it on the counter with a solid *thunk*, and glared at Auntie KiKi. "You stole one of these right out of my Grandpa Willie's pocket. I saw you do it, then asked around and found out who you were." The kid took out his cell phone. "I have a video of the whole Snickers thing right here. Want to see yourself? I can post it real fast on YouTube and Instagram."

KiKi jutted her chin and squared her shoulders. "I did not steal; I swapped. That video will show that I left a very nice Clif bar that is so much healthier. It was more a work of mercy."

"Grandpa's dead," the kid said as I kicked KiKi under the counter and added a "Did you really just say that?" look. The kid's lower lip quivered, his shoulders sagged, and he choked back a sob. "I loved Grandpa. I was named after him, and I promised him I'd get him a Snickers to take to heaven. He was allergic to peanuts and loved 'em as much as I do." The kid sounded more little boy than teen. "Now you made me break my promise and tomorrow they're going to bury Grandpa without the Snickers. You made me a liar, and it doesn't matter to you but it does to me." The kid's voice got louder, and customers started to stare. "I never lied to my grandpa. Never!"

65

"We'll fix it," I blurted before a barrage of "Don't shop the Prissy Fox because they're a bunch of grave robbers" tweets and messages flooded the media. "My Auntie KiKi here had a weak moment is all. Hey, we've all had weak chocolate moments at one time or another where we just couldn't help ourselves, haven't we?"

"I don't much like chocolate," Willie Junior sniffed.

"Okay, but I bet you like computer games and maybe you've gone a little crazy to get a new one that just came out and . . . and . . ." I was getting nowhere with this tactic. "What if my auntie and I put the Snickers back in your grandpa's pocket tonight? Then he'll have it for tomorrow." I added an angelic smile.

A customer came to the counter. "Is everything okay here?" she asked the teen. "You look so sad."

"He can't find a tux for the prom," I lied with a smile. "And there's a twenty-percent discount on those boots you've got in your hand." Nothing distracted like a nice discount.

I made the sale, then turned back to Willie. "So, are we okay here? We make the Snickers drop and all is good?"

The kid ran the back of his hand across his runny nose. "How do I know you're not lying to me, huh? Anyone who's a no-good Snickers stealer is a no-good Snickers liar."

I snapped a white straw flower off a purse headed for the donate bin. "We'll put this flower in that spray of white roses across your grandpa's casket. When you see it tomorrow you'll know we've been there and the Snickers is safe inside just like you want. Is it a deal?"

Junior gave me a hard look head to toe. "There's

something else. I know who you are and not just from the funeral. I saw your picture on Facebook with your dog and the cops." He pointed down at BW napping at the foot of the steps. "You're that lady who helped get the person who killed that rich dude they found naked in the bathtub a couple weeks ago. I want you to find out who killed Grandpa."

"Look, I know you're hurting," I soothed in my mommy voice that I usually reserved for BW. "But your grandpa had an asthma attack. He was old." *And he was cranky and obnoxious and if mean-to-the-bone caused death, he would have bought the farm years ago.*

"It wasn't asthma. His skin was blotchy. I could see it under all that makeup they had caked on him. Grandpa had bad allergies like me. I tried to talk to the cops, but they just said I was overwrought, whatever that is. My mom won't even listen because she just wants his money, so she's glad he's gone."

Junior held up his phone, his eyes more steely than sad. "Put the candy back and find who killed Grandpa Willie or I hit 'Send' to your favorite social media outlet."

"But your grandpa is getting buried tomorrow. The candy's doable but the other part takes time."

"Well, you better hurry up or else." Willie Junior turned and ran out the door.

"Sweet Jesus in heaven," KiKi gasped. "We're being blackmailed by Justin Bieber."

"How could you get us into this mess?" I growled under my breath, trying not to draw attention. "If this gets out, my business is ruined . . . again!"

"You? What about me? I'll be kicked out of the country club and the Daughters of the South will start a rumor that I have relatives in Ohio or one of those Yankee places. And Putter will blow a gasket that I'm eating sugar. If we don't come up with something right quick, that little pipsqueak will hit the send button like he said and we'll both be mincemeat. I hate mincemeat. I say we steal his phone."

"A teen and his phone are never parted. They sleep with the things under their pillow."

"Then we'll just have to call Mercedes." KiKi's eyes brightened. "She does all the makeup at the Slumber and that makes her a dead-person professional. We get her to write a note to Junior that it was asthma that killed Grandpa and not some allergy. 'To whom it may concern: Willie croaked 'cause he had it coming'?"

"*KiKi!*"

"Well, something like that. This is almost enough to make me give up chocolate." A sly grin slowly made its way across KiKi's lips, her gaze drifting to the Snickers on the counter. "Almost."

"You can't be serious."

"Honey, unless it has to do with family I'm never serious. Mostly I just drink martinis and have fun." Then my dear auntie snagged the Snickers on the counter, gave me a wink, and danced her way out the door.

Chapter Six

"Where are you going?" Boone mumbled as I slid out from under his warm protective arm into the cold loneliness of my bedroom. "It's the middle of the night."

"It's just going on ten." I nudged Bruce Willis at the end of the bed and he let out a sleepy groan. "I need to walk BW. I think he's having bad doggy dreams." *Mostly bad dreams of me kicking him out of bed.* I pulled on the jeans I'd dropped in my frantic haste to get into bed two hours ago . . . not that there was any sleep being had.

Boone pried open one eye. "I'll come with."

"You worked all day fixing my roof, thank you very much."

The moonlight shining in through the window caught the twinkle in his eyes. "You already thanked me for that."

"I'll bring back sweet potato pound cake from Mate Factors. They're open late tonight. Then I can thank you all over again."

"Don't be gone long. I'm a hungry man and I'm not just

talking about cake." Boone let out a soft sleepy laugh and rolled over. I got BW's leash off the dresser, hooked him up, and dragged him off the bed. We started down the hall, heading for the steps with doggy nails tapping against the worn hardwood floor.

"Trust me, this isn't what I want to be doing either, and you can thank your auntie with a Snickers fetish for this late-night disturbance. I know I didn't exactly tell your daddy the whole truth about this walk we're taking, but I'm kind of in a tight spot here. If I said I had an appointment with a corpse he'd insist on coming, and how many dead bodies can a guy take before he gets tired of it all?"

BW snorted.

"This is my last dead-person gig, no matter what. I have no idea where the heck Bonnie Sue is and that's fine by me, and maybe Mercedes really can convince Willie the Second his granddad died of natural causes. After tonight this dead-people thing is over and I'll go wedding dress shopping like a normal bride-to-be and all will be right with the world. How do you feel about being ring bearer?"

I snagged my denim jacket from the closet and closed the white paint-chipped door behind me. BW led the way down the sidewalk scented with cherry blossoms in full bloom as a breeze tousled the branches, sending white petals swirling around us in the silvery moonlight. In my very biased opinion, Savannah was always lovely, but a spring night like this was pure magic. "It smells like heaven out here," I said to BW.

"Talking to a dog?" Auntie KiKi drew up beside me.

"He's a very wise dog." I gave KiKi a quick once-over. "And why are you wearing your pink robe?"

With a flourish, she whipped off the terry cloth, tossed it into the bushes, and flung her arms in the air. "Ta-da! Now I'm badass-in-black girl with Putter's golf jacket and the yoga pants that his size-two sister gave me for Christmas. I gave her two pounds of pralines, so we're even. The robe's camouflage in case Putter caught me being up and about and started asking questions, though I got to say there isn't much chance of that happening. The man's off to a golf outing over in Augusta tomorrow, and to gear himself up for the occasion he's sawing logs to *Golf Is a Many Splendored Thing* blaring in his headphones."

"He really sleeps with headphones?"

"It's golf, honey; the reality ship sailed years ago." KiKi nodded at the street. "The Batmobile's gassed and ready for action. We can pick up a replacement Snickers on our way to the Slumber—and don't you be giving me that superior look. You know if I hadn't snagged the Snickers off the counter this afternoon, you would have done it yourself."

I sat BW in the back seat of the Beemer with the window down so he could stick his head out and look totally adorable in case we drove by the poodle's house. I took shotgun.

"I guess Walker isn't coming along?" KiKi asked as I closed the door. "You didn't tell him about Willie or the blackmail?"

Another burst of guilt slithered up my spine. "Do you see Boone sitting between us? Because that's exactly where

Savannah's version of John Wayne rescuing the damsel would be if he got wind of yet another body. And if he knew about the blackmail . . ." KiKi and I exchanged "God help us" looks and made the sign of the cross.

"But I've decided this is it on the dead-body front. I'm going cold turkey. Blue Hat Lady has vanished, getting the sisters off the hook, and that's fine by me. After the Snickers drop tonight and the dead-from-asthma letter from Mercedes gets delivered to Junior, I'm out. If any other lifeless remains flop across my path for any reason, I'm shutting my eyes and stepping right over the prone carcass and not looking back. I'm getting married, and I'm living happily every ever with the man I love!"

"We'll die of boredom."

"There is that."

KiKi pulled the Beemer to the curb in front of Mates. It was one of those local Savannah hole-in-the-wall places with a green door, cute yellow ruffled curtains in the windows, and food to die for. We got three helpings of sweet potato cake to go and picked up the Snickers and a chew toy for BW at the twenty-four-hour CVS. Then we did the stop-and-go thing, hitting every traffic light all the way up Broad Street.

"Not much action tonight," KiKi said while pulling into the Slumber's parking lot, empty except for Mercedes's pink Caddy next to the building. "Least there are a few lights on so the place doesn't look so . . . dead."

"Funeral humor? Really? Do you have to?"

"Like Cher says, 'Honesty makes me feel powerful in a

difficult world,' and there's nothing more honest than being dead. We can all learn from the book of Cher."

Right after college Auntie KiKi had been a roadie for Cher; she'd never quite left the stage and had been spouting unsolicited Cher-isms to the rest of Savannah ever since. KiKi, BW, and I headed for the back door marked "Deliveries," and I turned the brass handle.

"Mercedes said she'd be working on a customer and that we should come on in. And can you please refrain from dead-people humor? It's been a long day."

KiKi did the zip-across-the-lips thing and gave a little two-finger promise salute. We went inside, leaving the traffic noise behind us. Beige carpet cushioned the floor, and dimmed recessed lighting dotted the ceiling down the long hall. "Gives a whole new meaning to dead quiet," KiKi whispered. She held up her hands in surrender. "Not my fault; it just slipped out all by itself. And besides, we all need to realize death is a part of life and not get so freaked out about it like we—"

"Hey, ladies," Mercedes said, sticking her head out a doorway. KiKi screamed, tripped over BW, and sank against the wall, sliding down into a limp puddle. BW licked KiKi's face and Mercedes hustled over, her white official-looking smock flapping behind her. She knelt down next to KiKi. "What happened?"

I patted KiKi's cheek. "Comedy Central took a turn for the real."

"I think she's coming around." Mercedes smiled my way. "And she's not the only one who's come around. I hear tell you're marrying Mr. Boone. You done landed yourself the white whale, and with there being no whale in sight, my guess is you sort of forgot to tell him you were stopping by to drop off candy to a dead person?"

"I don't want Boone to worry."

"Or for him to go hiring bodyguards to protect your skinny self?" Mercedes was a great friend and sometimes my breaking-and-entering buddy. Back in the day she'd run a house of questionable reputation that was more dating service than the other kind of service. Now she was a respectable housekeeper by day, mortician beautician by night, and she had half of Savannah fighting over her for both reasons. Mercedes was a woman of many talents.

I steadied KiKi with one hand and fished the Snickers out of Old Yeller with the other. "Here's the deal," I said to Mercedes. "Willie's grandson made a video of KiKi and Grand Theft Snickers, and he's threatening to YouTube the performance if we don't get Grandpa's candy back in his pocket. You don't look surprised."

Mercedes rolled her shoulders. "Girl, you'd be plumb blown away by the stuff people want to be buried with around here. Hunting rifles, fishing gear . . . last week Sally Jacobs at the ripe old age of ninety-two was buried with a can of whipped cream and a picture of George Clooney. I don't even want to be thinking about it."

Mercedes nodded at the hallway. "You're lucky that old Willie's in one of our cheapo non-sealing caskets. The family laid him out in an expensive one; then they went and took a kickback to get him buried in the cheaper model. It happens.

The moral of the story is, don't tick off your family or they get back at you in the end, one way or the other. Willie's in what we call the limbo room where we keep caskets between hearse and heaven, if you know what I mean. A little funeral levity."

KiKi wobbled to her feet and managed to give me a superior look. "See there, even the pros do it. Dark humor is the sign of an intellectual mind."

"Or a demented one," I said under my breath.

The three of us followed Mercedes down another dim hall, and I pushed open the door at the end. It was cooler here, the AC cranked low and the floor not carpeted. Streetlight slipped in through the blinds, casting the whole room in stripes of grays and black.

"We need a flashlight," Mercedes said. "The windows here face the street, and we don't need to be drawing attention at midnight to overhead lights flashing on at the mortuary. It gives people passing by the creeps, and they go calling the cops thinking we got the *Walking Dead* going on for real."

Before my days of tripping across bodies, I'd never had a flashlight, but lately there always seemed to be a need. I reached in Old Yeller, grabbed the light, and clicked it on. The beam reflected off the stone floor, walls, and the casket waiting to get loaded up the next day. Mercedes slid the spray of white roses with a gold Styrofoam cross off the top of the casket, and I added the straw rose I'd brought along. "It's a sign," I said to Mercedes. "To prove to the kid that the Snickers is inside like we promised. He didn't trust us."

"And people say kids these days aren't smart." Mercedes grinned, her teeth white against her dark skin and the night around us.

I nodded at KiKi. "Okay, let's get this over with. Open it up."

"With my arthritis setting in like it is . . ." KiKi rubbed her shoulder and hunched over, though she'd never hunched a day in her life. "How can you ask your dear old auntie to do such a thing as lift a big heavy coffin lid?"

"You rumba," I grumbled. "You tango, do the tarantella with the greatest of ease. You can open a blasted box and you're the one who got us into this."

KiKi folded her arms and tapped her foot. I turned to Mercedes.

"Uh-uh. Don't go looking at me, no way. Once I close 'em up inside, my job is done and over with. Besides, everyone knows it's bad juju to go opening up a casket. Ever think of how DeeDee McCormak got to be called old prune face? Word has it she wanted one last look at her Tommy, opened the lid, and went totally gray right there on the spot. That woman shriveled up like a worm on a hot stove. Count me out."

"Well, that coffin isn't going to open itself, so it's rock, paper, scissors," KiKi said. "Like it or not, we're here now, and that makes us all in this together. On three."

I held out my right hand, KiKi and Mercedes doing the same. I counted, and since rock beat scissors and scissors beat paper, I was totally screwed.

"This is not fair." I stared at the long amber box with the flashlight reflecting off the shiny surface. "A shriveled bride? What will Boone think?"

Mercedes wrestled the gold cross off the spray of roses and wedged it into the front of my half-zipped jacket. "There you are, honey. You're done protected by plastic and the good Lord above. Nothing can beat that." She slapped me on the back. "Go get 'em."

I handed KiKi the flashlight, tucked my fingers under the lip of the lid, and pried up. "It's . . . really . . . heavy."

"That's so they can't get out," Mercedes said with a straight face. The lid creaked open, the flashlight exposing prone Willie bit by bit.

"He looks kind of sick," Auntie KiKi said to Mercedes.

"And that would be a vast improvement over his present situation. I had a devil of a time spiffing him up and trying to smooth out some of those wrinkles. Face like a road map."

KiKi handed me the Snickers. I held it between a shaky thumb and forefinger, plucked the Clif bar from the breast pocket of Willie's blue poly suit, then slid in the good stuff. "We should say a prayer. It just doesn't seem right to shut him back up and do nothing."

"Fine." KiKi cleared her throat. "Lord," KiKi started, eyes closed and head bowed. "Old Willie's your problem now and not ours. Amen and thank you very much for taking him off our hands like you did, but we sure wish you'd made it sooner rather than later as the man was a big old pimple on our backsides to be sure." KiKi cut her eyes from me to Mercedes, both of us staring at her in disbelief. "I said amen and thank you."

Mercedes shivered. "Heaven sakes, just close the lid before we get struck dead where we stand and there's nothing but a pile of ashes."

"Except . . ." I held the lid open. "We sort of got a situation." Auntie KiKi nodded to Willie. "There's a little matter of the grandson thinking granddad here didn't exactly die of asthma but that he was . . . well . . . murdered."

Mercedes's eyes rounded to the size of goose eggs. "Do you two stay awake nights dreaming this stuff up or what?"

"I'm sure the kid's got it all wrong," KiKi pushed on. "So I . . . we . . . just need you—"

"Me!"

"'Cause you're our friend and all. All you got to do is tell the kid that granddad died because it was his time."

Mercedes shoved back her bangs. "Do you see *coroner* written up here on my forehead? I'm just the nab 'em, slab 'em, and fab 'em girl around here. That means folks come to me and I make them look more fabulous dead than they were alive. The reason they went and got themselves dead and departed is not in my job description."

KiKi held out her hands. "Just meet with the grandson, have a milkshake and some fries, my treat, and tell him Willie was a victim of natural causes. Think of it as public service for a grandson grieving for the beloved grandpa he was named after. Touches the heart, don't you think?"

Mercedes struck a pose and tipped her head. She didn't say no right off, so that had to be a good thing, right?

"I want to be a bridesmaid. If I'm going to be part of all this here crazy stuff that's going on, I want to be part of the good stuff. I want to pick out pretty dresses and go to Bleu-Belle Bridal over there on Abercorn and drink champagne that they bring out to you on a little silver tray and treat you all special 'cause you're getting married and about to spend a boatload of money on dresses you only wear once. I look real good in fuchsia and something off the shoulder to show off the girls here." Mercedes thrust out her chest. "I do have mighty perky girls, if I do say so myself."

"I . . . I was thinking small wedding?"

"I just love weddings and never been in one." Mercedes glanced back to Willie in the coffin, then to KiKi, then back to Willie.

"Well, now you *are* going to be in a really terrific wedding," KiKi gushed, putting her arm around Mercedes, who was still staring intently at the coffin. "I tell you, Reagan doesn't know what she's talking about with that small-wedding stuff. Who in Savannah ever heard of a small wedding? Such things just aren't done around here. She needs to be having a big fancy Southern affair with all Walker's friends and her friends and her customers and her mamma being a judge, and I do believe fuchsia will be just dandy."

KiKi gave me a pleading look and added, "So now all we got to do is close up this here casket in front of us and tomorrow you can talk to Willie the Second and tell him granddad is at peace with the Lord and the angels singing above and—"

"Wait . . . a . . . minute." Mercedes put her hand up, and this time she held the lid open. She snagged the flashlight from Auntie KiKi and aimed it close. "Well, I'll be a monkey's uncle," she said in a breathy whisper.

"Does that take the place of being a bridesmaid?" I asked, KiKi giving me the auntie evil eye.

"Look right there." Mercedes pointed behind Willie's ear. "It's a rash. You know, I saw that before but didn't think anything of it. I just added another layer of makeup to cover the places you could see 'cause the new owner around here is having a hissy about wasting money. With the medical examiner giving Willie the dead-from-natural-causes stamp of approval when he was brought in, I figured all was well. Over there at Sleepy Pines they didn't find Willie till that morning. He was sort of bluish when they brought him in here. Bodies tend to lose color with no blood swishing around inside."

Mercedes aimed the light closer still. "Willie had an inhaler clutched in his hand to the point where I had to pry his cold stiff fingers off the thing—like he was hanging onto it for dear life. It said to use at bedtime, so I guess he took a blast before he went to sleep each night. That along with a history of asthma adds up to an asthma attack. Embalming pinks up the skin, making the rash more noticeable. I'm no doctor, but asthma does not cause a rash. Allergic reactions cause rashes. I doubt if Willie did this on purpose, so that means . . ."

"An unfortunate accident?" I ventured.

"That maybe had some help." Auntie KiKi harrumphed. "I hear they watch the dietary restrictions real careful over at the Pines. All his life Willie was a fast-talking, double-dealing scalawag, and my guess is somebody had enough and bumped him off just like the kid said. I say we call the cops and let them figure things out. You know, this is working out fine. Willie Junior will be so indebted to us for getting to the truth he won't be posting on YouTube. We need to celebrate and go on over to Jen's and Friends and order a round of strawberry martinis. I could do with a martini or two."

Auntie KiKi pulled out her cell and tapped in 9 and 1, but I snapped it away before she hit the next 1. "You know that part about somebody having enough of Willie and his dealings? Well, you can include Elsie and Annie Fritz. Willie got the sisters involved in some kind of con, and they were nearly doing the happy dance at his funeral. They work at the Pines and had to know about Willie's allergy and asthma, so that gives them motive, means, and the opportunity to do him in. That puts them on the let's-off-Willie list."

KiKi snatched back the phone and held it tight. "Look, if Willie lived up to his reputation, there's got to be others who wanted him permanently pushing up daisies. Maybe the sisters are innocent."

"Of course they're innocent, but the cops may think otherwise once they start connecting the dots. Willie took the sisters for a bundle."

KiKi yanked the Snickers from Willie's pocket and ripped off the wrapper. "This here is a full-out emergency, and I never met a situation that a two-olive martini or chocolate didn't make better." She caught a peanut on her tongue, her eyes starting to focus. "Okay, that's better." She squared her shoulders and smacked her palm against her forehead. "My neurotransmitters are firing up again to make sense of all this. I get that we can't call the cops because the sisters are involved, and I get that we can't be putting old Willie in the ground because that rash proves he was murdered in the first place, just like Willie Junior thinks. So the way I see it, all we have to do is reschedule Willie's sendoff till after we figure out who did him in for real. Once a body is planted, it's difficult to get it dug up, especially if the relatives protest. With that nice inheritance in her hand, Willie's daughter would put up a fight for sure and we'll never get the body back."

I gave KiKi a long, hard look. "Define reschedule."

"The old fart's all stuffed and mounted, so storage isn't an issue."

"Storage?"

Eyes gleaming, KiKi turned to Mercedes. "Here's what we'll do. You tell the family there's a problem at Bonaventure Cemetery with the backhoe breaking down and not able to dig Willie's final resting arrangements. The remaining Fishbines won't care two figs about that since they can be heading off to the lawyers earlier than planned for the reading of the will. Reagan here impersonates a secretary from the Slumber and informs the cemetery there's an issue with a relative coming to pay his last respects, so Willie's on hold for few days. I tell Willie Junior we're hot on the case and to give his itchy trigger finger a rest and not hit 'Send.'"

KiKi held her hands high as if she'd just kicked a touchdown. "Problem solved."

"Are you out of your ever-loving mind?" Mercedes screeched, stomping around the room and waving her arms like a possessed chicken. "A problem is having pie for dessert when you're on a diet or wanting to buy purple shoes when what you really need are boring black ones. If we get caught hiding a body, it's the three of us sharing a cell. Honey, I've been there before in my previous life, and it's no fun. And there's the fact that we're sending real bad vibes out into the universe by abducting a corpse. You know deep down inside this whole sordid affair is going to come back and bite us on the bare bottom."

KiKi pointed a stiff finger at Willie all snuggled in his blue satin slumber chamber. "If you ask me, it's not like we're doing anything wrong here. Fact is, I'd say we're doing something right in finding the killer, so that's good vibes we're sending out. Just think of this as Willie taking a detour for a few days. I ask you, now, who wouldn't welcome a little detour at this particular juncture of their life—or nonlife as the case may be? All we got to do is figure out where Willie's detouring to." KiKi looked from me to Mercedes. "And I just happen to have one doozy of an idea."

Chapter Seven

"If we lathered it in Crisco and shoved like the dickens, it still wouldn't fit," Mercedes said, the four of us staring at the end of the casket sticking out the trunk of the Beemer.

Auntie KiKi had moved the car next to the delivery door at the House of Eternal Slumber so that the Beemer was in the shadows and we wouldn't have to roll a casket perched on a cart clear across the parking lot.

"So what should we do now? And we better think real fast," Mercedes said in a panicky voice.

I snagged a brown tarp draped over a mound of mulch. "We wrap the end of the coffin in this and use BW's leash to hold it in place. I'll tie my yellow scarf at the end so what we're hauling looks legal."

"And then I'll park the Beemer in my garage," Auntie said. "I'll tell Putter that the car manual says BMWs need to rest every twenty thousand miles. He's a mighty fine cardio guy, none better, but he's not exactly a car expert."

"You want him to believe that *you* read a manual?" I gave KiKi a "Get real" look.

"If I add in that there's pot roast for dinner, the man will forget anything else I said. Pot roast is the abracadabra of the male species; say it and everything else vanishes."

Mercedes held the tarp in place while I wrapped the leash. KiKi added the scarf, a smile breaking across her lips as she took a step back. "Looks good to me. You know, I think this little plan of mine is going to work just fine and dandy."

"What's going to work fine and dandy?" Aldeen Ross wanted to know as she drew up beside Mercedes. KiKi grabbed my hand, I grabbed hers, and the only thing that kept us from fainting dead away was fascination with Aldeen's electric green nightshirt with "I See Guilty People" on the front in dayglow pink. Neither of us wanted to miss that or the police cruiser slippers strobing red and blue when she walked.

"What are you doing here?" Mercedes asked as her lovely mahogany complexion faded to latte brown.

"I got myself one of those app things for when the 'Hot Now' light goes on at Krispy Kreme over on Abercorn." Aldeen flashed her iPhone as she licked her lips. "See there, the app is blinking, which means a new batch of doughnuts is ready from the oven. I was heading on over and saw you all back here. I didn't want to be missing out on the fun." Aldeen slapped the tarp with a solid *whomp*. "What are you hauling at this hour? Dead bodies?"

Mercedes's laugh sounded like the Wicked Witch of the West. "It's . . . it's folding tables. Yep, lots of folding tables that the Slumber loans out to future customers." She hitched her head toward KiKi.

"Hey, just who you calling a customer?" KiKi snorted.

"The tables are for my shower," I blurted as Aldeen started to peel back the tarp.

"And I'm in the wedding," Mercedes said in a hurry as the tarp got inched up. "And . . . and Reagan here wants you to be in her wedding too. She told me herself."

"I did?"

Mercedes jabbed me in the back.

"I did!"

"And it's going to be a big wedding," Mercedes babbled on. "And we're going to pick out dresses out there at Bleu-Belle Bridal where they serve you champagne on the little silver tray and all kinds of stuff."

"Me? In your wedding?" Aldeen squealed, dropping the tarp back in place. Her eyes teared and she ran to me, the little red-and-blue lights strobing faster, and was that a siren sound now coming from the slippers? Aldeen threw her arms around me and hugged tight, making it hard to breathe—or maybe the gasping part was relief that the tarp was back in place.

"I've never been in a wedding before," Aldeen sniffed. "This will be a first for me."

"Girl, let me tell you, this here is a night of firsts." Mercedes retied the tarp. "I was thinking fuchsia for the bridesmaids' dresses. Don't you think fuchsia's a great color? I just know you'd look amazing in fuchsia."

Aldeen hugged tighter. "And gold shoes. Aren't gold shoes the best thing ever? Always wanted an excuse to buy gold shoes and now I have one."

"And there's no way you should be on a doughnut run tonight," KiKi said to Aldeen. "You want to look great in your new fuchsia dress."

Aldeen held me at arm's length, a determined look in her eyes. "I'm going on a crash diet. Maybe I'll meet someone. Weddings are great for meeting guys. I know, you'll just have to invite that new coroner the city hired on. I tell you, he's a real hunk and I think he's got his eye on me."

"And I'm sure he does." KiKi hooked her arm through Aldeen's and steered her back to the blue Honda parked at the curb. "Every wedding needs a coroner, and I'll teach you the rumba tomorrow at our dance lesson. I bet you can get in a workout tonight so you can get that diet on track."

Aldeen giggled, then bear-hugged KiKi. She climbed into the Honda, gave us a thumbs-up, and barreled down Broad Street.

"A coroner?" I choked. "At my wedding? I don't even know this guy. What if he drives his coroner-mobile to the wedding?"

"Better the coroner than having that wedding in a cell-block, you in jumpsuit orange, and Walker smuggling a hacksaw in the cake." Mercedes climbed in her Caddy and stuck her head out the window. "All I know is that this here is going to be a wedding to remember."

It was after midnight by the time BW and I helped KiKi berth the Beemer in the garage. In case Uncle Putter got curious about the car needing a rest and peeked in the garage window, we piled boxes around the back to hide the protruding casket. I then threatened my dear auntie with physical harm if she ever ate another Snickers, gave her a kiss on the cheek, and BW and I headed for home.

"Where have you been?" Boone mumbled as I crawled into bed. He snuggled up behind me all warm and sexy. "Did BW decide to walk to China?"

"I left the cake downstairs for breakfast, we're having a big wedding and Mercedes and Aldeen Ross are bridesmaids. They're wearing hot pink with gold shoes and a coroner is on the guest list."

Boone didn't move, but I could feel his body tense beside me.

"And we'll have pot roast at the reception."

"Pot roast?" I could feel Boone's mouth soften into a smile against my neck as he planted a lingering kiss, sending lightning bolts down my spine. He draped his big arm around me, drawing me close. "It's going to be a really great wedding."

* * *

"What did Walker say about where you were last night?" KiKi wanted to know as I handed her a cup of coffee that I'd brought out onto my front porch. We sat on the top step with the sun just tipping over St. John's steeples, a perfect breeze stirring the trees.

"Stealing a corpse isn't exactly pillow talk," I mumbled, still half asleep. "Thank heavens Boone left early this morning to start relocating his office to his house and moving his personal stuff into my house. The good news is he's okay with the big wedding."

KiKi winked at me over the rim of her coffee cup. "And we're having pot roast at the reception?"

"Along with biscuits and gravy—Boone just loves biscuits and gravy. And to add to the morning crazy, I called Bonaventure Cemetery. I thought I'd just leave a message on their machine, but they answered. I guess the line between day and night gets a little blurry when dealing with dead people. Anyway, the man said Willie has to take up residence in five days or they sell his hole to the next on the list, meaning you get Willie as a permanent guest forevermore in your garage. We now have less than a week to find out who else wanted Willie out of the way. For some reason, everything leads back to Sleepy Pines, so I've been thinking we should probably start snooping around there first."

I took a sip of coffee and peered at KiKi over the rim. "The only thing is, I don't think the Pines group will be all that willing to spill their guts to an outsider."

KiKi stopped midsip, her gaze fusing with mine. "Outsider?"

"We need an insider, and before you blow a gasket, hear me out. Uncle Putter's gone on that golf trip, so what if you sort of sprain your ankle? You can't take care of yourself in that big house with all those steps and you'll need help getting around."

KiKi plopped her mug down on the porch with a solid *thud*, coffee sloshing over the top. "I knew this day would come—you're putting me in an old folks' home!"

"Willie's room is available."

"You want me to stay in a dead guy's room!"

"Well, he's not using it any longer, and it was your Snickers addiction that got us into this mess."

"I can just tell that I'm going to hear about that Snickers for the rest of my life."

"If I have my way, you are, and so here's your chance at making things right. And with you having a sprained ankle, no one will think it's suspicious you're not driving the Batmobile, so it can stay in the garage. And you won't have to cook—think of that! You hate to cook. You're the bomb at canasta. You could be the canasta queen and get your picture added to all the ones in the hallway at the Pines, and you'll be waited on hand and foot, and you can use Uber to drive you around."

"I love to cook; you're the one who hates it and eats nothing but junk, and I want a hot driver. Tall, dark, Italian, who sings opera. Something Puccini would be nice."

"This is Savannah, not the Amalfi Coast, and where is all this coming from?"

"I was watching *Moonstruck* 'cause I wanted to see Cher again and decided I like opera. Take it or leave it. Hot Italian opera singer or forget your great idea." KiKi stuck her nose in the air and folded her arms.

"Okay, okay, and I'll cover your dancing lessons, and"—I gritted my teeth and sucked in air—"I'll take care of . . ." *Devil cat.* ". . . Precious." KiKi cut her eyes my way, a sly grin sliding across her lips. A queasy feeling pooled in my gut. "You played me?"

"Well, the *Moonstruck* part is true enough, and the Pines has happy hour with Mr. Jim making the best three-olive martini in all Savannah. They got a deal cooked up with Spa Bleu over there on Bull Street, and I've been wanting to go for months now. I hear they got a massage guy to die for."

"Where is all this coming from? You're a married woman, for Pete's sake."

"I'm just looking is all, and the way I see it, it's good for my heart. It gets it pumped up and going, kind of like aerobics but a lot more fun than going to the gym, I can promise you that. Aldeen's due for her rumba session any minute now, so I'm off to sprain my ankle." Auntie KiKi kissed my cheek. "Wish me luck."

KiKi started for her house, and I stared at her in disbelief. Auntie KiKi, the queen of making things come out just the way she wanted them to. Why hadn't I inherited that gene instead of the family sweet tooth? I stepped back inside to set up for the day at the Fox just as Aldeen swung her Honda into KiKi's driveway. She got out and fluffed her pink dancing skirt that flowed around her like a cloud, a really big cloud. She was twirling her way over to meet KiKi when Boone parked a red, slightly dented pickup truck at the curb. BW stuck his head between boxes piled in the back, and Big Joey waved from the passenger side.

Big Joey and Boone were brothers in all ways except parentage and skin tone. Big Joey was the Grand Poobah of the Seventeenth Street Gang and, whereas this wasn't exactly a step toward sainthood, the gang kept guns and drugs out of schoolyards and parks and Big Joey had given more than one kid a roof over his head and food at the table, kept him in school, and put him on the straight and narrow.

Boone lowered the tailgate for BW and he leaped off, heading straight for Elsie and Annie Fritz's house to do his business. Why oh why didn't dogs ever do such things in their own yard?

"Yo," Big Joey called, uncurling himself from the truck. His navy T-shirt hugged six-pack abs that had made more than one woman in Savannah weak in the knees. "Word is you got yourself a new roomie and I got myself a gig as best man. 'Bout time." He closed the truck door, grinned, and spread his arms wide.

"How do you like fuchsia?" Aldeen added as she wandered over. "And gold shoes. I just love gold shoes."

"And the Bar-Fighting Bulls are doing the tunes, so all's cool." Big Joey lifted me off the ground and swung me around. "My boys been practicing on and off for weeks now. Gonna be great."

Weeks? How did brides get away with eloping to Niagara Falls or running off to Vegas while I got a fuchsia wedding, man-food at the reception, and who knew what kind of music? Okay, I could pitch a fit, but it was a beautiful day in Savannah and Boone and everyone looked happy. If

Boone was happy, I could put up with anything, right? . . . maybe? . . . if I tried real hard?

Big Joey returned me to earth, then snagged two boxes from the truck and followed Boone up the sidewalk to the house. Tail-wagging BW joined the little parade with something clutched in his teeth. Usually he brought me a stick as a doggy present or maybe the neighbor's newspaper or . . . or . . . was that a blue hat hanging out of BW's mouth? *The* blue hat? It was covered in dirt. Why dirt? Oh, Lord, why dirt? With Aldeen front and center and a dead-body MIA, it was best to save any and all questions till later.

"Well, that little devil," I laughed, snagging the hat from BW as Aldeen and KiKi looked on. "He must have gotten this right out of the shop."

"It's kind of dirty to be selling here at the Fox," Aldeen said as BW headed off. "Maybe he retrieved it from your donate pile?"

"Yep, that's it," I chuckled, my stomach doing flip-flops. "Dogs. You never know what they're getting into. Once BW brought me a dead snake, and then there was the pink bra with rhinestones," I babbled on. "I had no idea where the bra came from, but somebody sure knew how to have a good time, and—"

"Is that a red purse in your dog's mouth?" Aldeen asked as BW trotted our way looking proud. I grabbed for the purse but Aldeen headed to BW and beat me to it. "I'm not exactly what you'd call a purse girl," she said, staring at the bag, "but I think I recognize this one."

She knitted her brows as she undid the clasp and pulled

out a gold compact, a comb, an inhaler, and a wallet covered in pink lipstick kisses. "Says here this belongs to Bonnie Sue McGrath. The address is over there at Sleepy Pines, and the Pines reported her missing just this morning. Seems they thought she might be visiting friends, but no one's heard from her. I got a picture of Bonnie Sue sitting on my desk, and she has this very purse clutched in her hands."

Aldeen looked from me to Kiki to BW. "What's it doing here all covered in dirt?"

Without saying another word, Aldeen followed BW as he headed for Elsie and Annie Fritz's backyard.

Chapter Eight

"Holy saints above," Aldeen sighed as Auntie KiKi and me stopped right behind her in Elsie and Annie Fritz's neatly tended backyard. BW continued on across the edged grass, rounding the wheelbarrow and continuing into the garden lined with sprouting veggies . . . some of them sort of plastic looking? He wiggled under the wire fence, his little black butt dancing back and forth till he got to the other side and resumed digging, dirt flying into the air.

"W . . . well, isn't this a nice surprise," Annie Fritz gasped as she stumbled out onto the porch, the screen door slamming closed behind her. She had on a wrinkled floral housecoat and a smile plastered on her dirt-smudged face. Her arm crooked in a come-here wave to get our attention. "I bet you all would like some mighty fine blueberry pancakes this morning? As luck would have it, you're just in time. Elsie has the griddle hot and ready and—"

"There's a hand sticking out of the middle of your

garden," Aldeen said in a calm voice, as if she came across such things every day.

"Hand?" Annie Fritz gulped. "What hand?"

"*That* hand," Aldeen snarled, jabbing a stiff finger at the exposed digits. "The one next to the dog."

"That there just happens to be a . . . a new vegetable Sister and I put in this year, and . . ." Annie Fritz's voice trailed off as Aldeen snagged a trowel from the wheelbarrow, opened the garden gate, gave BW her best "I am the police, so get lost" look, then bent down. She dug next to the hand, slowed, then stopped. She stared back at Annie Fritz and Elsie, both now standing on the stoop looking like death warmed over.

"Is there some reason Bonnie Sue McGrath is planted in your backyard?"

"Fertilizer?" Elsie ventured in a squeaky voice, and Annie Fritz added, "And just because Bonnie Sue happens to be in our yard does not mean we had anything to do with her getting herself there, now, does it? I mean, we're not the only ones who didn't have much use for her, and someone else could have hidden her there to frame two little old ladies for something sinister. I do declare, what is this here world coming to?"

"And that someone just happened to add plastic greenery to cover things up?" Aldeen held up a fake leaf.

Annie Fritz blushed and grinned. "Nice touch if I do say so. Bet it came from that dollar store over on Price."

Aldeen closed her eyes for a second, then stood and dusted her hands. "You're saying neither of you is responsible for this corpse and there will be no fingerprints or forensic evidence that will implicate you two in any way when we get Bonnie Sue to the morgue?"

"Maybe a teensy bit if you look real hard." Elsie let out a deep sigh. "You see, the truth is, we sort of found Bonnie Sue in our Caddy when we were parked over at the Pines yesterday. She was leaning over on the back seat. At first we figured she went and took a little nap and the nice warm Caddy seemed like as good a place as any to get away from the men always fighting over her. Then we tried to wake Bonnie Sue and she was as stiff as a mean dog's tail. We sat her up but then we didn't quite know what next to do with her."

"Like maybe call the police?" Aldeen arched her left brow.

"Except that Bonnie Sue makes it two who croaked over at Sleepy Pines in the last week." Elsie wrung her hands. "With this amount of dead people never happening there till Sister and I got into business with Mr. Jim, it looks like we're a big fat dead-and-gone jinx. That is not one bit good for business for either of us."

"This is about business?" Aldeen wanted to know.

"Honey, when you're living on retirement income, everything is about business," Annie Fritz said. "We happened to be putting in our garden anyway and it was the perfect resting spot. We figured that since Bonnie Sue was the queen of bed-bouncing bingo at the Pines, where jackpot takes on a whole new meaning, her heart couldn't keep up with the bingo part. More than likely she keeled over in the heat of the moment and that's how she got that there nasty bump on her head. Whoever she was messing up the sheets with then dragged her pitiful worn-out remains to our car that was parked at the curb and half hidden by the big fir tree. Our guess it was one of those married catting-around lotharios at the Pines who didn't want to get caught with his shriveled do-da in the wrong do-de and thought it best to get rid of the evidence."

"Isn't the Pines a retirement center?" Aldeen said, a confused look on her face.

Elsie wagged her finger schoolteacher-style. "Well, Bonnie Sue is living proof that they didn't retire from everything, though the living part doesn't count for much now. It took Sister and me a bit to dig the hole back here, and we moved Bonnie Sue from one place to the next so no one would get suspicious. Seemed fittin' to plant her in with the hot peppers."

"That's it." Aldeen tossed the towel to the ground and headed for the gate. "I need to call the coroner, and you two need to come to the station and write this down. If I tried to put it into a report, I'd get accused of drinking my breakfast, and I'm not just talking OJ. Didn't either of you think that someone would go looking for Bonnie Sue and start asking questions?"

"Asking questions doesn't mean that people have answers, now, does it?" Annie Fritz sniffed. "Believe it or not, we're good at keeping our traps shut when there's a real need." The sisters trudged along with Aldeen, and I whispered to Auntie KiKi, "Did you just hear what I heard?"

"That we were invited in for blueberry pancakes and now it's not going to happen?"

"That the sisters are good at keeping their mouths shut. What else are they hiding? I better get Boone before the sisters start talking their heads off down at the police station and say something about the Spring Chicken scam and getting taken for a bunch of money. That ties them to Willie in a big way and could get them into a lot more trouble."

"I think the trouble part is already in play, but we need to act fast and find out who wanted Willie dead before this all get worse. I'll give Bernard Thayer a call and start up his lessons again. He still thinks that being Mr. TV Weather for twenty years gives him a shot at *Dancing With the Stars*, and with Aldeen in official cop mode and on the sisters' trail, we need to get cracking. Everyone will believe Bernard and his two left feet sprained my ankle, and I bet the Pines will run right on over here to get me after losing two paying customers like they just did."

"Bernard Thayer? Really? Do you have to? You get his two left feet, but I'll get his roving hands and bad breath when I take over the lessons."

"If you feel the need to start whining about this, get it out of your system now before tonight when you bring me my things. We need to get a move on. Come around eight. I'm betting everyone at the Pines will be watching reruns of *Perry Mason* and we can have a look-see. I'm thinking that whoever did in Willie did in Bonnie Sue, with them both living at the Pines."

"Unless Bonnie Sue died of natural causes and it's a coincidence?"

"From your lips to God's ears, but I don't think the sisters are that lucky."

KiKi started for Rose Gate, and BW and I studied the hand flopped limply over the edge of the veggie grave. "You just couldn't be content with digging up bones like other dogs, could you? You had to go for fashion, a matching hat and a purse, no less. I guess this is what happens when you live in a consignment shop. Next time try to find something without a body attached, okay?"

We turned for the front of Cherry House and Boone standing by a pile of boxes at the curb, hair mussed, shirt dirty, eyes dancing, and without a doubt the sexiest man alive. "Big Joey's picking up the last load," Boone said to me. "And why were the Abbott sisters getting into the Honda with Aldeen Ross, and is that the coroner's van pulling up to the curb?"

Boone gave me a long, steady stare. "Sweet thing, we were apart for fifteen minutes. How could all this happen in fifteen minutes?"

"You know that dead body I told you about? It wound up in the sisters' pepper patch, and now they're off to the police station to explain how it got there. If you keep them out of jail, you might score red velvet cake for the rest of your life."

"Motive?"

"None that I know of."

"A body in the backyard is pretty damning, but for red

velvet cake I'll see what I can do. Big Joey can drop me off at the station." Boone kissed me on the forehead, then grabbed up a box.

I snagged his arm. "I love you."

He grinned.

I held tighter. "I mean I really love you, like in a corny, Valentine's-Day-sappy, can't-live-without-each-other kind of way. I just thought you should know."

Boone put down the box, snapped a daffodil from the patch by the Prissy Fox sign, and tucked it behind my ear. "Right back at you." He scooped me into his arms and kissed me long and slow and delicious until I heard . . .

"That's it, that's it," came Mamma's voice. "Don't let me interrupt." I cranked open one eye to an iPhone pointed my way. "This is a great picture for your wedding book. I got the guy who does the mug shots at the police station as your photographer; he gave me a great deal. Why is the coroner over there at the Fritzes' place?"

"Pancakes," I said, reluctantly breaking the kiss. I had to do something before Mamma scurried over to the sisters' house to check things out for herself. I thrust a big box into her arms to keep her attention. "No one does pancakes like Elsie Fritz, and since you're here, you can help move Boone's stuff inside. Many hands make a light load, and Boone needs to be hurrying off to meet a client."

"Your mother does not have to do that." Boone made a grab for the box, but I gave Mamma a little nudge to get her going. I needed to get her in the house. Any minute now Bonnie Sue's traveling bag would make an appearance, and

I didn't want to face another lecture on being a dead-person magnet.

"You know," Mamma said, juggling the box up the sidewalk. "We can use my car and KiKi's to help with this move. My car has a big trunk and so does the BMW, and—"

"No thanks." A trickle of sweat slithered down my back. "There's not much more to move and the Beemer needs to rest. KiKi read it in the manual."

Mamma staggered in the front door and made a right turn for the stairs. "My sister read a manual? How did I ever miss hell freezing over?"

I plopped my box in the hall, then went to the kitchen as Mamma's footsteps sounded overhead. I retrieved the cash from the Rocky Road container to get ready for a day of entrepreneurship-on-a-shoestring. I poured a cup of kibble into BW's blue bowl, which had his name scripted on the side in white in case he learned how to read and forgot where he dined. KiKi had bought the bowl for his last birthday. I wasn't sure of the exact date, since BW had been a rescue pup, so I'd given him my birthday. We shared everything else . . . house, food, bed, Boone . . . it just seemed like the natural thing to do.

"You know," Mamma said, coming into the kitchen while I put the money into the Godiva box, "Walker isn't the complaining sort, but it's kind of cramped up there." She pointed to the ceiling. "You don't even have a living area, and the man would probably like a desk or at least a nice chair, and my guess is Walker'll have to duck to get his head under the shower fixture in the bathroom."

I counted the tens and twenties, wishing there were a few more. "There's some room on the second floor to expand for a sitting area, and when business picks up, I can maybe relocate the Fox to a storefront. Then Boone and I can redo the downstairs and have plenty of room."

"I've got a better idea." Mamma's eyes twinkled. "Finish off the third floor up there in the attic and keep the Prissy Fox exactly where it is." She grabbed my shoulders and looked me in the eyes. "It'll be perfect for the children. You can watch them and run the store at the same time if you get in a little help to mind Gloria Elizabeth and Graham Robert with feedings and the like."

"Gloria? Graham?"

Mamma puffed out her chest. "Named after their amazing grandmamma and granddaddy, just like they should be."

"Boone and I haven't even set a wedding date!"

"We have an appointment for tomorrow to take a look at the Sugar Bell House over on Bull Street for the reception. If you ask me, there's nothing lovelier than a Southern wedding with crystal chandeliers and Victorian arches, and the two-hundred-year-old magnolias in the back should be in full bloom."

"The magnolias bloom next month!"

"I know. The girl I talked to said there was a cancellation." Mamma pressed her hands to her heart. "It's a pity your daddy's not here to see all this."

"There's nothing to see!" I yanked back the curtain on the back door to prove that today was just like every other day, at least on this side of the house where a dead body wasn't being carted away. Except things weren't normal here either.

"Why is the gold diggers' black Escalade parked in KiKi's driveway?" Mamma wanted to know. She pressed her nose to the window. "And why are they dumping her into the back seat like a big sack of potatoes? Heavenly days! I do believe those two girls have gone completely bonkers. They're sister-napping KiKi! Why would they do such a thing? Stop!" Mamma yelled, running out the back door, waving her arms and standing behind the Escalade so it couldn't go any farther.

Bella poked her head out the driver's side window and waved her hand, shooing Mamma aside. "Get out of the way. We have hair appointments in fifteen minutes at Miss Ida's, and if we're late we lose our spot and they charge us no matter what."

Anna shook a paper out the other window. "We got to drop this old gal at the Pines as part of our community service of driving old people around for free, of all things."

"I am not an old gal," KiKi bellowed from the back of the Escalade as Anna added, "It says right here that KiKi Vanderpool needs assistance, so we're assisting." Anna glared at KiKi. "And if you know what's good for you, you'll get better right quick and get the heck out of the Pines ASAP. You're not wanted there."

She gunned the engine. Mamma and I jumped out of the way as we watched KiKi's snarling face against the glass zoom past us.

"Okay, this is all a little strange, even for my sister. What in the world are you two up to now?" Mamma groused.

"Let's go with Auntie KiKi sprained her ankle, can't drive, and her house has all those steps and Uncle Putter is out of town so he can't help her?"

"And I'm sure it has nothing to do with the coroner parked over at Elsie and Annie Fritz's house. You two really need to get better at this lying thing if you expect to get away with it, but for right now I'll follow the Escalade. That Bella girl had a look of pure evil about her. Either that or her Botox is sliding around like a glob of Crisco."

Mamma hurried out of the house, heading for her hearse, and I felt a lot better that she'd be with Auntie KiKi. The gold diggers were always obnoxious and mean-spirited; the bedbug episode had proven that beyond a shadow of a doubt. But why would they care if Auntie KiKi went to the Pines and how long she stayed? What difference did that make to them?

And what was this about the mug shot guy as a wedding photographer and an appointment at the Sugar Bell House tomorrow? How'd that happened? It had happened the usual way by me not wanting to put my foot down, say no, and break Mamma's heart, that's how. I had to face it: I was a big fat wedding wuss. But it was sort of nice that friends and family wanted to get involved in my wedding; it meant they cared, right? My one consolation was that at least I'd gotten to choose the guy. Hubba-hubba to that!

I spruced up the displays, added a striped scarf to the chic jacket I'd put on Gwendolyn, then welcomed my first customers. I truly did have customers again, something Savannah Electric and Power, the waterworks, and the people down at the real estate tax office could all agree was a really good thing.

In between checking out shoppers and taking in new clothes to consign, BW and I lugged Boone's possessions off the curb and up the steps. I figured it was the least I could do with him off trying to rescue Elsie and Annie Fritz from the long arm of the law. What a guy.

"It is really crowded up here," I said to BW, sprawled across the boxes because there was no floor space to walk. "And Boone only brought in his clothes and a lamp. He does have other stuff, and this is his home too. How do you feel about moving into a doghouse?"

That got me a growl that suggested *I'd* be the one living in the doghouse.

BW hopped from box top to box top in the bedroom, then hopped down into the hallway. We passed the bathroom, which looked a lot smaller than it had yesterday, and trotted downstairs to find Boone behind the counter writing up a sale. In fact, there was a string of dreamy-eyed customers patiently waiting in line to check out.

"I can help someone over here," I said, snapping up another sales book, but no one moved to my side of the counter. Not that I blamed them. Who would want to be checked out by a hot and sweaty sometimes-blonde woman when a hot and totally adorable man could do the job?

"So what happened to the sisters?" I asked Boone after the last ogling female floated out the door.

"I'm happy to report that, at this very moment, Annie Fritz and Elsie Abbot are home sipping tea."

I threw my arms around him. "How did you pull it off? You are amazing. Another Perry Mason."

"It felt more like Homer Simpson. The sisters went into mourning mode, cried and carried on about how they were innocent, flimflammed—their words, not mine—and were being framed. In two minutes flat they had the whole police station, including the police chief, sobbing. I had to pass out tissues and even wiped my own nose a few times. The chief let the sisters go as long as they didn't leave town and promised to attend his grandpa's funeral on Saturday to give him a proper sendoff."

"They should franchise."

"The best news is that while I was at the police station, I got something that belongs to you."

"Better there than the morgue."

Boone took my hand and led me out the door, and I stopped dead in the middle of the sidewalk. "It's my pink scooter!" I ran full out to the curb and plopped on the cushy seat. I grabbed the handlebars, my pink helmet that smelled like cotton candy dangling off the side, and made *vroom-vroom* sounds like a two-year-old. Some things you never outgrow.

"I left it in a no-parking zone when I was on the run," Boone said, buffing a dirty spot on the front fender with his shirttail. "I knew the ever-vigilant Savannah police would tow the scooter, and they did. It's been in the impound lot and I bailed it out. I think the tires are low, but other than that it looks okay." He reached down, pushed on the front tire, and something slid out of his pocket.

"You dropped this," I said picking the gold ring off the curb. I held it up to the sun, the old ornate setting catching the light. "A ruby?" I looked to Boone, and—holy cow!— he was blushing.

"It's for you." He swallowed hard. "It was Grandma Hilly's wedding ring and the only nice thing the woman ever had in her life. I'm going to get the stone reset and add some diamonds and a platinum setting, going with that something old, something new. It was supposed to be a surprise, but now that you know about it, you can pick out whatever you want or we can shop for a new ring if you want and—"

I kissed him, dropping the ring into his palm. I held out my left hand.

"You . . . you want to wear it?"

"It's perfect. I wouldn't change a thing about this ring, Walker Boone, and Grandma Hilly did have something else really nice and absolutely wonderful in her life. She had you."

Chapter Nine

I t was nearly eight when I closed up the Fox. That was later than usual, but I wasn't about to toss out paying customers, and with Boone still at his place setting up his office, there was no reason to close. I left Boone a note telling him I was at the Pines visiting KiKi and her ankle and I'd explain later and not to worry.

"Hold down the fort," I commissioned BW as I spooned dinner into his bowl, adding a few green beans on top for presentation appeal. "And if you feel energetic, run the vacuum and straighten the blouses. The place needs a spruce."

Completely ignoring my housekeeping request, BW was asleep at the foot of the steps and snoring before I closed the door behind me. I got KiKi's hidden key and found the suitcase that she'd packed. I bungee-corded it to the scooter, slipped on my helmet, did a little jig because I didn't have to wait on a bus or cut through gross alleys containing wildlife, and zoomed off into the night.

I pulled into the Sleepy Pines parking lot that sat behind

a line of blooming azaleas. I untied the suitcase and started for the house just as Eugenia and some guy with blond hair stopped at the wrought iron gate by the patio. I guessed this was Mr. Up-and-Comer Dexter. Since my visit tonight was on the down-low so KiKi and I could sneak around, I scooted into the bushes to keep out of sight. This was a private moment between Eugenia and boyfriend, and maybe I shouldn't watch. Yeah, right, like that was going to happen.

They kissed good-night, then kissed again. Up-and-Comer got an A in expensive suit and a C minus in kissing. He was one of those wet-lip guys that made you want to get a towel, but considering the amount of giggling and suggestive body language going on, Eugenia must have liked it. She said something, giggled again, then opened the gate and did a really good sashay all the way across the patio to the back door.

I waited till Up-and-Comer left, counted to twenty, then slunk past the fountain, hit my head on a low-hanging flowering dogwood branch, tripped over the horseshoe post, and hobbled up to the back door. Normally I could have just gone to the front door and visited KiKi anytime I wanted, but with dear auntie and Operation Twisted Ankle, keeping my visit secret to get information seemed the best way to go. I'd turned the handle, hoping KiKi had it unlocked and I could just slip in, when the door cracked opened to reveal Auntie, finger to her lips in *shh* fashion. I crept inside and she pointed to a little alcove in the dimly lit hall.

Bits and pieces of *Perry Mason* drifted down the hall as she squashed me between the largest fern in all Christendom and an oak bookcase. I wedged the suitcase between my legs. "What?"

That got me another *shh*. Auntie KiKi jabbed her finger toward Mr. Jim in his office. He was sitting behind a cherry desk that looked as old and dignified as the house. "Why is Hollis here?"

"Only the devil himself knows," KiKi whispered back. Mr. Jim said something that got mixed in with Perry Mason's cross-examination. Hollis flipped a paper on the desk, then rocked back on his heels, looking smug.

"That's Hollis's evil look," I said.

"He looks like that all the time."

Hollis turned to leave and Auntie KiKi and I wedged back into the shadows, nearly knocking the obligatory Southern picture of blooming white magnolias off the wall. Mr. Jim snatched the paper from the desk, crushed it into a tight ball, and tossed it at the trash can, missing by a mile. He slammed his fist on the desk, making KiKi and I jump; then he got up, killed the desk light, and stormed right past us.

"We need to talk to Mr. Jim and find out why Hollis has got him in such a state. Maybe we can help." I started off but KiKi yanked me back, shaking her head. "First we need to find out what's on that note."

KiKi stuck her head around the corner, gave me a little nod, and we dashed across the hall and darted into the office. I closed the door and KiKi clicked on the brass desk lamp with a green glass shade. I parked the suitcase next to the desk, snagged the wadded paper from the floor, and smoothed it out on the desk next to the computer.

"Oh my goodness, it's official," KiKi gasped.

"You're right, it's a bank statement. Mr. Jim's flat broke. He's even behind on the mortgage. Hollis has friends at the bank, and I bet that's how he got this information. That rat was here to get Mr. Jim to sell before the Pines goes into foreclosure and—"

"Heavenly days, not that. This!" KiKi held up my hand, the ruby sparkling. "It's Grandma Hilly's, isn't it? I remember seeing it on her finger. That woman was the kindest and hardest-working woman I ever met, just like her grandson. I bet she'd be tickled pink over you and Walker getting married. It looks a little big, honey, and sliding around on your finger."

"I'll grow into it. This ring is not coming off."

Auntie KiKi kissed my cheek. "You got yourself a keeper this time, not like that first-time guy who just left here in all his pompous arrogant glo . . ."

Auntie KiKi stopped talking as footsteps sounded outside the door. Because we'd been in more than one tight spot in the last few years of sleuthing about, we acted together in perfect sleuthing harmony, dousing the lights and scurrying under the desk. That KiKi's elbow landed in my ribs and my foot jabbed her gut was not so perfect, but at least we were out of sight when the door closed with a click and the desk light came on.

"Where does he keep it?" whispered one guy, who sounded like a hundred-year-old version of James Earl Jones.

"Mr. Jim keeps the good hooch in the bottom drawer of

the file cabinet," whispered the male version of Betty White with a head cold. "And tonight that's what we need; it's what we deserve. Did you bring glasses?"

"I got the good ones out of the china cabinet in the library."

From our hideout under the desk and with noses nearly touching, Auntie KiKi and I watched navy Nikes and gray Adidas gym shoes cross the maroon carpet. Auntie KiKi poked my shin to get my attention and pointed up, mouthing, "The paper."

Oh drat, yes. Mr. Jim didn't need his financial problems to get out; the man had enough to deal with. I curled my fingers over the edge of the desk, felt around, and slid down the bank statement.

"We should toast two fantastic old fools for putting on such a good show and distracting everyone, even though it wasn't necessary. And here's to Willie and Bonnie Sue," Betty White said. "Good riddance to them."

KiKi and I exchanging wide-eyed looks. The two men chuckled, then clinked glasses. Willie? Bonnie Sue?

"Wasn't there a paper on that desk?" James Earl asked.

"Not that I remember, but it looks like Mr. Jim's planning a trip. Here's his luggage all packed and ready to go. Some fancy designer with those little Ls and Vs. Mr. Jim's living in the high cotton these days, I tell you. Finish your drink; we'd better get out of here before someone comes in wondering what's going on."

"No one will ever figure out what we've been up to, and we need to keep things going so no one suspects. We're right good at this. Hit me again with another shot to celebrate."

Glass clinked against glass, and Betty said, "What do you think of that KiKi Vanderpool?"

"Holy cow, the woman's dynamite. She can be the peach in my pie any time, I can tell you that." The file cabinet opened and closed, the light went off, and the door clicked shut. We waited a beat, then Auntie KiKi tumbled out from under the desk with me next to her.

"Peach in a pie? Dynamite?" I faced KiKi. "Who were those guys?"

"They're the killers! We should have jumped up and yelled, 'You're under arrest!' That's what Cagney and Lacey would have done."

"Cagney and Lacey are a million years old by now and not jumping anywhere, and if we did anything we could have gotten our heads blown off. These guys were not looking for company, except maybe Miss Dynamite." I shook my finger. "You had on that pink flippy skirt today, didn't you? You always get sassy in that skirt—and we couldn't have arrested those guys; we don't have any proof they did anything wrong."

"Are you kidding? 'A job well done'? 'Good riddance'? For whatever reason, they knocked off Willie and Bonnie Sue. They might as well have signed a confession, and, for your information, I did not have on the flippy skirt." Auntie KiKi pulled at her tan skirt. "This is the same thing I had on when the crazy Escalade sisters dumped me here like a

UPS package. What if Willie got these two guys into his Spring Chicken scam and they did the old boy in 'cause he had it coming? Willie Junior said granddad had a lot of money, and my guess is Spring Chicken is how he got it."

"Maybe, but how does bed-hopping Bonnie Sue fit into all this? Because you know she does. Two dead in such a short time is not a coincidence. You need to ask around and see what you can find out. From the sounds of it, everyone's been real friendly since you got here." I gave KiKi a hard look. "Especially the men?"

"Maybe."

"You did your Dancing Queen act, didn't you?"

"Mr. Jim makes a mean martini. Okay, three martinis, but not a drop more, and January Foot plays the piano and suddenly I was sitting on it and singing my little old heart out like I sometimes do, so what was the harm?"

"Uncle Putter's going to wring your neck."

"Honey, the way I see it I've already got a body sitting in my car trunk, so he can just add this one to the list. There's always a list. It's what keeps me young and peppy."

We stood and I handed KiKi the suitcase, holding on to it for a second, hoping she'd take me seriously. "You've got to be careful. I mean it. Don't let anyone see you with this bag or the bad guys might suspect you were in here when they were. You could be in danger, and what's another body at the Pines these days?"

"No one would suspect the Dancing Queen." She batted her eyes and fluffed her hair.

"Keep your phone with you all the time and look out for the shoes we saw. Keep an eye on Emmitt and Foley and who they keep company with. Our guys tonight know them pretty well and that might be a lead. If you get scared, call Boone, since I don't have a phone. Just say"—I looked around the office—"*apple*. He'll come running."

"I now have a safe word?" Her eyes twinkled.

"Not *that* kind of safe word."

"So, this means you're going to tell Walker what's going on? I'd leave out the part about Willie in the garage and pick up a meatloaf sandwich and a beer at Parker's. This will all go down much easier with food in hand."

I gave Auntie KiKi a hug. We doused the lights and checked the hall. I headed for the back patio doors and KiKi took the hall toward Perry Mason. I dug my scooter out of the bushes, then vroomed my way through the night, passing Anna and Bella along the way. They were in the back seat of a pristine red Lincoln Continental with two nice-looking men in the front seat. What the heck? Anna and Bella were stepping out on Clive and Crenshaw? Didn't they care if C and C found out? Because the kudzu vine was sure to pick up on this. I didn't like that the gold diggers had married for money but liked it even less that they were apparently two-timing their husbands.

I pulled the scooter into the little alley that ran behind Cherry House and parked it in the sort-of-white clapboard garage that could do with a coat of paint. I made my way up the overgrown sidewalk to the house, the first floor dark except for a little light in the kitchen and the display window in the front. I opened the back door. "Hello? Almost-husband, are you here?"

Something crashed over my head, and I took the steps two at a time. "Boone?"

I turned left and nearly tripped over BW, who was staring up at a hole in the ceiling with a jean-clad leg, no sock, and a worn brown boat shoe sticking out.

"Boone? Say something."

"I smell Parker's meatloaf. You're my hero."

"Hold that thought." In the unfinished room on the other side of the stairs, I spied a ladder leading up through the attic opening that usually had a wood covering over it. I'd always known the attic was up there somewhere but had never had the guts to check things out in a house nearly a hundred years old. I clamped the Parker's bag in my teeth, held tight to the six-pack, and climbed the ladder into dark shadows. "What are you doing up here?"

"Ruining your house."

A flashlight sat on an old dusty chest next to a stack of equally dusty boxes. I put the bag and beer on the chest and kissed Boone. He tasted warm and delish and like coming home. "What if we do this: I'll put my shoulder under your arm and you try to wiggle your leg free. Or we can call Big Joey and he can have a good laugh."

I bent down and Boone put his arm around me. "I think I've got a fat foot." He gave one last tug and both of us fell back on the flooring, staring at the rafters. Boone kissed the tip of my nose. "I think you have a leak in the roof, and it rotted out this part of the ceiling."

I looked down at Boone's leg. "You're bleeding!"

"It's just a scratch, and everyone knows that meatloaf from Parkers makes everything better."

"They need to put that on a sign." I sat next to Boone, got the bag, and pulled out one sandwich, two salads, two apples, and an oatmeal cookie, Boone's favorite. For me, anything with *cookie* in the title was my favorite, and there, in a nutshell, is why I'd only bought one.

"Where's the other sandwich?" Boone wanted to know as he unwrapped the one in front of him.

"At Parkers where it belongs. I need to fit into a wedding dress."

Boone tore his sandwich in half and handed me a section. "Buy a bigger dress."

Oh, for the life of the groom. "I'm fine with salad and an apple," I lied. I twisted off the cap of a water bottle and Boone did the ritual with the beer. We clinked bottles, though the plastic made kind of a *thunk*, and we dug in. "You're up here 'cause Mamma talked to you," I said around a mouthful of greens.

"Something about Gloria Elizabeth and Graham Robert that I didn't get, but she made it sound like they were coming to visit soon and we needed room and I should look in the attic. There *is* a ton of space up here."

I took a drink of water and chomped a cherry tomato, trying to pretend it was a meatball. "The thing is, I can't afford a lot of renovations and I just don't have time to do it myself and I'm kind of independent—"

"Kind of?"

"And I can't have you paying my way on things just 'cause you have a successful law practice, own the Old Harbor Inn, and business for me has been a little off lately. You and I are busy with jobs, so we'd have to hire someone, and you know how expensive that is."

Boone took a bite of sandwich, the yummy sauce dripping off his fingertips. "What about this: I'll buy half the house, you put my name on the deed so I don't feel like a kept man, and we use that money to pay for the rehabbing. We turn the attic space up here into bedrooms and storage and below into the kitchen, laundry, dining, and living room." He pointed through the hole and dropped a chunk of meatloaf to BW. "It's a big job and needs professionals. You and I can paint and decorate, but there's rot up here that needs big-time attention with contractors."

I stopped my fork halfway to my mouth. "You've thought about this?"

"We only do this if you agree. It's your house and you love it, and this way you keep the Fox on the first floor. You gotta admit that makes for an easy commute. No rush-hour traffic."

I put down my water and swallowed hard.

"Oh God, Reagan." Boone froze. "Please, I beg of you, don't cry. I can't take you crying. If you're upset, we won't do anything. We'll let the whole ceiling cave in and I'll step over the wreckage and I won't even care, I swear. It'll be a good conversation piece."

"I'm happy."

"This is happy?"

"Really happy. I'm not crying." I sniffed and swiped my nose. "I never cry. Finding Hollis on the dining room table doing the horizontal hula with my best friend, not one tear. Flunking organic chemistry and not graduating on time, the same. Slicing my finger to the bone while carving a pumpkin and twelve stitches later, nothing."

"So the little streams running down your cheek are not tears."

I wrapped my arms around Boone's neck and held tight. "Absolutely not. But you are one amazing man."

He held me tight back. "And you are one amazing woman."

"About that." I let go of Boone and smoothed the soft T-shirt over his rock-hard chest. Dang, was I a lucky girl or what? "I went to visit Auntie KiKi at Sleepy Pines. She's there for a sprained ankle that really isn't sprained."

"Does Uncle Putter know?"

"What do you think?"

Boone finished off his beer in one long drink.

"She's trying to see who else might have had a reason to knock off Willie and Bonnie Sue—that's the gal in the garden, and we think her death is connected to Willie's. We know the Abbott sisters didn't do the deed, so we need to find who did, and this is it for me on finding dead bodies." I made a cross over my heart. "No more. If I open a door and one drops at my feet, I'm stepping over it. Maybe I'll call 911, but I'm not paying any attention at all, no matter what."

"Even if that dead body has something to do with KiKi or one of your loyal customers at the Fox or the priest at St. John's who gave you First Communion or the gal at the Cakery Bakery who puts sprinkles on your favorite doughnuts?"

"I love the sprinkle lady. Her name's Lottie, and she has three kids in college. Can you imagine?"

Boone put down his sandwich and kissed me on the lips. "I don't want to change you, Reagan, I just want to marry you. You wouldn't have me give up the Seventeenth Street Gang, wear ties, or join the country club. All I ask is no secrets and if you need my help, ask."

"Well, since you brought up the help thing . . . when Auntie KiKi calls and says *apple*, she needs you quick, and as for secrets . . ." I opened another beer and handed it to him. "There's a casket in her BMW, Willie Fishbine's inside, and we think someone killed him with a peanut allergy, so we're holding on to him while we prove it."

* * *

"Are you all ready?" Mamma bubbled when I let her in the back door early the next morning. "We can't be late for the Sugar Bell. That cancellation date opening up is destiny knocking. It's a mighty lucky break that's meant to be. It's karma!"

Mamma had on a black-and-white flowered dress with a little jacket and a lovely black handbag. She looked every inch the quintessential judge. I had on a blue cotton skirt and white blouse, my hair pulled back into a knot because I'd just gotten out of the shower, and looked every inch the shopkeeper scrambling to keep it together.

"Our appointment with the hostess is at nine," Mamma added. "I got us the first available slot so we can put a down payment on that canceled date for next month. I have a check right here in my purse to secure the deal."

"I'll pay for it." *Somehow*, I added to myself.

"Nonsense." Mamma waved her hand, putting an end to the discussion. "I want to do this. The loveliest weddings are at the Sugar Bell House. It has that big porch, surrounded by live oaks and magnolias, and simply sublime Southern décor. I know it's going to be tight getting a caterer lined up on such short notice and finding you a nice dress—something long and in cream and not too much lace, since this is your second wedding." Mamma framed my face between her palms. "Oh, honey, we can make this work. You and Walker are perfect together." She glanced around. "So where is the groom? Is he sleeping in?"

"BW does the sleeping in around here. Boone isn't a sleep-in kind of guy. He's more a grab-a-protein-bar-and-get-the-job-done kind of guy."

I snapped up Old Yeller, swallowed a resigned sigh of *wedding out of control*, and headed for Mamma's hearse. "I got the Cakery Bakery working on a protein doughnut. If they figure it out, Boone and I got the happily-ever-after thing knocked."

Mamma powered down Bull Street and past Forsythe Park, speckled with morning joggers and walkers. The

Sugar Bell House was just beyond the Victorian district and out of the hustle and bustle of the historic district. Mamma pulled in front of the Foxy Loxy café next door, only slightly nudging the fire hydrant at the curb. She pointed to the once-upon-a-time white ornate house turned uppity wedding venue and sighed. "Isn't it exquisite? Just the right size for an intimate wedding of a hundred and fifty or so."

Truth be told, the Foxy Loxy was more my speed, but since Mamma had stood by me when I'd married Hollis knowing full well I shouldn't be marrying the jackass and never uttered a word of "I told you so" when I got divorced, I owed her this happy wedding of her dreams.

She opened the little gate, and we took the steps to the front porch with white wicker furniture and red geraniums spilling over white flowerboxes. Mamma knocked and the door swung opened to a petite thirty-something in a perfect blue knit suit, Christian Dior makeup, and a gold name tag etched with "Hostess Lou Ella Farnsworth." And Eugenia?

"But . . . but you promised us the first appointment for the cancellation date," Mamma blurted, looking from the hostess to Eugenia and clutching her purse as if it were a life preserver. "We are so counting on Reagan getting married here and—"

"Cancellation?" Eugenia gasped, hand to cheek in a horrified pose. She glared at Mamma and me. "I do declare, I have no idea what you're talking about. I'm here to reserve the Sugar Bell House for next year."

Lou Ella smiled at Eugenia and patted her hand. "Of course you are. Everyone knows you have to reserve an intimate wedding venue of this sort a year in advance, unless, of course, you wait for a"—she cleared her throat as if trying to dislodge a fur ball—"cancellation."

Eugenia parked her hand on her hip. "What kind of bride goes begging dates for her wedding? Why, I've never heard of such a thing."

"You're engaged?" I asked Eugenia. I felt more like saying "Drop dead and take the Sugar Bell House with you," but since Mamma was with me I went with good Southern manners. "Congratulations."

Eugenia slid her left hand behind her back and tipped her chin. "Any day now, Dex will pop the question, and I want to be ready and not caught off guard like some people around here." She nailed me with a sideways glance and exchanged sweet smiles with Lou Ella.

"Dex is such a find; we are soulmates and meant to be together. Everyone says so—with my volunteer work with the Savannah libraries and his status in the community." She hugged Lou Ella. "I'll have a deposit to you by the end of the week along with that little something extra we talked about. And don't you go giving my wedding day away now, you hear?" Eugenia gave Lou Ella an air kiss then floated down the steps.

Lou Ella gave Mamma and me a faux smile that nearly cracked her makeup. She held out her hand, took one look at me as if seeing me for the first time, then yanked her hand back. "I know you; you were married to Hollis."

"Sometimes referred to as Savannah's version of the Spanish Inquisition."

"He told me all about the pitiful way you treated him—how you tried to get him accused of murder, of all things."

"Actually, he *was* accused of murder and I got him off, of all things."

"That's a lie; you should be ashamed of yourself!" Lou Ella screeched. "Hollis and I are going to be married right here in August. Daddy can't wait to bring him into his real estate firm because Hollis is such a successful businessman with more prospects on the way. I wouldn't rent the Sugar Bell House to you no matter how much you pay me. There are ten people just dying to snap up this cancellation date who will probably pay more than you ever would. You should get married at Wall's Barbecue. I'm sure they have an opening, and it's much more your style." Lou Ella took a step back and, with a flourish, slammed the door in our faces, the glass rattling in the window frames.

Mamma turned to me. "Reagan, what in the world just happened here?"

I kissed Mamma on the cheek. "For once in his self-centered, lying, fornicating, miserable life, Hollis Beaumont the Third did me a favor."

Chapter Ten

I took Mamma's hand. "We should get coffee and a Danish to celebrate." I ushered my still-dazed mamma down the steps and across the sidewalk to one of the little white tables under a huge live oak tree outside the Foxy Loxy café. "Sit. Think happy thoughts, rainbows and unicorns."

"At a time like this?"

"I'll be back in a minute." I skipped inside and returned with two cappuccinos, the foam swirled into hearts—I loved how they did that—and two cherry Danishes the size of my hand. I'd probably have to jog to Beaufort and back to wear off the poundage from the pastry, but at the moment I didn't care. Some things needed celebrating. I sat across from Mamma and held up my cup. "Life is good."

"Reagan, that girl just ruined your chances to get married at the Sugar Bell, and it's the perfect place for you and Walker to start your life together." Mamma bit her lip. "I suppose we could wait till next year for an opening."

I took a sip and licked the foam from my upper lip. "I don't want to wait a year, and I don't want to get married at the Sugar Bell House." I put down my coffee and took Mamma's hands in mine. "I want to get married at your house. I want to get married where it means something, a place that has memories, good vibes, where I already know the furniture. I want you to marry Boone and me and I want to have Auntie KiKi as my matron of honor and Big Joey as the best man and BW as the ring bearer. I want the Abbott sisters to sing 'Ave Maria' because it's classic and pretty, and I want to wear strappy pink heels and a short pink dress with a twirly skirt for dancing. I want to eat pot roast and drink champagne and have a good selection of beer because Boone is more beer than champagne, and around midnight I want the Naked Dog food truck to pull up to the curb and us all to have loaded hotdogs with chili fries and sit on big blankets on the front lawn and eat because we'll be hungry again from all the dancing."

I crossed my fingers, held my breath, and studied Mamma with her judge face firmly in place as Dexter ambled up the sidewalk. He had his arm around . . . oh, you have got to be kidding . . . Arnett Fishbine?

"My house is too small," Mamma said in a slow, thoughtful voice, snapping me back to the moment. "But what about KiKi's house?"

"KiKi's house?"

Arnett was old enough to be Dexter's mother, though the skimpy yellow dress and exposed cleavage didn't suggest that a mother role was what she had in mind, and was that bracelet on her arm just like the one he'd given Eugenia? That rat-fink!

"Rose Gate is perfect." Mamma grinned like a kid at Christmas, her cheeks rosy with excitement. "Your aunt will simply love the idea. It even has the small ballroom KiKi converted all those years ago when she started teaching dance lessons. And there's that beautiful old staircase. I bet the fourth step still squeaks. And if you do an autumn wedding, all the mums will be out in force and it won't be so hot around here that we're all ready to pass right out, and that will give you and Walker a few months to enjoy the moment. Instead of summer pink, maybe you can go with autumn coral. I can make an appointment for us at Bleu-Belle Bridal. Just because you want a colorful dress doesn't mean you don't want something lovely. What do you think?"

"Think about what?"

"You? Walker? Filing a joint tax return? For heaven's sake, does any of this sound familiar? What in the world is so interesting that you keep looking over my shoulder?"

Mamma dropped her napkin to the ground, retrieved it, and discretely cut her eyes toward Dexter two tables over. She leaned across the table and lowered her voice. "I do believe that's the man who just bought the House of Eternal Slumber. There was a big article in the paper about him being Mr. Up-and-Comer, but from the looks of what's going on over at that table, it should have been Mr. Pucker-Upper."

"That's Eugenia's Dex."

"No!"

"Yes. What should we do? We need to tell Eugenia."

"What we need to do is drink our coffee and go home.

Honey, you can't tell Eugenia that her soulmate is doing kissy-face with . . ."

"Eleanor Roosevelt?"

"It's not that bad." Mamma grabbed another peek. "Well, maybe, but if you say something to Eugenia about two-timing Dex, it sounds an awful lot like 'I'm getting married and you're not, naaa na na naaa na,' and she'd never believe you. Besides, maybe Dex is here to break up with this woman and this is a last date?"

"Maybe she's adopting him. She has to be twenty years older."

Mamma set her elbow on the table, her chin resting in her palm. "Okay, you haven't touched your Danish and you're sitting there flipping your hair and your eye's twitching something fierce. Why are you obsessing over this Dex person? I know it's not just Eugenia; you two were never all that close. What's buzzing around in that brain of yours? Spill it."

"That woman with Dex is Arnett Fishbine. Her father lived and died at Sleepy Pines, and she's inheriting some serious cash. Okay, I get that Dex is hustling her for money, but why is he playing Eugenia? She's not wealthy and he can't really care for her if he's playing around like this. Then there's the thing about Eugenia and Arnett both being connected to Sleepy Pines. Doesn't that seem a little fluky to you? I mean, of all the women in Savannah, Dex connects with these two?"

Mamma sipped her cappuccino and bit into her Danish, not a touch of foam daring to cling to her lip or a crumb of pastry landing on her skirt. "Honey, a lot of people are connected to the Pines—even your auntie, of all people—and Dex is just a sleaze when it comes to women. All you can do is drop a few hints to Eugenia and hope she figures things out for herself, but right now we have a wedding to think about. *Your* wedding." Mamma held up her cup. "Here's to Walker and marriage and hoping you can focus long enough to put those two together."

Mamma headed off to Sleepy Pines to get Auntie KiKi up to speed on the latest wedding plans, and I headed for the bus stop. I needed to meet Boone at the bank to get things moving on the great attic venture before the rest of the ceiling caved in on us. I also wanted to tell Earlene about Bonnie Sue. Earlene could read about it in the paper, of course, but she seemed to genuinely care about the woman. I spied the bus two blocks away and waved my hand to make sure Earlene saw me actually standing at an officially designated location like a good law-abiding citizen.

Earlene got closer, then closer still, not slowing down one lick. She stuck her nose in the air and powered right past me, stopping a block away. Good grief, now what?

"Well, this sure is a surprise," Earlene snorted when the bus door slid open and I stepped inside huffing and puffing. "Look who it is, that snooty Reagan Summerside person who thinks she's too good for the bus now that she's got herself a hot pink scooter to buzz around town on. Don't think I didn't see you the other day flying right by me."

"What about now? I was standing where I was supposed

to be." I pointed out the window. "Right back there alongside the orange oval with 'BUS STOP' stamped right in the middle. Why didn't you pull over for me?"

"I did pull over, just a little later than I should. Makes you appreciate the bus more if you have to run after it once in a while."

I dropped change in the box and sat down. "I have bad news."

Earlene hit the gas. "Your wedding better not be called off, girlfriend. I already bought a dress that's going to have Big Joe salivating like a hound dog."

"The wedding is still on, but that little old lady you wait for each week over by Sleepy Pines? Well, she's sort of kind of dead." I totally sucked at delivering bad news.

"What's sort of?"

"Beyond sort of; she's just . . . well, you know what I mean."

Earlene made the sign of the cross and I joined in. "I suppose I should have seen it coming," she sniffed. "Every Tuesday she and that little old man with the goatee who got on at the next stop, catching the 8:43, would sit side by side and laugh and have such a good time together."

"Goatee?" I sat up straight. "Short, bald, gray . . . are you sure about the laugh?"

"Well, he only laughed with her and no one else. He tried to put a button in the fare box once, thinking I wouldn't know the difference, and now that I think about it, it was more of a sneaky kind of laugh than a belly laugh, if you know what I mean. They'd get off at the same place every week at the corner of Oglethorpe and Bull. When he passed away, I guess she did too. I hear this happens—one goes and then the other just can't cope. She must have died of a broken heart, though she did have friends at River's Edge Retirement Community. She'd catch the bus and visit there once in a while. When you find out when the wake is," Earlene added, "let me know. I'd like to pay my respects."

I got off the bus at Oglethorpe and Bull Street and watched Earlene fade down the street, meshing into morning traffic. I looked around, wondering why Willie and Bonnie Sue always exited here at Chippewa Square. It was nice enough, but Savannah had twenty-three really nice parks. Why here all the time? You'd think they'd mix it up a little. Maybe they wanted to grab lunch at Six Pence down the street—except the restaurant didn't start serving till elevenish. Two hours was a long time to wait for lunch even if the Pence did have the best shepherd's pie on the planet.

I crossed Bull to Savannah Bank and Trust, pulled open the heavy glass door, and spotted Boone already seated on one side of a desk with a yellow-bowtied bank official on the other. Boone had on his usual jeans but, in honor of the occasion, wore business attire in the form of a blue button-down shirt. He'd once told me that a suit made him look like a hitman for the mob so the judges had given him a special dispensation not to wear one in the courtroom. My guess was that this dispensation had had a lot more to do with tickets to the Atlanta Braves and a case of Johnny Walker Red.

"So you're getting married," the banker said as I parked myself beside Boone. "When's the big day?"

Boone smiled, signed some joint bank account papers, then passed them over to me. "We're not sure; we're just enjoying the moment."

"Well, don't wait too long." The banker tapped a newspaper and leaned back in his chair. "That's what this little old lady did, and now she and the man she came in here with all the time are done and gone. You think you're going to live forever and then suddenly somebody's burying you in their garden and there's a really bad picture of you on the front page of the *Savannah Times*."

I started to add my signature below Boone's, then stopped and grabbed the newspaper. There was Bonnie Sue staring back at me. "You mean *this* woman and Willie Fishbine came in *here* together?"

The banker drummed his fingers on the desk. "I need to keep customers' business confidential, but now that they're both gone . . . Every Tuesday those two were here when we first opened the doors. They'd get off the bus across the street, make deposits, and then leave. He had checks, and she always had a check from him; that's why we all thought for sure they'd tie the knot sooner or later. It looked as if he was kind of supporting her. Then they both went and kicked the bucket before anything came of it. Darn shame. You better get that date set before something happens and you wind up like these two."

"October, and we're having pot roast," I said, scribbling

my name. I thanked the banker, grabbed Boone's hand, and hustled him out the door.

"October? When did this happen?" Boone wrapped his arm around my shoulders and we started down Bull Street.

"When I got us out of getting married at the Sugar Bell. Now it's Auntie KiKi's house, October is nice weather, six months off gives us time to get organized, and Mamma's doing the ceremony, and none of this is cast in stone if we want to change something. What do you think?"

Boone planted a kiss in my hair. "Sounds perfect, and now that we got the wedding all figured out and ready to go, what do you make of Bonnie Sue and Willie Fishbine together? I gotta say I never saw that one coming."

Again, oh, for the life of the groom. A venue and date did not a wedding make, but at least he hadn't said "let's get married at Abe's on Lincoln and do shots and chicken wings." "I took the bus to get here and Earlene said Willie and Bonnie Sue got on the bus at different stops. That means they didn't want anyone at Sleepy Pines to know they were an item, but why? What difference could it make?"

We stopped in front of Six Pence, and Boone rested his hip against a little red VW. "You said Willie bit the dust over a peanut allergy? I got the coroner talking about the two deaths at the Pines and he didn't say anything about peanuts in Willie's stomach, and it would have come up because of the allergy. How could Willie die of a peanut allergy without peanuts? The coroner did say that Bonnie Sue was suffocated probably three days ago."

"You talked to the coroner?"

"It seemed only fitting I should meet this guy, since he's coming to our wedding, plus getting to know the coroner is always a good idea. Amazing how coffee and doughnuts gets people talking. Bonnie Sue was suffocated by a down pillow, probably an old one. Yellowing feathers were found around her collar and one in her mouth. She had a tassel clutched in her hand."

"Pink tassel?"

"That sounds like more than a lucky guess."

"The sisters have an old pink pillow with the stuffing coming out, and it has tassels. They sit on it in their Caddy to see over the hood during their shrinking years. With them as prime suspects, Ross and her merry band of law enforcers are sure to search the sisters' house and car right off. Call Uber or Big Joey or someone to come get us. We need to get that pillow before Ross does. We need a car!"

"Or we can take this car." Boone patted the fender he leaned against. He reached in his pocket and pulled out keys dangling from a purple puffball. "The Chevy won't be ready for another week, and Jimmy over at Car Spa said I could borrow Henrietta here. It's her daughter's car and she's away at school."

"It's a freaking ladybug. It even has the black spots. Are those eyelashes over the headlights? Is that a big key sticking out the back? You're really going to drive around in a car that looks like a giant toy?"

"This from a woman who owns a pink scooter." Boone puffed out his chest. "I'm secure enough in my manhood to handle it."

"That makes one of us." I snagged the puffball. "I'll drive. If the other kids see you behind the wheel of this thing, they'll beat you up—unless they're laughing too hard." Boone curled himself into shotgun and I cranked the ignition. "Elsie and Annie Fritz are minding the Fox. Text them to keep Ross away from the Caddy at all costs."

"I've seen those two in action. Are you sure you want to add that last part?"

"We got to get to the smoking pillow—that's like a smoking gun but softer and prettier and just as deadly. If Ross finds it, the sisters are toast, and I know that taking the pillow is obstruction of justice, so it's a darn good thing I got a heck of a great lawyer to get me off if I get caught."

I gave Boone a quick kiss and we barreled off, or at least did as much barreling as a pimped-out VW bug could muster. I only ran two yellow lights—okay, one was kind of orange-ish, but we needed to hurry. We screeched to a stop in front of Cherry House as a police cruiser pulled up right behind us. Annie Fritz stumbled out of the Fox into the front yard. Her hand to heart and a herd of shoppers following.

"I think it's safe to say that the sisters got my text." Boone got out of the car and I did the same, Ross and two cops hustling right behind us.

"It's her little old heart," Elsie bellowed as she raced down the steps, waving her arms in the air. "You all need to do something right quick before it's too late."

"It's acting up something terrible." Annie Fritz patted her chest and gulped in lots of air. "Thank the Lord above you're here," she said to Aldeen. "I need an ambulance. I need a doctor. I desperately need a nice dress to be buried in. Save me, save me." Annie Fritz did a quick spin and, eyes fluttering, collapsed against one of the cops. He did the heroic catch, and a sobbing Elsie grabbed Ross by the front of her navy polyester jacket. "It's a true blessing you arrived when you did."

As if on cue, BW let out a mournful howl, Boone tried not to laugh, and I inched my way toward the back of the sisters' house. The Caddy sat in the driveway, looking all nice and innocent. I opened the door and yanked out the pink pillow minus one tassel. Mission accomplished! I congratulated myself on a job well done and was quietly clicking the door closed when a firm hand landed hard on my shoulder.

"I'll take that," came Ross's voice from behind me.

I spun around and gave her a big toothy grin. "My, you're looking skinny. You'll be amazing as my bridesmaid, the prettiest one for sure."

"There're laws against bribing cops with wedding party status, you know." Aldeen held out a plastic evidence bag and I dropped in the pillow. "I've been dieting two days now and it's killing me. I had doughnut meltdown this morning and dunked a roll of masking tape in my coffee."

"Look, you can't lock up Elsie and Annie Fritz; they didn't knock off Bonnie Sue, and all you have is some flimsy circumstantial evidence connecting them to a crime they didn't commit."

"I have the murder scene." Aldeen tapped the car hood. "The weapon." She held up the pillow. "And Bonne Sue was buried right here in this very garden, sprouting plastic leaves. I still don't know how to classify that one."

"What about desperation over getting sent up the river for something you didn't do? And what was their motive in knocking off Bonnie Sue? Tell me that, huh? Why would they do such a thing? Those two poor old souls—"

"You mean those poor souls who just put on an Oscar award–winning performance out there on the front lawn to keep me and the boys busy while you snuck back here to get rid of crucial evidence? Personally, I thought the howling dog was a bit over the top."

"Maybe a little, but BW likes to ham it up, and the truth is that Elsie and Annie Fritz just happened to find Bonnie Sue in their car and had to get rid of the body so it wouldn't seem like they're a jinx. With all the people dropping dead over at the Pines since they started their Premium Woeful Weeping Package for the residents, the sisters didn't need another body to make people feel nervous. They had to hide Bonnie Sue. Think about it. It makes perfect sense that they'd want her alive, not dead, because of the jinx. There's just no motive for knocking her off."

"That you know of." Aldeen folded her arms, giving her girls some much-needed support. "You think these old-sters are all walkers and hearing aids and they sit around and sip liquored-up sweet tea and play canasta day in and day out? Well, that's not all they're up to. I've heard stories, lots of 'em, and Elsie and Annie Fritz aren't in the middle of this mess by accident. They're involved in something, and you need to quit interfering or you'll wind up getting married at the courthouse—and not in the fashion that will make your mamma smile."

Aldeen thrust out her hip and tossed her head. "But now that you mention it, I do believe I've lost a pound or two. Let me know when we're all going dress shopping. I just ordered some new Spanx to smooth out my womanly curves so I'll look right fetching."

I followed Aldeen back to the front of the house, where the sisters were being herded into the cruiser and a news team from WSAV was pulling to the curb. Boone headed for the Bugmobile, no doubt to follow Elsie and Annie Fritz and somehow save their behinds yet again. I had serious doubts he could pull it off, and the sisters' sobbing theatrics probably wouldn't work a third time.

I followed a group of customers back into the Fox, and by late afternoon the curious crowd and TV cameras had thinned out and my Godiva candy box was fuller than usual. At least there was some good to come of all this. The bad part was that the sisters and Boone had not returned, dark clouds hung over St. John's, and Willie Junior was heading up my sidewalk. "Where is he? What did you do with my grandpa?"

"I'm sure your grandpa is just fine," I said in a cheery voice to reassure a lady looking at two new straw hats on the dining room table. I hooked my finger at Junior to get him to come behind the counter. I lowered my voice, hoping he'd take the hint. "Your granddad's safe and sound, and we need to keep him that way till we find out what's going on. Do you have any idea who'd want to harm your grandfather?"

"Are you kidding? My mother, that's who." I gave Junior a finger-across-the-lips sign to quiet him down. "Grandpa made money on some vitamin deal, and she wanted him to pay for a facelift. She couldn't talk him out of the money, no matter how hard she tried, and believe me, she tried a lot. Now Grandpa's dead and she's acting stupid and running around town with a flashy dude half her age. She got a new credit card and she's spending money all over the place like a crazy person. She thinks she's really hot."

"Did your grandpa ever talk about someone named Bonnie Sue?"

"Who's Bonnie Sue? What does she have to do with my grandpa? I thought you were supposed to be a big-time crime solver, but you're stupider than my mom. You got three days to find out who killed Grandpa or I'm putting that video I have on YouTube and telling everyone *you* murdered him 'cause you didn't like him and you hid his body and you're nothing but a big old dumb liar."

Junior stormed out of the Fox, the hat lady giving me the evil eye, just as a smiling Boone balancing two Vinnie-Van-Go-Go's pizza boxes with a six pack on top strolled in. I was always beyond glad to see him, but now his timing was perfect. Nothing got a woman out of a bad mood faster than a great-looking guy in the room. The lady's "Eat dirt and die" look instantly morphed into a sweet smile and she pranced past Boone and out the door. I quickly locked it behind her.

"How'd it go with the sisters?" I asked.

"I got them out on bond using my house as collateral.

We're skating on some pretty thin ice here, and if they go on the lam, I'm setting up my law practice here between the blouses and the sweaters."

"Well, it'll improve my business, that's for sure."

He tapped the pizza boxes. "I figured you'd be off to visit KiKi and her ankle tonight, so I have two contractor guys coming over to take a look at the attic and see what's going on up there. It's raining hard, and maybe we can find that leak before you, me, and BW are sleeping in a moat instead of a bed."

Boone put the boxes on the counter, gave me his devil smile, and pulled the purple puffball with keys out of his pocket. "It's starting to rain hard out there." He nodded to the window as a crack of lightning lit up the sky. "Someone could get really wet riding around on a scooter."

"Really wet?"

"Really, really wet."

"You're enjoying this, aren't you?"

"Heck, yeah."

I grabbed the keys, kissed Boone, and ran out the door.

Chapter Eleven

Rain slapped the windshield, sending the wipers into hyper-mode as the light from streetlamps and neon signs reflected off the drenched pavement. Traffic sucked; everyone had suddenly forgotten how to drive because water was falling from the sky. I made a right onto Barnard and pulled to the back of the Pines. Trying to remember where the low-hanging branch was and not trip over the horseshoe court again, I sprinted past the fountain, heading for the back door, and tapped the glass window. The door flew open and KiKi threw her arms around my neck, sobbing as she dragged me inside.

"What happened?"

"You're getting m . . . married at my house, of all things, and I'm your matron of honor." She blubbered harder. "You're the daughter I never had."

I kissed her forehead and hugged her tight. "With you, Uncle Putter, and Mamma, I was sort of communal property. So I'm guessing all this means the wedding plans are okay with you?"

"I couldn't wish for more, and Princess can be the flower girl. I'm just betting that BW's going to be ring bearer, so Precious gets equal time." KiKi looked up at me, eyes glistening. "We'll put a daisy garland around her little neck, glitter in her fur; she'll look adorable."

Auntie KiKi snagged an old wooden cane leaning against the wall and hobbled down the hallway with me following, leaving a trail of wet footprints on the hardwood floors. A bluesy rendition of I Found My Thrill on Blueberry Hill warbled from the living room. Candles lit the room. "No *Perry Mason* tonight?"

"It's a wake for Bonnie Sue. The geography of the song might be off, but the thrill part is right on. Everyone's chipping in to cover funeral costs; seems she was having a tough time making ends meet these last few years. And we had some more excitement with Issy Ledbetter's daughter wanting to move her mother out of the Pines with all that's going on and people dying like they are. Issy pitched a fit right here in the hall, saying she wasn't going anywhere, but truth be told, these deaths and suspicions of murder can't be helping poor Mr. Jim's pocketbook one bit."

We turned right to the first room with a plastic forsythia wreath decorating the door. Auntie KiKi opened it to a double bed with a pink-and-green floral bedspread, matching drapes, a Queen Ann desk and an overstuffed chair on one side, a loveseat on the other, and Anna and Bella gaping at us with tape measure in hand. All four of us froze, staring at each other.

"Well, hi, there," Anna finally managed. "This is such

a . . . a nice room, don't you agree? So spacious and accommodating, with a fine southern exposure and French doors right out there to a little patio, of all things."

"We thought you'd be at the wake." Bella nibbled her bottom lip. "So we're here to . . ."

"Measure for new drapes and not disturb you," Anna filled in.

"Yes!" Bella held up the tape measure and grinned. "Mr. Jim's having all new drapes made for the place, and we're helping him get the numbers together because he's so busy and we got all that community service to do. Well, we got what we need and we'll be on our way." Bella gave KiKi a squinty-eyed look. "So tell me, exactly how long do plan on staying around? I mean, you are looking kind of banged up today; maybe you need a more help-oriented facility like Senior Moments over there on Hull Street? Bet they'd love to have you."

"Think about it," Anna added. "Fact is, you need to think real hard."

Anna and Bella closed the door behind them, and I gave KiKi a long look. "Holy cow, they're right."

"Are you kidding? Measuring for drapes? Do those two think I'd actually fall for that whopper of a lie? What are they up to now, and why are they always up to something? Besides, I'd rather have blinds in this room and some nice curtains to let in the light. What's the use of having big doors like this if I you cover 'em all up. I'll talk to Mr. Jim myself and—"

"Forget drapes." I grabbed Auntie KiKi by the

shoulders. "KiKi, you have a bump on your forehead and your ankle's swollen for real and your hair looks like a bird's nest and you don't have on a speck of makeup. You never go anywhere without makeup. You're a complete mess!"

"Remind me not to have you write my obituary." KiKi flopped down hard on the loveseat and propped her foot off the end. "It's just a little accident is all. After your mamma left, I was sunning myself out there on the patio with a Key Lime Pie martini. I got up to get another lime slice to try and pep it up, and before I knew what was happening I was face down in the fountain, the thing suddenly spluttering and spitting. The plumbing around here is a mess." Auntie KiKi dropped her voice. "I do believe it was Bonnie Sue's ghost that pushed me in."

"Sounds more like the ghost of martinis past and present."

"One little very weak drink is not enough to make me stumble about like a drunken sot, and there wasn't a soul in sight when Mr. Jim dragged me out. Not only did I get this here bump and gimpy leg, I ruined my new iPhone that Mr. Jim now has sitting in a bag of rice, of all things. With my luck I'll get it back served up next to a chunk of boiled white chicken and steamed butterless, saltless broccoli. I even lost my drink when I fell, though I do think the koi fish seemed a lot happier the rest of the day."

Auntie KiKi leaned closer and whispered, "The way I see it, Bonnie Sue doesn't like that I've taken over her room and the old hussy's still hanging around. I keep hearing things."

"Heavy breathing?"

"Footsteps. I can still feel her cold hands on my back as she gave me a good hard shove." Auntie KiKi shivered and rubbed her arms.

"That's it." I grabbed the suitcase sitting next to the dresser and flung it on the bed. "I'm packing you up and getting you out of here." I yanked open a dresser drawer and started pulling out clothes. "It's raining like no tomorrow, so I'll bring the car around closer to the back. Though you've got to try not to fall over laughing when you see it; you have enough bumps and bruises."

KiKi grabbed a floral nightgown out of my hand and tossed it back in the drawer. "I can't leave now. What if it wasn't Bonnie Sue but Anna and Bella who shoved me in the fountain? They sure enough want me out of here—and maybe they wanted Willie and Bonnie Sue gone too for some reason. And what about those gym shoe boys? We still don't know who they are. We're not going to get answers with me limping around Rose Gate, now, are we?"

KiKi folded her arms. "I'm staying put till we figure this all out and get Annie Fritz and Elsie off the hook. They've been neighbors for years and I can't just walk away now, can I?"

"Well, you should know that the hook just got a little sharper. Bonnie Sue was smothered by the pillow the sisters have in their car, and Willie was writing checks each week to Bonnie Sue."

"He was paying her?" KiKi sat up straight. "For being . . . friendly. She was a right friendly woman, to be sure, but with Willie?" We both shuddered. "See there," KiKi went on, "I can't be leaving here with all these questions needing answers. I'm your mole, honey, the inside man on the job. I'm James Bond, martini and all. This was meant to be and you can't change fate."

Lord give me patience and hurry! I took KiKi's hand. "I'll get you a new phone so you can stay in touch, and Mamma, Boone, and I will stop by and check on you every few hours to see how you're doing."

"Seems excessive."

"Have you looked in the mirror?"

"Well, don't be bringing me flowers, I'm putting in an order right now for something fried. Make it dead animal, crustacean, or filled pastry and something chocolate. All this healthy living is sapping my strength and I won't be able to spy for diddly. I bet James Bond never ate rubber chicken and wilted broccoli."

I handed Auntie KiKi the cane. "Fried will have to wait, but I have it on good authority that Mr. Jim hoards not only bourbon but chocolate brownies. With the wake still going on, what say we raid the pantry?"

KiKi stood and started for the door. "Maybe we can fry the brownie."

We headed down the hall and I flipped on the kitchen light, the overhead fluorescents flickering to life. "Sit here," I said to KiKi, pointing at a little oak table and window seat with blue cornflower cushions. I found the brownies next to the mugs and got an apple from the fridge for me, wishing it had the word *tart* attached to it. I lit a fire under the teapot as Eugenia floated in through the back door, whisked off her raincoat, and flung it onto the counter.

"Well, now, I just seem to be finding you everywhere these days," Eugenia said to me. She twirled across the white tile floor, her spring green chiffon dress floating out around her as she hummed "I Could Have Danced All Night." "In spite of this dreadful weather, I had the most wonderful evening. It would still be going on, but my darling Dex has a business meeting in the morning and needs to get ready for it. He's such a hard worker and he's doing it all for us." Eugenia stopped by the door and snapped up her coat. "Good night, now. Enjoy your girl time and your tea. How cozy."

"Eugenia," I said. "Maybe Dex doesn't have a meeting tomorrow? I mean, how much do you really know about him? The man runs a mortuary; early morning is not rush hour."

"I know plenty. I'm not stupid." Eugenia's lips thinned. "I Googled Dex. He's from Atlanta and moved here because he has friends in the Oglethorpe Club and business connections and wants to make his mark." She stuck her nose in the air. "In case you haven't heard, he's taking Savannah by storm, and I just happen to be part of that storm and you need to butt out of my life, Reagan Summerside." Eugenia spun around, jutted her chin, and stomped out of the room.

Auntie KiKi took a bite of brownie. "So what do you know that the rest of us don't? 'Cause you are definitely up to something, bringing up old Dex like that."

I took a bite of apple. "Dex is burning the candle at both ends. He's canoodling with Eugenia and the new and improved and suddenly rich Arnett Fishbine. He gave them each the same gold bracelet Eugenia had on tonight."

"I say we hunt him down and neuter him."

"According to Willie Junior, mommy dearest spent a small fortune getting new and improved and wanted her daddy to pay for it, but he turned her down flat, leaving her with some hefty bills and no way to pay them off."

"And then Willie ate a peanut and solved all her problems." KiKi and I exchanged looks and KiKi added, "Arnett knew how asthma and allergies look alike because of her son having the same condition, and last I heard she didn't give a flying fig that Willie's burial was postponed. Sounds like another who-knocked-off-Willie candidate to me."

Thunder rattled the windowpanes and I gripped my mug. KiKi patted my head. "You should go before this storm gets any worse."

"Worse?" I dug around in Old Yeller and pulled out death-by-pink lipstick, a purple brush with sparkles in the handle, my trusty flashlight, and a canister of pepper spray. I gave KiKi the flashlight, pepper spray, and lipstick, hoping it looked better on her than it did on me. "It is vitally important to point the pepper spray away from you when activating it or you'll hate me forever. Be sure to lock your door and wedge that desk chair in your room under the knob. Tomorrow I'll get you a phone and the cavalry will descend."

"Tell them to be discreet so I just look like any other little old lady with a cane."

I gave KiKi a kiss on the cheek. "You are always a lady, you will never be old, and KiKi Vanderpool will never, ever be *just*."

By the time I reached the Bug, I was soaked through and scared spitless. A little rain, a little thunder, and I was fine. But this storm had left *fine* about an hour ago and headed straight to terrible. I drove at a snail's pace, trying not to short out the Bug's electrical system, which would turn the car into a dead bug and me out into the night alone. *Sweet Lord, spare me that!* I took a right onto Abercorn, lightning crackling around me. I had the steering wheel in a death grip, my ring sliding around on my wet finger. The streetlights blinked, blinked again, then died, casting all of Abercorn into a sea of black.

Sweat slithered down my back and I turned onto Gwinett, the streetlights and houses there having no better luck with electricity. I pulled the Bug to the curb, decided that waiting for the rain to ease up was not going to happen anytime soon and that being alone in a storm was a lot worse than being with someone. My special someone just happened to have a candle burning in the bedroom window. I made the sign of the cross, then dashed for the house, chanting the Lord's Prayer as I splashed my way to the porch. I slammed the door behind me and nearly passed out from relief.

"Hurry and get up here," Boone called from the second floor. "There's a flashlight on the steps. My fiancée's due home any minute now and it's going to be hell to pay if she catches us fooling around."

"You better make it worth my while, big boy," I called back, kicking off my shoes so as not to drip everywhere. I was chilled to the bone and shivering, and not just because of the rain. I had a feeling, a bad one, that someone was here in the house besides Boone. I knew what Boone felt like . . . warm, protective, familiar. This was different. Scary different.

Dredging up my last bit of courage, I spun around as another snap of lightning illuminated the dining room. Someone darted into the kitchen . . . maybe? With this much terror bottled up inside me, it was hard to separate fact from not-fact, right? Besides, who would want secondhand clothes enough to raid the place on a dark and stormy night? It made no sense, not one little bit. I must have imagined the whole thing, and in my present state, that wasn't hard to believe. I looked around again to see nothing but more lightning and thunder.

"Reagan?" Boone called down again. "Are you okay? You need me to come down there and throw your sweet ass over my shoulder and haul you up here?"

Another rumble of thunder shook the house to its foundation. I darted up the steps to find Boone sitting in the middle of the bed, shirt off, sexy as hell, reading something that looked like rolls of blueprints by flashlight. BW lay sprawled across his lap. More lightning zapped overhead, and I dove headfirst under the covers.

Boone lifted an edge of the blanket and peeked in. "Hello?"

I cracked one eye open and peeked back. "I'm not a thunderstorm fan."

"Never would have guessed. How's KiKi?"

"Can you visit her tomorrow and bring a fried cow?"

"Whatever the lady wants." Boone rolled up the blueprints, and clicked off the light. The single candle in the window danced shadows across the walls and ceiling. He snuggled down beside me as more thunder rumbled through the city. "Now let's see if we can think of a way to get your mind off the storm."

"It's not going to work. Nothing works."

Boone laughed deep in his throat and snuggled closer. "Wanna bet?"

By noon the next day we had blue skies, birds chirping, and Boone had made a pretty good dent in my thunderstorm phobia. Fact is, I was looking forward to more thunderstorms and more cures. He had afternoon meetings with clients, so he volunteered for morning Auntie KiKi duty and to get her a phone.

After I wrote up a sale for the cutest blue Kate Spade handbag that I'd had my eye on but could never afford, I hung up a brown skirt, catching my ring on the belt loop. I so needed to get the ring sized before I lost it, and I didn't even want to think about that happening. With the Fox empty for the moment, I had time to pair the skirt with a peach blouse for the display. I was just finishing when Elsie and Annie Fritz shuffled in the front door.

"It's mighty nice that you asked us to mind the place while you visit KiKi," Elsie said in a quiet voice. "We're so embarrassed with all that's going on, we don't dare leave the house, and we're missing seeing everyone over at the Pines. We always helped Mr. Jim out with things, and I'm sure he's shorthanded now. Finding Bonnie Sue in our backyard made the front page of the *Savannah Times*' home-and-garden section, of all things. Whatever are we going to do about all this?"

"Well, you sure don't have to be embarrassed while I'm around," Arnett Fishbine said, elbowing her way past the sisters and dumping an armload of clothes on the counter. "Fact is, if you ladies really did the old hussy in, I'm deep in your debt and thank you kindly."

Chapter Twelve

Arnett picked up a jacket from the pile of clothes she'd dropped on the counter. "Can you believe that Daddy wrote that tramp into his will? Thank heavens that now that she's hanging out over there at the morgue, all that money that was supposed to go to her goes to little ol' me. To celebrate my good fortune, I'm headed to Atlanta to refresh my wardrobe."

She dropped the jacket back in the pile. "Sell what you can and donate the rest. In fact, take my profit from these things and give it to the sisters here for their lawyer fees. They got it coming along with my best wishes for a speedy acquittal. You all have a good day now, you hear? I sure am. Retail therapy is therapy for the soul, and right now my soul is singing up a storm."

Elsie and Annie Fritz stood perfectly still, mouths open, as Arnett left the building. Elsie finally managed, "I do think Willie's daughter just thanked us for knocking off Bonnie Sue so she could go on a shopping spree?"

"Not that we did any knocking, you understand," Annie

Fritz added in a rush. "But what truly doesn't make sense is why Willie would include Bonnie Sue in his will, of all things. She spent time with the fellows at the Pines, to be sure, but I don't remember her ever making nice with Willie Fishbine. Best I can remember, they didn't have anything to do with each other at all."

"Bonnie Sue was hard up for money, so maybe Willie felt sorry for her?" I ventured, not quite believing the words I was saying. "Maybe she invested in Spring Chicken and Willie felt guilty that he took her money for a rotten deal and wanted to help her out?"

Elsie harrumphed. "Feeling sorry? Helping out? All Willie ever thought about was making money and getting rich. Fact is, that's how he convinced Annie Fritz and me to invest in Spring Chicken in the first place. He said he only invested in winners and he was letting us in on the ground floor. It was all very hush-hush and he only let in people who could afford this sweet deal. He knew we had some money with the house and our pensions and now the Woeful Weeping deal cooked up with the Pines. When things went belly-up, we were too embarrassed to talk about it, and no one else mentioned it either. I think we felt like old fools you see on TV who are so stupid and get scammed and taken advantage of. None of us wanted to believe we were like that. After a while we got an attorney and he looked into things, but there was nothing illegal going on. The contents weren't toxic or harmful, and proclamations in the brochure of 'miraculous rejuvenation' and 'youthful vitality' aren't against the law, since what makes for 'youthful' and what's a 'miracle' are anyone's guess. The vitamins sounded like something that would sell, and they did at first—till people realized they didn't feel better at all. Then Sister and I were left with a bad investment and plumb sunk."

"If it's any consolation, you weren't the only ones. At least two men at the Pines got taken for a ride and were none too happy about it. Do you remember Willie spending time with some of the men at the Pines more than others? Maybe taking them aside and chatting or going out for lunch? They might have spent time with Emmitt and Foley too."

Both sisters giggled and Elsie said, "The men around there were Bonnie Sue's turf, but maybe KiKi will find out who these two other investors are now that she's over at the Pines. That reminds me; she called us and left you a message." Elsie pulled a neon pink Post-it from her pocket and read, " 'First off, you got to get yourself a phone or take up raising carrier pigeons so people can get a hold of you. And you need to remember to feed Precious.' And KiKi said she wants a"—Elsie flipped over the paper—"Cajun catfish sandwich from over there at Bayou Café."

Elsie stuffed the note back in her pocket and Annie Fritz pulled a hankie from hers and dabbed her eyes. "I don't know how Sister and I are ever going to repay you two for all that you've done for us. You are truly a blessing to take on our problems the way you have."

I took each of their hands. "We haven't found the killer yet, but we're working on it, and besides, you two were with me through Hollis and the divorce from hell and I'll never forget that. But if you'd like to make KiKi's day, she'd sure appreciate some of your amazing chocolate doughnuts, and as for me"—I held their hands a little tighter—"how about a red velvet wedding cake?"

I left the Fox to the sisters, now chatting about cake and cream frosting and in better spirits than when they came in. I retrieved my scooter from the garage and putt-putted off to River Street and the Bayou Café. The thing with a scooter is that you can zip around cars and pedestrians and tour buses and sightseeing trolleys. With narrow streets, clueless tourists, and cobblestones, Savannah had been made for scooters—unless someone opened a car door onto the street and sent you flying.

I parked in the shaded lot next to the river as a behemoth container ship from Panama growled its way to the busy deep ports beyond. Back in the day, pirates had docked here, liquored up men at the local bars, then loaded them onto their ships. The Pirate House still had the underground tunnels to the river to prove it. That's one way to get a crew together.

I crossed River Street, heading for the café nestled in with the other tourist shops, until I spotted Cassandra's Jewelry store. It was really more upscale fashion jewelry for tourists than for brides-to-be, but I'd gone to school with Cassandra, had been in her wedding, and knew she could size my ring. Besides, I wanted to show it off.

"Well, look with the cat dragged in," Cassandra gushed as I entered the garden-themed boutique with cherub fountain gurgling in the center and potted palms all around.

She lowered her voice to keep the conversation between us and not the shoppers. "What brings you to the snobby side of the tracks?"

I held out my hand. "I need to get it sized."

"Oh, it's beautiful!" Cassandra scurried around the glass counter glittering with shiny bobbles and bands, her blonde ponytail swishing side to side. She gave me a hug. "I heard you got the man. That chin, those eyes, enough chest hair to carpet the family room. Hubba-hubba, girlfriend. The high school yearbook said you were the one most likely to win the lottery but lose the ticket. Well, I think you found that ticket."

I laughed, slid the ring off my finger, and placed it in Cassandra's palm. "It needs to be a size smaller."

"Daddy takes care of jewelry repair, and he and Mamma are in New Orleans soaking up cool jazz and warm baguettes. They'll be back this weekend. I can keep the ring till then or you can take it to another jeweler."

Having my lovely ring with a stranger felt like abandonment, and being without it for a week felt worse. "I'll bring the ring back."

"Except you might lose it with it rolling around on your finger like a doughnut. Do what I did when I went steady with Princeton Wellington and he gave me his high school ring. I wrapped dental floss around the back to make it smaller. It's waterproof, clear so it doesn't look horrid, and if you get caramel stuck in your teeth, you're covered. It should hold you till Dad gets back, and best of all you won't come in here crying your eyes out over losing a lovely heir-loom that can't be replaced."

"I'll do it, and now that I'm here, maybe I could buy something nice for Boone. Something meaningful. It won't be as sentimental as this ring, but do you have any suggestions?"

"Cufflinks for the big day are always nice." Cassandra reached into the case and brought out several pairs. "A pocket watch. This is a nice one, and you can engrave it." She put the watch on the countertop.

"Boone's not a cufflink or watch kind of guy. He's more of a bacon-of-the-month-club kind of guy." I heaved a sigh. "I have no idea what to give him, but you do have nice things." I pointed to a gold bracelet with a crystal heart. "I know a guy who bought two of those and gave one to each of the girls he's dating."

"I had a customer the other day who bought *three* of them." Cassandra leaned across the counter. "It was that up-and-comer they wrote about in the paper. I recognized him right off. I bet he was giving one to each of his girlfriends. He's a class-A player. I see them all the time in here. They give the same jewelry so they don't have to remember who they gave what to. Total sleazebags. Makes you appreciate Walker and my Archer, that's for sure. We got the winners."

I thanked Cassandra, collected one really delicious fried fish sandwich and one broiled piece of soggy cod from the Bayou, made a stop at CVS for dental floss, non-minty, and headed off to the Pines. Since this wasn't an after-hours clandestine visit like my other outings, I parked the scooter in the back lot and used the gate.

"You better have something fattening in that there bag," KiKi called from her lounge chair on the deserted patio. "Or consider yourself written out of the will."

"How about grub and gossip? You can't beat that now, can you?" I dragged a wrought iron chair from the little white round tables that decorated the patio and sat beside Auntie Kiki. I handed her the sandwich bag and stopped mid-delivery. "Holy mother of pearl! You look worse. Boone couldn't have seen you like this or he would have called me." I picked up the phone sitting in her lap and waved it in the air. "Why didn't *you* call me? You have a black eye, for Pete's sake!"

"I bumped into a door that was suddenly open right in front of me for no good reason." KiKi pulled the sandwich out of the bag, unwrapped the paper, and took a bite. "And as for calling, honey, you don't have a phone," she said around a mouthful. "And to tell you the truth, I didn't call anyone 'cause you'd all go fretting up a storm and want me to leave here, and that's not going to happen. I finally got Mr. Jim making the martinis the way I like them, I finagled two sausages for breakfast from Lemar, I got a spa appointment at four, and I need to find out why I keep having accidents that are not accidents."

"Are you kidding? Someone's on to you snooping around, that's why. The killer knows you're looking into Bonnie Sue's demise and wants you out one way or the other!"

"Maybe, but there's something else going on around here, and I can't put my finger on it. I'm not going to just run off like a scared puppy."

Auntie KiKi took a bite of sandwich, and for a second I shamefully forgot about her injuries as I watched the spicy sauce dripping deliciously off her fingers and onto the napkin. Forget spilled milk; I was really close to crying over spilled sauce.

"Besides," KiKi continued, snapping me back to the moment, "no one messes with KiKi Vanderpool and gets away with it, but I will promise to keep in contact and call. Fact is, I bought a phone cover to match my luggage. I got it online and the boys around here helped me get the shipping right. Emmitt and Foley even stopped bickering for five minutes to try and figure things out so I'd get the case in one day and not three. An LV case is a mite extravagant, but it gave me a chance to talk to the guys and I got some information. Every man likes helping a woman in distress."

KiKi leaned a little closer. "First of all, none of them trust Dexter, and they've tried to warn Eugenia to steer clear of him. But she's not listening. She's in love with him. None of them said much about the great Spring Chicken scam, but I got the feeling some of them were involved. I just have to find out who." Auntie KiKi bit again into the sandwich like the shark from *Jaws*. "So now tell me about this gossip."

With all this going on at the Pines and KiKi right in the middle of it, there was no way I could get her out unless I called in the Marines. Since capturing stubborn aunties wasn't exactly in their job description, KiKi would stay at the Pines, at least for the moment. I took out my broiled, bunless, sauceless cod with a sprig of wilted rosemary. The Styrofoam container it came in probably had more flavor. "I detoured from getting your sandwich and went into Cassandra's Jewelry to get my ring sized."

"And maybe show off a bit."

"There is that. Her dad who does the jewelry work is on vacation, but Cassandra just happened to mention that someone we know and loathe bought not two gold bracelets with crystal charms but three. Our very own local Romeo has three women on the string: Eugenia, Arnett, and some mystery lady. How does he find the time?"

"Honey, the real question is, how does he find the stamina?" KiKi licked sauce from her fingers as the double French doors leading out onto the patio suddenly burst open and Emmitt backed our way.

"I've had it with you, Emmitt Gilroy, you old fart," Foley bellowed, shaking his cane, his Cubs cap tilting as he chased Emmitt across the pavers. "*I'm* the one who's giving the first eulogy at Bonnie Sue's wake on Friday, and you can just go straight to Hades for all I care."

"Bonnie Sue was my girl," Emmitt yelled back, shaking his walker at Foley. "And I'm giving the first eulogy 'cause you'll be too busy trying to get that there cane off your hand, 'cause it's there forever." Emmitt stopped and rocked back on his heels, a smug grin tripping across his face as Foley held up the cane. He shook it once, twice, three times.

"It . . . it won't come off!" Foley's face reddened, his

eyes bulging, the vein in his forehead ready to rupture. "I can't let go of the dang thing! What did you do to me, you lily-livered varmint?"

"The wonders of superglue, and it's exactly what you had coming for putting that whoopee cushion on my chair in the dining room last night. Everybody was laughing at me thinking I did something unseemly. Well, I got the last laugh this time, you old coot. That there cane's attached to you like a third arm." Emmitt laughed. Foley growled deep in his throat, swinging the cane as Mr. Jim hurried through the door.

"Hold on, you two." Mr. Jim jumped between the men.

Foley shook the cane at Emmitt. "I'm the one who's holding on, if I want to or not, and this is the last straw. We're having it out once and for all. I'm challenging you to a duel. I demand satisfaction."

"Something you never gave Bonnie Sue."

"I'm going to blow your head clean off your shoulders!"

"Not if I blow yours off first!"

"No one's blowing anything." Mr. Jim grabbed the cane and the walker. "The three of us are having some brandy and talking things over like civilized people."

"Hang civilized," Foley bellowed, waving his Cubs hat in the air. "This is war, Gilroy." Emmitt thumped his way back inside, yelling, "And I'm gonna win. You better be sleeping with both eyes open if you know what's good for you."

Mr. Jim sat Foley in a chair. "You stay here and calm down now. I'll get something for the glue and a nice glass of apricot brandy. You know how you love that apricot brandy I order special."

Mr. Jim patted Foley's shoulder and left. Foley gave one more shake of his cane, frowned that it didn't release, then pulled in a deep breath. "I'm mighty sorry you lovely ladies had to witness that scuffle, but Emmitt and I have been battling over my lovely Bonnie Sue since she got here almost a year ago now." Foley's voice hitched. "I can't believe the light of my life, the song in my soul, the gravy on my mashed potatoes is gone, never to return."

He swiped his eyes and Auntie KiKi handed him one of her napkins with a sauce smear. "Bonnie Sue was a lucky woman to have you care so deeply about her. I hear she was right friendly with Willie Fishbine too."

"Bonnie Sue and Willie?" Foley shook his head. "I keep my eyes open, and I know what goes on around here. My corner room is great for seeing what everyone is up to. I see who's coming and going, like when January Foot smuggled in a stray cat she found. My little pumpkin didn't even like Willie at all—told me so herself on more than one occasion. Bonnie Sue was mine, truly mine, forever mine and no one else's, no matter what Emmitt Gilroy has to say. Just because he has the big room at the end of the hall, he thinks he's some big shot around here."

Foley stood, blew his nose into the napkin, and stuffed it into his pants' pocket. "You ladies have a nice afternoon, now. I'm going to go see about getting this cane off. If you hear gunshots, don't you be alarmed none. Sooner or later

Emmitt and I are going to put this to rest once and for all and it ain't gonna be pretty, I can promise you that."

Foley hobbled back inside. KiKi waited till the door closed, then said to me, "Foley might think he knows everything that goes on around the Pines, but he doesn't know about this here." KiKi reached into her pocket and held up a blue paper with gold edges and an embossed chicken.

"He doesn't know that next time you want me to bring Kentucky Fried Chicken extra crispy? I don't think the old boy cares."

KiKi shoved the paper in my face. "Take a closer look. This is a stock certificate for fifty shares of Spring Chicken, and you'll never guess where I found it."

Chapter Thirteen

"It was stuffed in the back of the closet in Bonnie Sue's room," Auntie KiKi said around a mouthful of fried fish. "Wedged tight between two shelves. I found it when looking for a place to hide the pralines Walker brought for me. I had to hide them, 'cause if your mamma finds them she'll take them, saying my health is going right to the dogs. Easy for her to say; I'll be the one back to Putter and the land of healthy living in no time. I need to enjoy the moment while I can."

I snagged the Spring Chicken stock certificate out of KiKi's hand. "Bonnie Sue bought into the Spring Chicken scam like the sisters did? I can't believe it. Old Willie must have had a big heart after all. Who knew? He actually felt bad that Bonnie Sue lost money, and he was helping her out financially and that's why he gave her a check each week."

KiKi dabbed sauce from her lips. "Honey, if something sounds too good to be true, then it is, especially in the case of double-dealing Willie Fishbine. Besides, where would

Bonnie Sue get the money to invest in the first place? She was skint, and everyone knew it."

"Okay, so she could have borrowed money from one of her male friends to buy in, figuring it was a good deal and she'd make money on her investment?"

"The sisters said Willie only let investors in who could afford it. My guess is that rotten excuse for a human being wanted his money fast so that when the vitamin scam blew up, he had his cash safely tucked away where no one could get their hands on it. This Willie–Bonnie Sue connection just doesn't add up. Maybe I'll find something out at the spa this afternoon. It's amazing what people talk about when they're wearing fluffy robes, sipping lemon water, and sitting around with seaweed smeared on their faces."

KiKi grabbed her cane and wobbled to her feet. "You best be off; my appointment's in twenty minutes and I got to get myself presentable." She fluffed her hair and batted her eyes. "Anthony's picking me up and I don't want to be late for that, now, do I?"

"Anthony?"

"Did you know that Uber stands for *you'll be eternally thankful*?"

"Uh, U is y-o-u and *thankful* does not begin with R."

"Don't be picky, dear; it's mighty unbecoming."

Auntie KiKi headed inside and I started for my scooter. I cut across the patio and around the cherub fountain spitting water at the sun, cut through the break in the azalea hedge, and stopped. There on the sidewalk by the street and next to the Pines was none other than old Dex with Hollis right beside him, both taking a stroll. Two of the sleaziest guys in Savannah in the same place at the same time was not a coincidence. I ducked down and crept closer, then darted behind a white concrete bench to—

"Playing hide and seek?" came Boone's voice at my side.

I slapped my hand to my heart so it wouldn't jump out of my chest and yanked Boone down beside me. "What are you doing here?" I whispered.

He held up a white cord. "Phone charger for KiKi. I forgot to give it to her when I dropped off the phone, and why are you hiding in the bushes?" Boone wagged his brows. "If you can't think of a reason, I can. You look awfully cute today." He tucked a curl behind my ear. "Fact is, you look awfully cute every day. I think we need to celebrate that fact."

I felt a blush creep into my cheeks and pointed to Dex and Hollis. "Those two are up to something."

I felt Boone's breath on my neck. "Forget them. I'd like to be up to something."

"What do you know about this Dexter guy?"

Boone exhaled a resigned sigh of *not getting any now*. "He likes good cigars, Maker's Mark on the rocks, and nice-looking women. I've seen him at Abe's on Lincoln a few times with some hot babe."

That left Arnett out. "Eugenia?"

"Older, late thirties, looked like money. I didn't recognize her."

Hollis and Dex moseyed on around the corner toward

the front of the Pines, and Boone and I stood. I dusted pink azalea petals from my backside and Boone added, "You know, if Dexter is here with Hollis and they're scoping out the Pines, my guess is that real estate's involved."

"Of course!" I grabbed Boone by the front of his shirt and kissed him hard. "That's why Hollis was after Mr. Jim to sell the place—he's got a buyer lined up. Dexter! He probably met Dexter when he came to visit his uncle Foley. Two dirtbags found each other. Mr. Jim doesn't want to sell, but with all this bad publicity, he might start losing customers and be forced to. Maybe Hollis even caused the bad publicity."

"Hollis is a lot of things, most of them not good, but a murderer?"

"Maybe not on his own, but I ran into his fiancée and she said Hollis was looking for a big deal. Maybe this is it? Maybe she pushed him into it—she's a pushy kind of person, and thoughts of murder do cross your mind when you're around her. I'm sure Hollis wants to marry her and get into her daddy's real estate company, and this would be a big score, showing he's worthy. Hollis visits his uncle at the Pines, so he knows the layout and the people there. And this Dexter guy wants the Pines bad enough that he's juggling three women at once, two probably for the money. I don't have a clue as to why he's dating Eugenia."

"Three at once, huh? I can't keep up with one."

"We need to find out more about Dexter. Maybe he's a total badass and talked Hollis into knocking off Willie and Bonnie Sue to get the negative publicity going and buy the

Pines? Dex and Hollis are here, so Dex isn't at his office at the Slumber. What say we wander on over to the Slumber and talk to the help and figure out what he's up to?"

"I have a meeting at four. Wait an hour and I'll go with."

"Dex could be back by then. I'll go on my own and . . . and you got a funny look. What's this meeting you're going to all about? Is everything okay?"

Boone gave me one of his sexy grins, but this time it didn't quite reach his eyes. "There's this lawyer–client confidentiality thing and there's nothing you need to worry about—and don't go changing the subject. Without me around, you're not going to be content with asking some questions; more like breaking and entering."

"Let's go with snooping and sneaking."

Boone tweaked my nose. "One of these days, sweet stuff, you're going to get caught with your hand in the cookie jar, so I got you something you might find useful." He reached into his pocket.

"You got me a flip phone!" I pried it open.

"You are now officially on the grid. It cost a buck; I swear that's what they're going for these days. I knew you'd have a fit if I bought you an expensive iPhone, but a dollar keeps that independent steak of yours intact, and now we can stay in touch in case that cookie jar thing happens. I even put in some phone numbers like KiKi's, your mom, Elsie and Annie Fritz, and Big Joey if you get into a real bind and I'm not around. But I'm number one."

I gave Boone a kiss and slid the phone into my back pocket. "Now I got junk in my trunk like all the cool kids."

I wiggled my behind. "But to put your mind at ease, number one, there won't be any problems today. Mercedes is probably at the Slumber, it's broad daylight, the cat's away and the mouse will be careful and very quick, Scout's honor." I crossed my heart and held up a two-finger salute.

Boone took off for the house, sunlight glinting in his dark, recently cut hair, no doubt styled but refusing to stay in place. A strand always fell across his forehead, another curling at his left ear. He walked a bit stiffer today, not carefree, not Boone-like at all. Something had him on edge, and it took a lot to get Walker Boone there. My guess it had something to do with this meeting at four.

Concerned, I headed for my scooter, wondering what to do. I didn't want to nag, but I didn't want Boone to think I didn't have his back. I'd always have his back.

I scootered off for the Slumber, passing Green Square, named after Revolutionary War hero Nathanael Green. I dodged a group of tourists following a leader wielding a pepto-pink umbrella to keep everyone together, turned left onto Broad, then followed two cars into the Slumber's parking lot. I had lucked out. There was an early evening wake and I could blend right in with the crowd.

I parked behind a clump of oleander bushes in case I needed to make a fast, inconspicuous getaway and fluffed my hair from helmet head to trendy—or at least that was the look I hoped for. I tucked in my blouse, tucked Old Yeller under my arm, and joined two funeral-goers trooping in the front door.

I pretended to sign the "Yep, I'm sorry he's gone too"

book, but instead of seeking out Dennis "Bingo" Mulvane in the Heavenly Pastures slumber room or hitting up the tea table for windmill spice cookies, I hung a left down a hallway marked "Business Offices."

"You're here!" Mercedes gushed, giving me a quick hug. "I was trying to find you and have been calling all over the place. You need a phone, girl."

"And I now have a phone." I held up my flip.

"Who made it, Fisher Price?" Mercedes grabbed Old Yeller's strap and yanked me into a room that—thank you, Jesus—was body-free, containing only stainless steel shelves of stuff and a long, empty table. She had on her white do-up-the-dead smock and her forehead was dotted with sweat.

"Girl, our luck is running out on Willie. I was in Mr. Dexter's office getting the 411 on my next client due in when Bonaventure Cemetery called. They started to leave a message 'cause he's out and the secretary and director are busy with the funeral going on out front. When I heard Willie's name mentioned, I freaked and picked up the phone. Bonaventure wants to know where he is!"

"I think heaven would be a stretch."

"I faked being the secretary this time around, but if they call back we're doomed and I can kiss my job here good-bye. I told Bonaventure that the family was waiting on a long-lost cousin to come in and pay their respects, but the cousin can only be lost for so long. We got to find who whacked old Willie and get that boy in the ground pronto. How close are you to finding the killer?"

"How well do you know your boss?"

"Mr. Pretty-Boy is a suspect?" Mercedes's eyes shot wide open. "Well, I'll be; I never saw that one coming. He's all smiles and slick-dressed, but he has cut me back to using the cheap makeup that turns orange on the dearly departed. And he said to only style the front of their hair these days to cut back on my hours, but I just bet Mr. Dexter's charging for the premier treatment. And another thing—my last paycheck bounced like a big rubber ball."

"Boone and I saw Dexter keeping company with Hollis over at Sleepy Pines, and they were checking out the place. Dexter plus Hollis adds up to a real estate deal with Dexter wanting to buy the Pines and Hollis doing the big-commission happy dance. If Dexter's having money problems, knocking off two residents would do a lot to drive down the price, and he could get the Pines for a song."

"A cane-to-casket operation?"

"Never thought of it that way, but it fits. Right now all we have on Dexter is guesswork. With him out and about and the secretary and director busy, we can have a look-see on what's really going on. Where's his office?"

"You know, just one time I'd like to meet up with you and we go shoe shopping or do some normal girly thing." Mercedes stuck her head out the door, then hooked her arm at me in a "Come on!" gesture. We slunk down the hall, past an open room with a garden mural, fake trees, flowers, and real caskets on display. Some were wood, some gray metal, others copper, all with tops open to blue or white satin lining.

"Pillows in coffins? They take this eternal rest thing seriously."

"Props the head up and holds it in place so it doesn't go flopping around like a dead fish."

"I am so sorry I asked." I followed Mercedes inside the last door, marked "Private," late afternoon sun spilling in through a bay window and a door leading to the back parking lot. A blue-and-mauve rug covered polished hardwood floors; a cherry desk sat to one side facing overstuffed club chairs. It was a typical business office except for two caskets against the back wall, top halves open wide exposing white silk and ruffled lace.

"Okay, Columbo," Mercedes said to me. "What are we looking for?"

"Anything that tells us how bad your boss wants the Pines, just how broke he is, or some connection to Willie and Bonnie Sue, and why in all that's holy does Dex have coffins in his office? You'd think one room of the things was enough."

"It's all about the Benjamins." Mercedes tapped the dark ebony casket. "This little beauty here is the JFK Original, the other is the Elizabeth Taylor, and both are exact replicas. At these prices, they are not coffins or caskets but eternal rest dwellings. Mr. Dexter makes a bundle off them, and when a customer sees JFK and Lizzy sitting all special here in his office, the other cheapo dwellings in the other room look pretty second-rate. No one wants to bury mamma or dear old granny in second-rate digs."

"Celebrity coffins?"

"This is nothing; you should see the Fairway. It has a green Astroturf interior, golf clubs inlaid on the top, and golf balls on the sides. With this being spring and golfers out in force, there's not a Fairway to be had in all of Georgia."

"You know a lot about this stuff."

"Too much."

I gave Mercedes a hug. "You're right, next time it's shoe shopping and martinis."

Mercedes hunkered down and yanked open the bottom desk drawer; I settled into the maroon leather desk chair and flipped up the laptop. I heard papers shuffling and Mercedes said, "Well, we got a thank-you note from Howie Baker saying how nice his wife's funeral was and how he just got a dog and named him Dexter. Here's an overdue dentist bill. Sweet heaven, root canals cost the earth; I'm buying myself a new toothbrush today. I got ten copies of that *Savannah Sun* article featuring Mr. Up-and-Comer—somebody sure does love themselves mightily—a financial report from Elder Planning Industries LLC, and a box of new Slumber brochures. Looks like Dexter's raising his prices . . . again." Mercedes held up the Elder Planning report. "What do you think this is all about?"

"Eugenia said Dex wanted to grow his company, Southern Way. Maybe this is a model? Dead and getting there is big money these days, and adding the Pines to the Slumber makes sense. You're having better luck finding stuff than I am. Everything on this laptop is password protected, the sign of a guy with a lot to hide. The only thing I have up here is a blinking light on the desk phone saying there's a message waiting. You don't think it's Bonaventure calling back, do you?"

"Reagan, honey," Mercedes said as I handed her back the report. "We got ourselves a body sitting in a Beemer and some kid blackmailing KiKi over a Snickers bar. I'd say anything's possible at this stage of the game."

I picked up the phone and hit speaker, then messages. "Dexter!" the phone barked, making me drop it on the floor. Mercedes and I stared at it as if it were a giant roach. "This is your father. For God's sake, grow up and be more like your brother. No way am I going to cosign a loan for another one of your harebrained ideas."

Mercedes plucked up the phone with two fingers and handed it to me. "Dang. I guess old Dex isn't everyone's idea of an up-and-comer, and if the Pines is on Dex's radar, he's going to have to do it himself." She waved a paper from her perch on the floor. "I got a letter here from Savannah Savings and Loan about the Southern Way Company LLC not having sufficient collateral for a loan at this time. I'd say my boss, your suspect, is in a serious financial situation."

"And that is exactly why he's dating Arnett Fishbine."

"Woof. Have you seen her latest facelift? I didn't know she had money. Word is she maxed out her credit cards for her new face and boobs."

"Arnett's financial situation has most dramatically improved recently, and I doubt if Dex gives a flying fig what she looks like. My guess is he's more interested in the bundle she inherited from her skinflint dad and how to get his hands on some of it."

I sat back in the leather chair. "Okay, so we have Dexter in a financial bind and wanting to buy the Pines to grow his business. That gives him motive to knock off Willie and Bonnie Sue to give the Pines a bad name, drive down the price, and persuade Mr. Jim to sell. And just for the record, he's not only playing Arnett; he's putting the moves on some hot out-of-town babe and no doubt hitting her up for money too."

"Two women at once? That's risky business." Mercedes closed the bottom drawer, pried herself off the floor, and sat in the club chair.

"Try three women; he's got Eugenia on the string too. I get Dex making up to the rich gals to further his agenda and feather his nest, but then there's Eugenia, and why her? No money, no connections to speak of. Family name goes back generations but Dex is from Atlanta. Why would he care about an old Savannah family? Dex is all about following the money."

"If Dexter is after the Pines, then maybe he's using Eugenia to persuade Mr. Jim to sell? Like you said, the Pines has been in his family for generations and he's not likely to part with it easily, that's for sure. But Eugenia is his only daughter and pretty much gets what she wants."

"That's got to be it! You're brilliant."

Mercedes batted her eyes. "And I'm a fine-looking woman to boot, but the only thing is, Mr. Dexter might have bitten off more than he can chew with Eugenia. I heard she chased her ex down Bull Street with daddy's Buick when she caught him cheating. Good thing Dex owns this mortuary, 'cause if Eugenia finds out he's doing the deed with those other gals, he could wind up being his own best customer."

A ringtone of "Grandma Got Run Over by a Reindeer" filled the air and Mercedes slid her phone from her smock pocket. "Duty calls; I'm being summoned to the delivery door. My customer has arrived. COD probably isn't a reindeer—more like fried chicken, gravy, and butter biscuits—but I couldn't find a ringtone for that. I'll keep my ear to the ground for news on my boss, and you need to get out of here too. Mr. Dexter's Mercedes isn't in the lot now, but if he finds you snooping, he'll bury the evidence so deep you'll never find out what's happening and he might see fit to bury you right along with it. If he's knocked off two to get what he wants, what's one more to add to the list?"

Mercedes left, the door closing with a soft click, leaving the room eerily quiet, dust motes floating in the afternoon sunlight, JFK and Elizabeth lurking right behind me. The place was beyond creepy. With all the dead bodies invading my life lately, I should be getting used to this funeral stuff, right?

Wrong! But it wasn't the dying part that got to me so much as the murder part. People were winding up here at the Slumber before their time. They should be out getting a double-dip spicy mocha cone at Leopold's or having a strawberry shortcake martini over at Jen's and Friends instead of lying in lookalike coffins that cost a bundle.

Giving my snooping abilities one last shot, I typed in "corpse" for the computer password. Then I tried "tombstone" and "six feet under" and had started with "casket" when voices sounded out in the hallway. They got louder. Someone was coming! See, this was my problem, or at least one of them—I never knew when to fold my tent and walk away, or in this case, keep an eye on the parking lot for Dex's car, which I now saw was there. I always had to press my luck, and my luck had just run out.

I closed the laptop and darted for the door to the outside. Locked! Dead-bolted and no key? *Are you kidding me?* Dexter was afraid someone would walk off with Lizzie and Jack? The desk had an open bottom, so there was no hiding there, leaving me with one—make that two—less-than-great . . . no, make that totally horrible, possibilities.

The doorknob turned and my mouth went dry. I stood on the leather chair, hitched my leg over the ebony side, hugged Old Yeller to my chest, grabbed a handful of white lace to balance, then slid into the soft white silk. Taking a deep breath, I pulled down the casket lid.

Chapter Fourteen

I will not freak out! I will not freak out! I chanted with both eyes closed tight. I finally got the guts to pry one eye open, hoping that the JFK box had a light inside like a car. You know how you close the car door and the light stays on for a bit till you get things going, and since this was a superduper model coffin, why not? But there was no light, not even a glimmer. Black and nothing but black.

I could hear movement and muted voices. Someone was out there, so I wasn't alone, I reassured myself. Hey, I wasn't under dirt, no tombstone on top; I was in an office. *Breathe, just breathe! Try diversion. Think of how nice and comfy the silk is, how the pillow holds my head so it doesn't flop around like a dead fish.* And something was ringing? My ears? Oh, right, my phone! And it was loud! I wiggled my hand into my purse and maneuvered the flip to my ear, "Hello," I whispered.

"Reagan," came Boone's voice. "Why are you whispering? Where are you?"

See, this is one of the reasons I'd never wanted a phone: anyone could get me anytime. "I'm in a coffin. How's your day going?"

The lid flew up, Dexter and Mrs. Jones-Brown staring down at me. Holy mother of pearl, I had a corpse-eye view of what it was like to be dead and at your own wake. "I'll call you back," I said to Boone. "I have company."

Mrs. Jones-Brown screamed, Dexter screamed, and I joined in because it seemed like the thing to do at the moment. Mrs. Jones-Brown faded backward and I heard a thunk onto the floor. I bolted upright, the casket teetering then tipping over with a loud crash, rolling me out onto the carpet. I snagged Old Yeller and stumbled to my feet.

"Who . . . what . . ." Dexter turned white as the satin inside the coffin. He sat down hard in the club chair.

"Are you okay?" I asked him.

"Asthma. Stress triggers it. People jump out of cakes, not coffins." Dexter pulled an inhaler from his suit pocket and took a puff.

"I . . . I . . . I was trying it out for my dear auntie." I pushed back my hair, then pointed to the JFK. "I wanted to see if it was a comfy coffin."

"Eternal rest dwelling," Dexter muttered, his eyes still wobbling round in their sockets.

"You're KiKi Vanderpool's niece," Mrs. Jones-Brown muttered, pushing herself to a sitting position. She straightened her pink flowered hat and smoothed her dress over her knees. "I heard KiKi was over there at Sleepy Pines with a sprained ankle. If you're here looking at caskets, she must be in mighty terrible shape. I need to go visit her before it's too late."

"She's getting better; I'm just taking precautions." I took Mrs. Jones-Brown's arm and helped her into the other chair, then turned for the hall. "I'll have someone bring you water."

"So how was it?" Mrs. Jones-Brown asked.

I stopped and turned back. "How's what?"

She nodded at the JFK. "My Wesley's making eyes at the cashier at the Piggly Wiggly again, so I'm doing a little early reconnaissance in case the situation doesn't reverse itself right quick."

"Overpriced. Put him in a cheapie from the next room and take the rest of the money and go on a cruise."

I hustled down the hall, elbowed my way past two incoming Bingo mourners, and ran out onto the porch. This was one of those best-of-times, worst-of-times moments. Best in that JFK and I weren't bonded together for all eternity and worst in that Dexter would have no problem figuring out who I was. He didn't seem like a stupid guy, so my trying-out-the-casket-for-auntie spiel wouldn't fly. I'd been in his office to snoop around, and he knew it. Maybe not right now after being so taken by surprise, but it would dawn on him sooner or later.

The question was, what would he do about it? I inhaled the beautiful spring early-evening air, then redialed Boone.

"A coffin?" Boone said when he picked up.

"Eternal resting chamber. I was helping Mrs. Jones-Brown plan her philandering husband's demise."

"Glad you're having a productive day. My meeting's taking longer than I expected; we've hit a few snags. I'm grabbing a bite at Wall's, so do dinner without me and look at the blueprints I left on the counter and see what you think."

"I think I miss you."

"Right back at you." Boone disconnected and I made a beeline for the scooter. Savannah was always Slow-vannah, part of the city's charm, but when the schools let out or when there was rush hour traffic, it was more crawl than rushing anywhere. I gave up on Broad Street, which looked more like a parking lot, and zoomed across State Street till I got to Green Square, where things came to another standstill. The twenty-three city squares were lovely mini-parks draped in history and Spanish moss, and traffic flowed—or didn't flow—around them as if they were cobblestone rotaries.

I got trapped behind a horse-drawn carriage, resigned myself to a clip-clop pace, and was that Uncle Putter's black Beemer parked at the curb? But he was playing golf, and Auntie KiKi hadn't said he was coming back early.

I couldn't see the telltale license plate TEE4ME, but there was a hospital decal in the window and the little scratch on the hood. Of course, there had to be more than one black Beemer at St. Joseph's Hospital and more than one with a scratch from Auntie KiKi's misplaced martini glass at the Happy Halloween Country Club Dance, right? The carriage turned onto Houston and I spotted an opening in the crawl, aced out a Honda Civic, and zipped onto Price, passing the heavenly aroma of Walls barbecue as I zoomed by.

"Well, there you are," Elsie said as I hustled into the Fox. "It's been a whirlwind day, though it doesn't look like it now with no one here." She gave me a big wave when I came in the door, BW running up, whining and smiling as if I'd been gone a month. That's one of the great things about dogs—you're always tops on their list.

"You're here just in time to close the place up," Annie Fritz added.

"Not before I shop," Aldeen Ross wheezed, running in behind me. She leaned heavily on the counter, catching her breath. "I jogged all the way here from Forsythe Park; that's a whole two blocks and I'm just betting I lost another few pounds, and I aim to celebrate by buying something sexy. Do you know how hard it is to impress a coroner? If you're not prone on the floor and not breathing, they have no interest in you."

Annie Fritz reached for a pink blouse with a ruffled collar from the pile of just-brought-in clothes lying on the counter. "Those running shorts you got on," Annie Fritz said to Aldeen, "and your sweating like a cold beer on a hot day are enough to make me forget you're the one who put that ugly yellow tape around our garden and impounded our Caddy and put us in jail."

"Not for long, and I was just doing my job." Aldeen took a swig of water from her bottle.

"What I want to know is where you were when that snake Willie Fishbine swindled Sister and me in that Spring Chicken vitamin scheme. I sure didn't see any crime scene tape then, did I? That scum-sucking Willie sure got what he deserved, all right, no thanks to you. Glad to be rid of him."

Annie Fritz stared at Elsie and me, all of us open-mouthed. This was a bad slipup and we all knew it. The last thing we needed were the sisters connected to another dead person, especially with the word *swindle* tossed in.

"Right now I'm just like any other well-rounded woman," Aldeen panted. "I'm trying to lose a little of the rounded part and not die along the way. I think I'm going to pass out right here on the floor." Aldeen wobbled and I got a chair from the dining room that had once actually been used for dining.

She crumpled into the chair. The good part was that Aldeen didn't collapse on the floor; the really good part was that she was so worn out that the Willie connection didn't seem to have sunk in.

"That's better." Aldeen gulped more water. "You know, Willie's grandson's been down at the police station all hours, night and day, insisting his granddad was murdered." She faced Annie Fritz. "So, tell me about Willie and this Spring Chicken scam."

Holy cow! So much for not sinking in. "I am so glad you're feeling better!" I scooped my arm under Aldeen's, yanking her to her feet. "I got in the cutest floral sundress that I bet is just your size, and I guarantee it will get that handsome coroner you're after more interested in you than something dead on the floor."

Ten minutes of talking nonstop plus giving Aldeen the deal-of-all-deals on the adorable dress to keep her mind on shopping and not on Willie and murder and the sisters got Aldeen out the door without her asking more questions. I flattened myself against the door after I closed it and sucked in a deep breath.

"That was close," I said to the sisters. "I think, between the jogging, the coroner, and the new dress, she'll forget about Willie and the Spring Chicken scam and you connected to all of it. It was a fast conversation, just a few words, so there's really not much to remember."

"I just sort of got running off at the mouth," Annie Fritz whined. "I was making conversation, you know how I do, and everything just spilled out all at once and I couldn't stop it."

She nodded to a Snickers sitting beside the Godiva cash box. "And you know how Aldeen said Willie's grandson goes to the police station and gives them grief? Well, he was here and left this. He said you'd know what it meant and that the clock was ticking. I told him we didn't have any clocks here at the Fox at the moment, ticking or otherwise, and he should stop back in a few days in case one came in."

"Was he smiling?"

"Snarky, like he knew something I didn't, the little punk. Walker called to give us your new phone number, and your mamma stopped by and said she'd pick you up at ten sharp to try on wedding dresses. We'll be glad to cover for you, but right now we've got to go."

Elsie fluttered her eyelashes. "All this here publicity does have its perks. We're meeting with Sassy Savannah Canasta Club over at Sweet Potatoes and having peach-glazed chicken. We're sort of celebrities around town and suddenly in high demand; who knew such a thing could happen? We thought we'd be the bane of society, but being this close to a murder is like being a rock star. Bunch of ghoulish folks out there, I tell you. We just got to remember not to say anything that would link us to the murders for real." Elsie gave Annie Fritz the big-sister stare. "But now, before we go, we want to see that there phone Walker was talking about. I can't believe you finally have one."

I pulled the flip out of my back pocket. "Ta-da!"

Elsie and Annie Fritz exchanged looks, burst out laughing, gave me big sympathy hugs, then strolled out the door arm in arm.

I wrote up two sales and kept the Fox open, hoping to catch the evening shoppers while I straightened the place up. I ran the vac, dusted, added a cream blouse to a linen jacket, and wrote up three more sales. I would have written up more, but when shoppers realized the sisters weren't around to gossip and talk about Bonnie Sue getting planted in the garden, they lost interest and left. Elsie had been right about the ghoulish part.

I counted out cash, put it in an envelope to pay the sisters, and stashed the rest of the money in the Rocky Road container. I ladled out a cup of cottage cheese, a cup of tuna, and added a tomato for me, then spooned out kibble for BW. "Don't give me that 'I'm starving' look. I'm on a diet, so you're on a diet. You don't want people to be calling you Chubbers the ring bearer, do you?"

I day-dreamed of Oreo cookies and ate the cottage cheese instead. I tried, I really did, to make sense of lines drawn on blue paper, failing miserably to distinguish windows from doors and closets. I rerolled the papers, leaving it up to Boone, then headed upstairs to change into a hoodie and yoga pants left over from a time when I'd actually tried yoga. I'd toppled over on downward dog, broken the instructor's arm, and been banned from the yoga studio forevermore. Now the pants were relegated to evening walks with BW, and so far, I hadn't broken anyone else's appendage.

Knowing the sisters wouldn't take pay for helping me out at the Fox, I slid the envelope through their back kitchen window that didn't latch tight, then BW and I headed up Lincoln. The sky was ablaze with pinks and blues rapidly fading into dusk, streetlights blinking on, making Savannah oh-so-romantic and always a little mysterious.

We cut up Abercorn, and I spotted Dex and Arnett coming out of Cuoco Pazzo's, the best Italian in the city, with a take-home bag in hand. So that's why Dex had told Eugenia he hated Italian food; he took Arnett there! Using every ounce of willpower I possessed, I refrained from tackling Dex to the sidewalk, running off with the delicious bag, and being done with dieting. Instead, I slowed down so he and Arnett wouldn't see me. I didn't need to have Dex thinking

I was spying on him twice in the same day. Once was more than enough, even if it was from inside a coffin.

BW and I rounded Lafayette Square with the lovely lit fountain, one of the obligatory spots for all Savannah wedding photos. Would Boone be up for that? I didn't want to dictate our wedding day; I really wanted it to be *our* wedding day, and I still had no idea what to get the man to mark the occasion. Having a skywriter script out "Yippee" in white smoke was a possibility, but I wanted something more lasting.

We headed down Charlton, the massive live oaks forming a canopy of leaves, and started across Madison Square. As much as I loved this walk, tonight it wasn't a random choice. I'd had a niggling feeling ever since I'd seen Uncle Putter's Beemer, or what I thought was his Beemer, earlier in the day near Wall's Barbecue where Boone was having dinner. If there was one thing I'd learned from my dead-body affliction of late, it was that coincidences didn't exist.

Lights were on in Boone's house that was now his office, the Bugmobile parked at the curb. Right behind it sat Uncle Putter's Beemer, this time the TEE4ME license plate in full view. I stopped dead right in the middle of Madison Square, two tourists bumping into me. I muttered an apology but couldn't take my eyes off the Beemer.

"Yo, girl and dog," came Big Joey's voice right beside me. "What's up?"

"I'm supposed to be home reading blueprints, and Boone's in there." I pointed across the street. "And my uncle's in there and he's supposed to be playing golf and he's not playing golf and my aunt thinks he is and instead he's here talking to a lawyer, *my* lawyer. Nothing good comes from talking to a lawyer, even it is Boone."

"You getting married; bet it's that. Some big surprise headed your way."

"But why wouldn't my aunt know that her own husband is in town?"

Big Joey took my hand, his big dark one engulfing my much smaller one. He led me to a wood bench, the old iron park lights casting a golden glow around us with BW lying at our feet. " 'Cause," Big Joey said to me. "Auntie and you like this." He held up two crossed fingers. "If she knows the 411, she tells you what's happening; then no surprise."

"She'd blab."

"It's in the gene pool, babe. You got to trust the husband."

"I do trust him, but . . ." I sucked in a deep breath. "But what if that's not it? What if it's something bad and Putter's had enough of Auntie KiKi's shenanigans and sneaking around doing crazy things? That's in the gene pool too and not always easy to live with. She's over at Sleepy Pines right now with a fake sprained ankle, snooping after a killer. And then there are all the other times, like when we swam with the alligators and she jumped off a fire escape and Boone caught her, and the time we nearly got burned alive out at that lumber yard fire, and then switching Clif bars for Snickers, and—"

"Snickers?"

"The gene pool again, and we've done more break-ins

than you can imagine or the cops need to know about, and Uncle Putter's smart and I just bet he knows some of this stuff has gone on. Maybe he's had enough of Auntie KiKi sneaking out at nights and hunting killers."

"Or maybe he's changing his will, selling property, anything that needs a legal eagle."

"KiKi would be around for those things."

Big Joey put his finger across my lips. "Doc Putter's a righteous dude; fixed Granny's ticker pro bono before the Seventeenth Street Gang arranged for health insurance. KiKi's a handful, but she cool."

I jumped up. "I need to see what's going on."

Big Joey shook his head. "Bad idea. Gotta trust."

"I have to be ready to help KiKi if something bad's happening, and I know Boone can't tell me anything because of lawyer/client privilege."

"Walker sees you, he won't be happy."

"I won't get caught."

"Uh-huh."

I handed Big Joey the leash, crossed Charleston, rounded Boone's house, and cut down the narrow walkway separating Boone's house from the one next to it. The dim light shining out the kitchen window guided me along as I stepped around the garbage cans, praying that nothing slithered out. I crept up the back wooden stoop and felt over the back door for the hidden key. *Bingo*, it was still there.

I turned the lock and entered the kitchen with original porcelain sink, scarred countertops, and red retro Formica table and chairs that any fashion-crazy millennial would kill for. I slunk down the hall, voices drifting my way, and stopped by the dining room that had once housed the ugly dining room furniture but was now being converted into Boone's office.

There were no doors yet, but two polished oak ones leaned against the hall wall ready for installation. I side-stepped the doors and peeked in at Boone and Uncle Putter staring at papers scattered across the cherry desk, two half-filled glasses and a bottle of Johnny Walker Red between them. No smiles in sight, not a one.

Voices were hushed. I caught pieces of conversation saying that KiKi not being a Vanderpool would kill her, that Uncle Putter didn't want to hurt her like this but they'd get through it if it came to that and Boone promising to help any way he could.

Freaking hell! This was no fun wedding surprise pack-age! This was a horrible divorce package! I backed out of the house the way I'd come in, replaced the key, and joined Big Joey, BW sitting on the bench beside him.

"Give it."

"My uncle is definitely divorcing my aunt. Uncle Put-ter's from a distinguished family, I think he's had it with thirty-nine years of crazy and recently a lot of this is totally my fault. I talked Auntie KiKi into this latest scheme to find out who killed Willie and Bonnie Sue so the Abbott sisters don't get sent to the gallows."

"Gallows?"

"And now KiKi's headed for divorce court. I was the final straw. I need to get KiKi out of Sleepy Pines right now and . . . and turn her into the perfect wife. If she's president of the Garden Club and sings in the church choir on Sundays and volunteers at the hospital every day maybe Uncle Putter will change his mind. She'd be lost without him. And . . . she can't have anything more to do with me. I'm a bad influence."

Big Joey put his arm on my shoulders surrounding me in hug of comfort.

"I mean it." I stifled a sob. "No more me and Auntie KiKi. It's cold turkey. You know I thought it would be hard for Boone to put up with my dead-body affliction and the stuff I get sucked into, but it's tough for me not knowing what he's working on and realizing he can't say anything about it no matter who or what."

"All about trust, babe. You and Walker, meant to be."

Big Joey and I sat together for a few minutes, Big Joey being the hero and me being a total mess. I finally managed, "You roaming the streets tonight looking for a damsel to rescue?"

"Seventeenth Street Boys buying up Pinky Masters right around the corner. Needed to check out night foot traffic. It closed last year, we're all missing the Tabasco popcorn, and adding it to our real estate holdings gives the young guns employment and some business sense."

"And it has that really sweet old jukebox from the fifties."

"Aces on the box." Big Joey planted a soft kiss in my hair. "Got my digits?"

I pulled the flip from my hoodie pocket.

Big Joey laughed. "Babe." He gave me one last hug, BW a pat, then left.

BW and I headed home, taking the long way around to Troop Square where there was a doggy fountain and BW could do a little canine communing and get a drink. It gave a whole new meaning to local watering hole. We headed up Habersham and spotted Dex and Eugenia entering the Firefly. *Really? First he's out with Arnett, now Eugenia? Two dates in one night? You've got to be kidding!* And Eugenia was clearly getting the short end of the dating stick. The Firefly was nice and had great jerk chicken, but it didn't hold a candle to upscale Italian and amazing pesto sauce.

By the time I got home, I was more depressed than ever. I felt terrible for Auntie KiKi, terrible for Uncle Putter because he was so unhappy, and sorry for Eugenia because Dexter was playing her like a well-tuned fiddle. Damn the man.

I checked the front display window to make sure the light was on so passersby could see the cute stuff I had for sale, then headed upstairs. I showered and crawled into my fave Hello Kitty nightshirt. It wasn't sexy, even had a chocolate stain from where I'd spilled cocoa when I hadn't been calorie crazy, but Kitty and I were pals and tonight I needed a friend. BW curled up at my feet.

"Are you sleeping?" Boone whispered in my ear as he crawled in beside me an hour later.

"Not really." I sat up and stared at him through the dim light shining through the window from the streetlight outside. "I know you met with Uncle Putter and I know he's divorcing Auntie KiKi and it's all my fault for getting her involved in my dead-body problems, but we have to stop the divorce no matter what it takes and I don't give a rat's behind about your confidentiality promise. This is serious, Boone, and you got to help me fix it. Uncle Putter and Auntie KiKi cannot get divorced no matter what!"

Chapter Fifteen

Boone propped himself up on his elbow, his dark eyes black as the night around us. "Eavesdropping can get you in a lot of trouble, sweet stuff."

"You knew I was at the office?"

"I've lived in that house for a few years now and pretty much know every old creaky board in the place. Besides, I saw your reflection in the window. And for the record, Putter and KiKi are not getting a divorce and that's all I can say."

"Why?"

"Because Putter is my client and—"

"Not that *why*, but why aren't they getting a divorce?" I shoved my hair that needed bleaching bad out of my face. "I mean, Auntie KiKi jumps first and wonders where she's going to land midair, and I'm not exactly a good influence. Uncle Putter is a surgeon. He's grounded, settled, methodical."

"And KiKi is his reason for living. She keeps life

interesting and fun and he loves her." Boone kissed me and it was a really good kiss. "I can relate."

I felt a sappy smile slide across my just-kissed lips. "I make your life interesting and fun?"

"Sometimes I feel myself turning gray right on the spot, but yeah, you do."

This time I kissed him. "But if it's not a divorce, something else has Uncle Putter upset and it involves KiKi and I can't let people I love swing in the breeze when I can help them."

Boone snagged me around the waist and flipped me on top of him, our noses touching, his smile meeting mine. "This time you're on the sidelines and I want you to promise me you won't tell KiKi there's a problem when you don't even know what it is. You'll get her upset for nothing, Reagan. Putter and I are on this; you have to trust me."

"I'm not much of a sidelines kind of girl."

"Do tell."

"And when you said *nothing*, you didn't look convinced, so there is something and it's important and about the family or you and Uncle Putter wouldn't be meeting in the middle of the night with your heads together over a bottle of bourbon."

"Just this once, stay out of it. Do it for your Auntie KiKi."

* * *

"Well, are you ready?" Mamma asked me as she barged

through the front door of the Fox. She held her hands high and danced around the hall, BW barking right beside her. "This is going to be a wonderful day and . . ." Mamma put her hands down. "Reagan, you look like death warmed over. What's going on? You can't go trying on wedding dresses with a frown on your face and bags under your eyes."

I forced a smile; the bags were ironed in. "I had a restless night."

"Couldn't you and Walker restless some other night than the one before wedding dress shopping? This is a big day." Mamma sat me down on the third step that led upstairs. She unzipped her purse and got out her makeup bag. She tipped my chin to face her. "Make kissy lips."

She added lipstick like she had when I was fourteen and going to my first high school dance. She smoothed on foundation, blush, and a dab of mascara, then she and BW stood back and admired her handiwork. "Better." Mamma sat down beside me on the step. "Now what's wrong? Are you and Walker okay? Ohmygod, you found a lump."

"Boone and I are good and I did not find a lump."

"You're pregnant!" Mamma squealed. "Not a problem; we can push up the date and—"

"I am not pregnant." I scratched BW behind the ears. Having BW beside me was always comforting, especially when things got messy and I didn't know what to do next. "There's a situation. I promised Boone I wouldn't get involved, but telling you isn't getting involved, it's sitting and talking, right? There's something going on with Uncle Putter and Auntie KiKi but I don't know what. All I know is divorce isn't the issue and Boone made me promise not to upset Auntie KiKi and tell her something was up with her husband. I'm out of the loop. Most of the time I *am* the loop."

Mamma's face changed from wishful mamma to serious judge. "If Walker's not telling you what's going on, then Putter's hired him and what they discuss is between them and that's not going to change." Mamma took my hand. "You do have to trust Walker, honey. If he says not to tell KiKi, then we won't. But . . ." She tilted her head, the sister side of Gloria Summerside brightening her eyes, "It doesn't mean we can't find out what's happening on our own. If we find anything important, we can let Putter and Walker in on it, but we need to sniff around. They won't be happy about what we're doing, but they'll have to deal and it's what they would do if they were in our shoes."

Mamma gave me a hug. "We Summerside girls, and dog, stick together. So what's going on lately besides the wedding? Maybe that has some bearing on this KiKi/Putter situation?"

"Auntie KiKi and Uncle Putter are hosting the wedding, but they've had big parties before, so nothing new there. Boone and I are finishing the attic and expanding Cherry House and the place will be torn up for months, but that involves Boone and me and the workmen. KiKi hasn't mentioned anything out of the ordinary, though what's ordinary in the life of KiKi Vanderpool is anyone's guess."

Mamma stood and hauled me to my feet. "Well, something's got your uncle in a state if he's talking legal stuff with Walker, but right now the Summerside girls have a wedding dress to shop for and that takes top priority." She smoothed back my hair. "We have to look and act normal or KiKi will know something's not right." Mamma and I slapped big smiles on our faces. "Ready?"

"Ready."

I opened the door to find the Abbott sisters standing on the front porch. "Lord save us," Annie Fritz gasped as she and Elsie walked in. "What's happening now?"

"I think we need to dial the smiling back a notch." Mamma gave BW a pat good-bye and we headed for her car parked at the curb. When we got to the Pines, Mamma slowed, craning her neck as we passed a shiny red Mustang convertible, top down, circa sometime before I was born. "Now that's a car, the muscle car of all muscle cars."

"What do you know about muscle cars?"

"Believe it or not, I too was twenty and wild and reckless."

The twenty maybe, the wild and reckless part, never. She was my mother! The car was parked behind a moving van that was parked behind the Goodall Plumbing truck. Mamma tooled around all three, then glided into the lot. She killed the engine and we took the path between the glorious azaleas, Mamma pulling me to a stop before we got to the patio.

"We are in serious need of a *normal* check since we didn't do so good with the attempt at smiling. We can't have KiKi thinking anything's up or she'll grill us till we cave. No one grills like your auntie. She'd make the CIA proud."

"Put your judge face on; that's normal for you."

Mamma's brows knit together, eyes beady, lips thin, jaw set.

"Less *Judgment at Nuremburg*, more 'Did you really run that red light?'"

Mamma softened her features. "What about you?"

"I'm a bride; I can look any way I want and it gets chalked up to wedding jitters and 'He better show up or else.'" We crossed the patio. The double doors leading inside the Pines were propped wide open.

"Coming through," bellowed Anna with Bella behind her, pushing a wheelchair with Clive—or maybe it was Crenshaw—on board. "We got a delivery here," Anna added. "And we're in a big hurry, so move it."

Mamma and I jumped out of the way, letting the three pass followed by two swanky-looking forty-something gals strutting their stuff and wheeling in suitcases. These gals took moving men to a whole different level. Auntie KiKi stood inside, cane in one hand, a tote bag over her shoulder, the black eye still visible under layers of makeup, and an arm in a sling. A sling? What the—

"We can't talk here," KiKi said, cutting Mamma and me off before we could ask questions. KiKi hitched her head toward the patio. "Let's get in the car. These walls have ears."

"But—"

That got me the evil auntie eye, so I shut up and trailed

behind Mamma and Auntie KiKi thump-stepping out into the morning sun. We dodged two more movers in tight jeans, red silky tops, and heels hauling in a double bed and wicker headboard. We loaded KiKi into shotgun and I took the back seat. Mamma powered up the hearse and turned to KiKi. "All right, we're here in the car. Now talk!"

"I'm faking it. At least the arm part is a fake." KiKi flashed a big grin, pulling her arm out of the sling and waving it around. "See, good as ever. My bed collapsed and I rolled out and hit the floor, and don't either of you start with the 'You're coming home now' lecture."

"Why on earth," Mamma yelped, "would you fake a broken arm, and beds just don't collapse on their own." Mamma backed out of the parking space not bothering to look behind, making two walkers jump out of the way.

"I had to add the arm 'cause the cane just wasn't cutting it anymore," KiKi said. "Everyone here has a cane, and the bed collapse was a good excuse to up the stakes. I promised Doc Abrams that Putter would give him one of his standing Saturday tee times out there at the country club if he'd come over and put me in a sling."

"And Doctor Abrams went for it?" Mamma asked, sliding to a stop at a traffic light.

"For a weekend tee time at the club, I could have gotten Charlie Abrams to cocoon me in a full-body cast. And there's more," KiKi bubbled. "You saw Clive, or maybe it was Crenshaw, coming into the Pines this morning. Well, Emmitt told me that Anna and Bella aim to get their antiquated husbands—who are suddenly having accidents"—KiKi added air-quotes to *accidents*—"into the Pines, come hell or high water. Seems it's the only place C and C consented to go. So, suddenly there are two openings at the Pines, or at least there were until I swooped in and snatched one."

I sat up in my seat to be closer to the conversation. "And I saw Anna and Bella tooling around town with two guys, older, good-looking, not C and C. You think they're ditching C and C at the Pines and looking for newer husbands? The car they were in was vintage sweet, and the two guys in front were good-looking dudes."

"All I know," Auntie KiKi said, "is that a few weeks ago C and C were on a fishing trip, and now they're hobbling around needing help. How did that happen, huh? And two openings were needed at the Pines, and suddenly now that happened too. Plus Anna and Bella were around the Pines doing their volunteer work, so they had time to soak in what was going on around there. Suffocating the bony Bonnie Sue and dumping her in the sisters' Caddy would be easy enough, and it fits right in with C and C and their accidents. They had to know about Willie's peanut allergy."

"We did catch them snooping in your room," I said to KiKi. "They had that measuring tape, and I bet it was to see if furniture would fit, and they made it clear they wanted you out of the Pines or else. Maybe all your accidents are the *or else*?"

Mamma jumped the curb and squealed into BleuBelle's parking lot. She drummed her fingers on the steering wheel.

"So now we have two sets of suspects who could have done in Willie and Bonnie Sue: the gold digger sisters to make room for C and C and the smelly-shoe guys, whoever they are."

"And Dexter Thomas," I added. "He's in a hurry to buy the Pines, and fallout from the two recent deaths makes the place much more affordable. We've got suspects with motives, but we don't have proof. Nothing we can take to Aldeen Ross to get Elsie and Annie Fritz off."

"That's my job," KiKi beamed. "I'm your mole and I saved the best bit of information till last. You know how you just mentioned the gym shoe guys? Well . . ." Kiki reached in her tote bag and pulled out gym shoes, a gray pair and the navy. "I found these by the trash cans last night. Now we know for sure those two we saw in Mr. Jim's office are from the Pines and they're starting to get squeamish about what they did."

"When I dropped KiKi off that first night," I said to Mamma, "we heard two men toasting the demise of Willie and Bonnie Sue, but all we could see were their shoes moving around the room."

"Well, this isn't good at all." Mamma turned off the car. "The shoes in the trash means these two guys realize KiKi saw them."

"I think the gym shoe guys were just not taking any chances," KiKi said, "No way could they have known we were there, but I'm getting closer to finding out who they are, that's for sure. But enough of suspects and murder." KiKi pulled her iPhone from her purse. "Now it's on to finding Reagan a great wedding dress. I want to take pictures and remember this day." KiKi made the phone do a dance in the air.

"Holy cow!" I yelped. "That's it. The gym shoe guys know you were in Mr. Jim's office, or at least they suspect you might have been there. They saw the Louis Vuitton luggage there, and you bought the iPhone cover to match it. That's why they got rid of the shoes; they're afraid you're on to them. They're getting too close. You need to get out of the Pines right now."

"Are you kidding? When we're so close to finding the killer? It's got to be these gym shoe guys or the gold diggers or Dexter. No way am I moving out of the Pines till we figure this out, and that's final." KiKi folded her arms and did the stubborn Summerside glare.

"I agree," Mamma said, a suspicious glint in her eyes that I didn't like one bit. "And there's only one thing to do—I'm moving into the Pines with KiKi. With both of us together, what could happen?"

"Do you want a list?" I protested, my hair feeling as if it were on fire.

"I can sleep in that big chair in the corner of your room," Mamma rushed on, steamrolling right over my objections. "I'll tell Mr. Jim you need special care with your arm in a sling."

"It'll be like a sleepover. It's our chance to help Annie Fritz and Elsie, who are always there for everyone else. Now it's our turn to help them." KiKi did the high-five thing with Mamma, both beaming like kids on Christmas morning. I started to object again but got the no-nonsense look from Mamma, so I shut up. All kids know when they've lost the battle, and this was my Waterloo to be sure. I was no match for Mamma and Auntie.

"You have to call me," I insisted. "You have to check in."

"We'll call, we'll call. Stop nagging. Now let's go shopping."

Still beaming, Mamma and Auntie opened the car doors to get out and a bolt of panic ran up my spine. This time it had nothing to do with dead bodies or suspects or sleepovers and everything to do with the steamrolling part of our last conversation.

"Stop." I held up my hands. "Now it's my turn. You two are getting your way on staying at the Pines and now I am getting mine. I don't want a long wedding dress with yards of tulle. I am so over tulle, and lace; no lace anywhere. I did all that with Hollis and we saw how that ended up."

I faced Mamma. "Remember the conversation we had at the coffee shop about a nice short coral dress with a frilly skirt for dancing? That's what I want." I reached in Old Yeller, pulled out a wrinkled paper, and held it up. "Like this one. I tore it out of a J.Crew catalog. If we can't find something in BleuBelle, I can order this one online."

"An online wedding dress," KiKi gasped, making the sign of the cross. Mamma following suit.

"Repeat after me," I said, adding a bit of stern for good measure. "Simple dress."

"Simple," Mamma and Auntie KiKi said at the same time with no enthusiasm whatsoever.

Feeling immensely better about my little coral dress, I climbed out of the back seat and led Mamma and Auntie KiKi into BleuBelle Bridal. The little blue bell over the door tinkled merrily as we entered, the aroma of silk, taffeta, and never-ending tulle washing over us. A crystal chandelier sparkled in the center. Blue-carpeted raised platforms and big gilded mirrors were scattered here and there with changing rooms behind, giving each bride her own space to feel special. I wouldn't need that, of course. A normal-sized skinny mirror hanging on a wall would do for a short coral dress suitable for a fall wedding.

"Miss Frances will be with you in a few minutes," the blue-smocked lady behind the counter said to us. "You're welcome to peruse our sample dresses and get a feel for your own personal wedding style. Do you want a train, no train, pearls, beads, sequins, floor-length veil, tiara, a hundred butterflies released when you say 'I do'?"

"I already know my style." I held up the crinkled dress picture. "Something like this, short and sensible for fall and a second wedding."

The smocked woman blinked a few times. "Short?"

"Coral would be nice."

"Miss Frances will not be pleased."

"Miss Frances can go—"

"Can maybe have another color in mind?" Mamma interjected before I said something I shouldn't and got us thrown out of the BleuBelle.

Smock lady pointed a stiff finger toward the back. "A bridesmaid dress might work. We keep a few on hand. The bridesmaid dresses are in the far corner by the restrooms. This must be one of those arranged marriages," she added under her breath.

"It is not an arr—"

Mamma hooked her arm through mine and yanked me toward the back. "Just breathe, honey. We'll find . . . something."

We passed lovely cupboards, doors wide open, adorned with sculpted flowers and bows and bursting with wedding gowns from white to off white to cream to blush to taupe to—

"Eugenia?" I gasped. Mamma, KiKi, and I stopped in front of a platform showcasing Eugenia in a white dress that looked as if it were painted on except for the flair of organza puffed out at the bottom. She sort of looked like one of those white bottle cleaner brushes you buy at the grocery store.

"Don't you just adore this dress?" Eugenia smoothed her hands down her sides. "It's the modern look. Dex will love it. It's expensive, but I want the best because Dex says I'm the best."

"He proposed?"

Eugenia jutted her chin. "Soon, and this is the dress for our wedding. I have to order it in my size, of course; Miss Frances is writing up the sale now, and it will take extra long to make it as it's a specialty dress. I think one of the Kardashians wore this dress, and I simply must have it!"

Eugenia's face pulled a frown. "Miss Frances likes this one." Eugenia snagged a dress draped over a chair and tossed it, the yards of tulle billowing out, covering me, Mamma, and Auntie KiKi. "It's a closeout, so last year; who would wear a last-year-model wedding dress, of all things? It's a cupcake dress and it's blush." Eugenia made a gagging sound. "Everyone knows it's white for wedding . . . white, white, white, no matter how many times you walk down the aisle, we all deserve white."

Miss Frances came up to Eugenia and whispered, "Your card won't go through, dear. It was declined."

Eugenia jabbed her hands on her hips and tossed her head. "Your machine is broken or there's a mistake at the bank. Unzip me now so I can straighten this out and you can order my dress today. I simply must have this dress!"

Eugenia tiny-stepped her way to the changing room since there was no room in the dress for her legs to move normally. Mamma, KiKi, and I fought our way from under flounces of material. I got the hanger off the floor, hung up the gown, stepped up on the platform to put the dress away, and stopped dead when I looked in the mirror.

"Come on," Mamma said, she and Auntie KiKi trudging to the back of the shop. "Time's a wastin'."

I held up the dress to my front, the shimmering blush tulle floating around me like a soft cloud. I tucked a narrow strap over my left shoulder, then did the same with the right. I straightened the bodice that fit snug in the middle with a slight plunge that enhanced the bustline and accentuated a narrow waist. I had a plunge and a waist. Who knew! "This is it."

"This is what, dear?" Mamma turned back to me, KiKi nearly colliding right into her.

"This is *the* dress."

"Honey, it had you at cupcake. It's diet transference; you're sugar-deprived and a little delusional."

"Boone would love this dress."

"I don't think it comes in his size," Mamma sighed. "It's beyond lovely and you would look lovely in it, but it's long and you don't want long, probably had the tulle manufacturer working nights, and there's even—God forbid—a touch of lace at the bodice."

"It makes me look . . . pretty." I spun around, the dress swooshing and gliding with me. "What do you think?"

Mamma and KiKi glanced at each other and KiKi asked, "What happened to the little coral dress?"

I looked at myself in the mirror again. "What little coral dress?"

It took two minutes for me to fall in love with Sabrina (I decided a gown this lovely must be named) and way more time to pin the alterations and configure the bustle (what century was this?) with Mamma and KiKi fussing over who would pay for the dress we all loved that was on sale and marked down as it was last year's model. Normally the bride just ordered the dress in her size, but this was the one and only one left on the planet, or so Miss Frances said.

The clock in Mamma's car flashed twelve when we pulled into the Pines parking lot. We helped KiKi rewrap her arm and adjust the sling to make her look pathetic. The bruised eye was pathetic enough without any enhancement. "It's showtime," KiKi said, leaning heavily on her cane as we headed toward the back door.

"With you it's always showtime," Mamma quipped, then opened the door to Mr. Jim heading down the hall. "Could we have a word?" Mamma asked, heading Mr. Jim off.

"As long as none of those words are *duel* or *I'm going to blow your head clean off*." Mr. Jim spread his arms wide. "Welcome to the nuthouse. You hear all that ruckus from the living room?" He hitched his chin in the direction of the yelling. "It's now official. Emmitt challenged Foley to a duel on Friday at noon at Washington Square."

"Official as in glove smacked across the face?" Mamma gasped.

"Official as in Atlanta Braves cap smacked across the butt, and I'm guessing the effect is the same, especially since Great-Granddaddy's dueling pistols are now missing from over the fireplace and no one seems to know where they are, or at least they aren't telling me about it. I can't exactly rifle through everyone's room doing a search, now, can I? There's a pool on who's going to win; odds are two to one in favor of dead-eye Foley over sharpshooter Emmitt."

"Don't worry," Mamma soothed. "They're old guns; they're probably useless."

"Old guns still have a lot of killin' in 'em, and Emmitt and Foley were part of the reenactment company for years. They know about old firearms and how they work. I've shot the pistols myself a few times, kind of a family tradition on New Year's. Believe me, they work just fine."

Mamma patted Mr. Jim's hand. "I'm so sorry. Sounds like you got your hands full. Is it okay if I stay a few days with KiKi? She'll have a hard time getting dressed and cutting her food with her arm the way it is."

"And holding her martini glass, no doubt." Mr. Jim swiped a bead of perspiration from his forehead. "Judge, you can stay as long as you like. I just wish *I* could leave." Mr. Jim glanced up. "And to add to the joy of the day, here comes my daughter looking like a thundercloud in pink heels. Sweet mother, now what does she want?"

"Daddy!" Eugenia elbowed past me and Mama, getting right in her daddy's face. "We need to talk."

"Later, sweetheart. It's been a day and I have a lot going and—"

"Now, daddy dearest."

Daddy dearest was pretty much like *bless your heart*; sounded good, meant bad. Mamma, Auntie KiKi, and I watched Eugenia march Mr. Jim toward his office, then all trooped down the hall toward Auntie KiKi's room. I glanced back at the office—door closing, Eugenia bellowing—and doubled back, leaving Mamma and KiKi to settle in. Eugenia might not be the killer, but she was keeping company with the biggest suspect on my list and I wanted to know exactly what Dex was up to and just how he was playing Eugenia.

Chapter Sixteen

I had gotten closer to Mr. Jim's closed office door, trying not to be conspicuous about eavesdropping, when I looked up to—

"Hi, sweet thing. How'd wedding dress shopping go?"

I patted BW, standing at Boone's side, then threw my arms around him. "Kiss me."

"I like this dress already." Boone started to backtrack to the outside patio where there was more privacy, but I held him in place.

"This spot is good and you'll hear why in a second."

"Ah, eavesdropping again, are we?"

"I think you'll like this time better than the last." Boone's oh-so-fine lips met mine as Eugenia's muffled yelling seeped out into the hall.

"We keep having this same conversation, Daddy," she said. "I need money, and we never have enough. I want a wedding dress; I already have it picked out. I want to get married at the Sugar Bell House and need a down payment.

I need new clothes if I'm going to marry Dex, and I *am* going to marry him!"

"Has he proposed?" came Mr. Jim's voice, Boone's eyes widening at the conversation.

"Why does everyone keep harping on that?" Eugenia yelped, making Boone's lips smile against mine.

"Because—" Mr. Jim started till Eugenia cut him off.

"I'm tired of waiting on old people, Daddy. I'm tired of picking up prescriptions and running their errands and handing them this and that and getting stuff for them and waiting on them hand and foot. I'm tired of this house. I want something new and fresh. I want Dex. People are dying all the time around here and it's happening a lot lately, in case you hadn't noticed, and the Pines is getting a bad reputation. I think it's a sign to sell. Your friends are here now, but pretty soon you won't get anything for this place. Sell the Pines now, sell it to Dex and we'll have money; finally, we'll have money."

"Honey, if Dexter truly loves you," Mr. Jim consoled as one of the residents ambled by Boone and me grumbling something about getting a room, "let him put a ring on your finger and he'll marry you no matter what."

"I want to prove to him just how much I love him, that I want to be part of his life. I do volunteer work, he's a smart businessman; we're the perfect Savannah couple. I want to show him I can make him happy and be an asset to his work."

"By selling him our home?"

"He got the Slumber, and the Pines would be a great

addition. He worked for a company in Atlanta that invested in funeral homes and retirement homes and now he wants to do the same thing here in Savannah. He has big ideas, and he wants me to be part of them. If you sell the Pines, you could pay the place off and have money left over for retirement, and Dex would see that I have his back and we're a good team, and, for crying in a bucket, he'd marry me!"

"Dexter can find another retirement center to buy."

"He wants the Pines. He has his heart set on it. It's the right price range and a good location and has room to expand. He's got it all worked out. He loves this place."

"So do I, Eugenia, so do I."

"You're impossible, Daddy. Totally impossible," Eugenia sobbed. Footsteps inside approached the door. Boone broke our delicious kissing session, then hustled BW and me out onto the patio. We ducked behind a yellow hibiscus bush and heard Eugenia stomping down the hall in the other direction.

Boone craned his neck to see if anyone was listening, then whispered, "Eugenia's right about one thing. Dex really does have this all figured out; he's playing her and using Arnett and that other gal I saw him with. You got to hand it to the guy; he's got major cojones."

"Do you think his major cojones included knocking off Willie and Bonnie Sue to drive down the price? Hanging around Eugenia and being at the Pines, it would be easy enough for him to pick up on Willie having money and know that Arnett would inherit and that Willie had a peanut allergy and asthma. And Dex would know something about asthma, since he has it. I found out when casing out caskets for Mrs. Jones-Brown. But why knock off Bonnie Sue? The link between Bonnie Sue and Willie has always been a problem."

"Maybe she was on to Dex? And it would be easy enough to frame the sisters with their Caddy always being at the Pines. What we need is evidence."

"Maybe I can talk to Hollis. He's in with Dexter, and I bet he knows something."

"Maybe you can poke yourself in the eye with a sharp stick. It would be less painful, and you know that Hollis won't tell you anything if it puts his real estate deal in jeopardy."

"He might let something slip. At least I might get a feel for just how ruthless Dexter is and maybe find out other sleazy stuff he's done and then take it to Ross." I placed my hands on Boone's chest, his amazing heart that loved me beating strong and steady. "About the wedding dress. Her name is Sabrina and she's very pretty."

A cute grin tipped the corner of Boone's mouth. I was getting to know this grin as the fun grin, the one he saved just for me. "You named your wedding dress?"

"Special things deserve a name." I patted Old Yeller hanging off my arm. "So, what brings you and BW to the Pines?"

"I have business with Anna and Bella. I've been their husbands' attorney for years. Everyone at the Pines loves BW, so I brought him along. Our pup is turning into a bit of an attention whore."

"I know better than to ask about the business, but I'm guessing it has something to do with a flashy red Mustang I saw them with, and don't let BW's fan club feed him a bunch of treats. We don't need him waddling down the aisle. You'll probably run into Auntie Kiki and Mamma; she's moving in for a few days, and when you see KiKi you'll know why. Can you tell them I'm walking home?"

Boone tucked a strand of hair behind my ear. "Be careful, sweet stuff. I don't think Hollis is dangerous in that he'd hit you over the head with a club, but if you ask questions, it's bound to get back to Dexter and he could be a killer. That man's all about money and nothing and no one is standing in his way, including you." Boone held up the leash. "Wanna take BW for protection?"

"Hollis isn't much of a dog person, and since I'm going for information I don't want to ruffle feathers. I'll need to be discreet."

Boone laughed.

"I can always play the I'm-thinking-about-selling-Cherry-House card. Hollis has wanted to list my house—*our* house—forever."

Hollis's real estate office was over on East Wayne, and I hadn't visited the place in years. As always, it had great curb appeal, with pink and white petunias overflowing the window boxes, a trimmed walkway, and perfect grass where no weed would dare to grow. When Hollis and I had first been married, I'd helped him out at the office. Even had my own desk—but then so had Janelle. I got a computer on my desk; Janelle got Hollis.

"You're not the last person I expected to see in here today but pretty darn close," Hollis said as I came in the door. "What do you want now?"

Hollis, the ever-charming man-about-town. "No receptionist today?"

"Out to lunch." Hollis gave me a curious look. "You're finally selling Cherry House and came to list it? 'Bout time you got rid of that piece of crap."

I wouldn't list Cherry House with you if you were the last realtor on earth was not the way to get info, so I went with, "I met your fiancée and thought I'd stop by to say congrats."

"She said you were a first-rate pain in the rump with no taste, but then what else is new?"

"And . . ." Having been married to Hollis, I knew his one soft spot besides his gut. Flattery! "I hear business is booming and you're a real . . . up-and-comer." I forced a congenial smile. "Word has it you're going to be named Mr. Realtor this year. Way to go."

Hollis sat up straighter. "I'm doing okay." He leaned a little closer as I took a chair on the other side of his desk. "Did you really hear the Mr. Realtor thing or are you just yanking my chain?"

"Hey, you've had some great sales lately, everyone's talking, and with clients like Dexter Thomas you're a shoe-in. I hear he's a wheeler-dealer first-class and will do anything to drive down the price . . . anything."

"You really are thinking of selling Cherry House?"

Time to reel in the fish. "Is he interested in buying it?"

"If the price is right. You do realize that Cherry House

needs a lot of work done to it, and that has to be reflected in the price."

"I heard Dexter has his eye on buying Sleepy Pines. With all the bad publicity lately, he could get that for a song as well. He's racking up some nice properties around town and, with you as his realtor, it's a feather in your cap."

Hollis preened. "We met at the Pines. He's dating Mr. Jim's daughter, and I visit Uncle Foley from time to time. Dexter Thomas has got his eye on a lot of properties and he likes that I know the area. Last week we were in the Beaufort/St. George area driving around, looking at sites for a retirement village, a whole community. Some farms are going bust and he can swoop in and get them for cheap. The man has deep pockets."

As long as they're someone else's pockets . . . but . . . but . . . This time I sat up straight. "Last week you and Dexter were gone? As in, you both got back seven days ago?"

"Four days ago. We got back on Tuesday, and why do you care?"

"Dexter was with you the whole time?"

"It was business, good business. The man can drink like a fish, especially on my dime, and you're looking weird. Are you having an aneurysm or something? Well, do it outside so you don't mess up the office, I don't want the paramedics in here shoving things around, and I just had this carpet cleaned."

I jumped up and headed for the door. "I wish you and Lula Bell every happiness, and I mean that. Thanks for the help."

"Her name's Lou Ella."

I got to the sidewalk, rummaged around in Old Yeller for the flip, and hit speed dial 1.

"What did Hollis do now?" came Boone's voice on the other end.

"Dex isn't the killer. He was with Hollis driving around Georgia trying to see who he could swindle next when Willie and Bonnie Sue bit the collective big one. I guess he could have rented a car, driven back at night, and knocked off Willie then Bonnie Sue, but that's two trips back and forth, no sleep, and it seems pretty far-fetched."

"He could have paid someone."

"That would cost him, and we know he's operating on a shoestring. Mother of pearl, how could I be so wrong about this guy? I thought he was such a creep that knocking off old people for money fit him to a tee. Maybe he's not that bad and will marry Eugenia. Tell me you found something out on your end. I need good news."

"Well, your mother and KiKi just put fifty bucks on old dead-eye whoever-that-is, and they're making plans to go visit the gym shoe guys."

"You have got to be kidding."

"Sweet thing, I don't have enough imagination to make this stuff up."

"See you later, alligator." I disconnected

Walking on autopilot, I headed for home. So now who was the killer, and how could I tell Elsie and Annie Fritz things were not going well? They were counting on me. *I* was counting on me. Maybe the gym shoe hunt would turn up who these guys were, or maybe Anna and Bella *had* knocked off Willie and Bonnie Sue? The two openings at the Pines just when the gold diggers needed them most really did seem too good to be true. And what about Arnett? She needed daddy's money, and the only way she was going to get it in a timely fashion was to take action. Maybe Arnett, having no intention of sharing the loot with Bonnie Sue, had just gotten rid of her too.

So far the Abbott sisters still had top billing for knocking off Bonnie Sue with her being found in their garden and the tassel pillow in the car. The good thing was that they had no motive to knock off Bonnie Sue. When it came to Willie, the sisters had mucho motive, but so did others, thank heavens. That there was no smoking gun that tied the sisters to Willie's murder helped a ton. Anyone could have served him peanuts, though there were none in his stomach.

The police still thought Willie's death was down to natural causes, so at the moment I knew more about Willie and Bonnie Sue's deaths than Aldeen did, and that gave me time to find the killer. I just hoped this was a really long moment, since my number one suspect had just alibied out.

"Thank you kindly for the money in the envelope you left for us," Elsie said as I came in the door at the Prissy Fox. "It'll come in handy." She clasped her hands together and giggled. "Now you have to tell Sister and me all about the wedding dress."

"It's lovely," I sniffed. "Mamma took pictures, but you're sworn to secrecy." I walked behind the counter and kissed Elsie on the cheek, then Annie Fritz.

"Whoa," Elsie said, holding her hands up as if in surrender. "What's gone wrong, honey?"

"Nothing." I forced a smile. I was doing a lot of that lately. I couldn't tell these two lovely ladies how desperate things were. Why worry them when I was worried enough for all three of us? "I'm just getting sentimental about the wedding is all." But unless I got lucky, the only way Elsie and Annie Fritz would see the wedding was on Instagram.

"Well, that is understandable, with marrying a lovely man like Walker and having the affair at your auntie's house," Elsie said. "And Sister and I have some great cake ideas. I know you said red velvet, but we'll set up a little tasting so you and Walker can decide what flavor suits you. You just might change your mind. Brides have the right to do that, you know."

"And we got our eye out for the perfect cake topper," Annie Fritz added. "But right now we're headed off to Narobia's Grits and Gravy for another fan appearance. Seems everyone wants to hear about us and the body in the garden. And business sure is good when we're here at the Fox. We're thinking you should put our pictures on one of those bus benches, something like 'Sisters . . . saints or sinners? Come see at the Prissy Fox.'"

"Aldeen Ross would have a canary."

"Honey, Aldeen Ross would rather have the coroner." Elsie and Annie Fritz laughed all the way out the door and my heart sank. Who was the blasted killer?

Business was good, taking my mind off the Dexter fiasco. Another mannequin for display would be great; a charge card machine would be terrific, or even one of those things you hitch onto your phone that takes credit cards. Of course, that meant an expensive iPhone, and right now that was not in the cards. This was my first week doing well financially and I needed a few more before considering a phone upgrade. And besides, I didn't want to give my flip an inferiority complex.

I took in a cute pair of yellow sandals, white denim capris with rhinestones on the cuff that I loved, and a navy-blue polka dot rain jacket that would look adorable on Mamma.

"We got a problem," Mercedes panted as she stumbled into the Fox. "And, yes, it needs to be on a T-shirt, I get it."

"You could have called. I have a phone, remember?"

"Girl, this is way beyond a phone conversation." Mercedes cut her eyes side to side to see if the customers were listening, then whispered, "Grab your purse and get the keys. You know that certain someone cooling his heels in KiKi's garage as we speak? His presence is needed back at the Slumber right now! Aldeen Ross is on a hunt for Willie Fishbine!"

Chapter Seventeen

"We can't drive a Beemer down Broad Street in the middle of the day with a casket sticking out the back, and what's going on?" I said to Mercedes. "Why in the heck does Aldeen want Willie now?" I smacked my hand on the counter. "I know why. Willie Junior went to the police pitching a fit again that his granddaddy was murdered and they finally listened to the boy. That and the fact that Annie Fritz just happened to mention that Willie was involved in a scam and she was taken to the cleaners by the old goat might have spurred Aldeen's sudden interest just a bit."

"Sweet goodness, you think!" Mercedes came to the other side of the checkout counter. "Now Willie's death is looking suspicious and Aldeen's got a right to exhume. Seems she contacted Bonaventure; Bonaventure said 'What body?' and called the Slumber. The secretary freaked out, started to call Dexter, who happens to be out of the office. She has a hot date, so I told her I'd look into this mess. But unless we kidnap Aldeen Ross or she's abducted by aliens, she's going to come looking for Willie and that's bound to lead her right to us. There are not that many people interested in these murders, and we are definitely at the top of that list."

"It's getting late, going on dinner time. There's a good chance Aldeen will wait till tomorrow and we can do our magic tonight and make Willie reappear."

"It's just a little after four and Aldeen's on a diet, so forget dinner. Right now she's more dog with a bone, and the bone's missing and she's got to be wondering why and most of all how."

Think, Reagan, think! "We need something to distract Ross. She needs a new focus. How well do you know the coroner? Can you get him to do you a favor, a really big favor, like ask Aldeen out on a date tonight? Tell him we'll pay."

"We?"

"Tell him it's Be Kind to a Detective Week and . . . and taking her to dinner would make her really happy, and a happy detective is good for everyone and . . . and I don't know, just promise him anything else you can think of."

"Our distraction is a coroner?" Mercedes rolled her eyes, then pulled out her phone.

"You have him in your address book?"

"We're in the same business. He finds 'em, I fix 'em."

Mercedes hustled out the door and onto the porch as a customer came up to check out. I kept one eye out the display window watching Mercedes pace back and forth and one eye on my sale pad as I wrote up two pairs of jeans and a blue paisley blouse. Mercedes laughed, then looked serious, then laughed again. She came in as the customer left.

"Okay, we're on, he'll do it. And he wants to be in the wedding."

"Invited?"

"Wedding party. You said promise him anything. He likes Walker, and with him being new in town, he thinks being in the wedding will be fun and a good way to meet people that talk back to him. He's got a sense of humor."

"I got a funny coroner in my wedding party?"

"Better than a bun in your oven."

"Not according to my mother. Meet me back here at nine. I'll get the spare keys for the Beemer, but we need muscle to move the coffin. When we were at the Slumber, we could just roll the thing and push it into the trunk. Now we got to haul it and get it out of the trunk. I'd ask Boone, but transport of a body in a Beemer is probably against some kind of law and he's an attorney and that's a no-no. I'll think of something. Hey, we got this far, didn't we? We're on roll."

"On a roll to where?" Boone came in the door, balancing two grocery bags.

Mercedes folded her arms and hitched her hip onto the counter. "This explanation I gotta hear."

I gave Mercedes an evil look that didn't make her budge one inch, then turned to Boone. "You know how you liked that coroner guy? Well, he's now in the wedding party. I needed him to ask Aldeen Ross out on a date tonight, and being in the wedding party was part of the bribe. He's got a sense of humor, so that's nice, right? And remember that client–attorney confidentiality thing you have going on?

Well, maybe this time we could go for a what-you-don't-know-can't-hurt-you confidentiality. Sometimes being in the dark isn't all bad. You could be asked questions it would be best you didn't know the answers to.

"I'll take my chances."

I took a deep breath. "Think of this as part two of part one. Aldeen is looking for that certain guy I told you about who's chilling out in Auntie KiKi's Beemer. Many think he's supposed to be in a certain cemetery, but when he turned up MIA, that certain cemetery called the funeral home wondering what the heck's going on. Someone needs to get MIA back where he belongs before Aldeen sends out a search party and certain people wind up in deep doo-doo. The names have been changed to protect the guilty and to keep you out of this mess as much as possible."

"I appreciate that, but your mess is my mess." Boone kissed me on the forehead. "Maybe the MIA guy simply got lost in that certain cemetery. The place is big, there're coffins everywhere, it's pretty much coffin central. Most are encased in concrete with angels and the like on top, but it doesn't mean they all have to be. Things do go missing or get misplaced and then suddenly they're found. It happens."

"You mean—"

"I mean I'm going to fix dinner and then work on the attic tonight so we can get the expansion going and not live in sawdust and plaster for the rest of our lives. That leaves you to maybe . . . wash your hair."

"I can wash my hair."

"And I bet Big Joey would like to help you wash your

hair. Sometimes hair can be hard to manage and heavy. You'll need help with the heavy." Boone held up the grocery bag. "How does stir-fry shrimp and salad sound? It should be dark, really dark, when you wash your hair, so you have time to eat now." He turned to Mercedes. "Hang around; there's enough for three."

Boone walked off toward the kitchen, Mercedes watching as he went. "Dibs."

"Too late, honey; he's all mine."

*　*　*

A crescent moon slipped behind the clouds, the only sounds crickets and birds without enough sense to be asleep at midnight. I killed the Beemer headlights and Mercedes, Mamma, Auntie KiKi, and I stared at the stone entrance to Bonaventure Cemetery, black iron gates chained together and padlocked shut. During the day and evening the historic place was crazy with tourists and guides and buses and snapping cameras. In the dead of night it was, well . . . dead.

"You shouldn't be here," I said to Mamma, sitting in the back seat. "What if we get caught? You're a judge. You could get . . . de-judged."

"I'll plead temporary insanity. With a casket in the trunk, it won't be a hard sell, and you should thank your lucky stars KiKi and I volunteered to help. How did you and Mercedes plan on getting Willie out of the trunk with Big Joey and his muscles tied up at a nephew's bar mitzvah?"

"How was I supposed to know about the bar mitzvah?

It's not exactly a seventeenth gang ritual now is it." I heaved a sigh. "All I wanted was for you to bring me the Beemer keys 'cause I couldn't find the spare set over at Rose Gate. I didn't expect you both to show up on my doorstep and wind up here."

"Beats reruns of *Mash*, and Mr. Jim ran out of martini olives. What's a girl to do for the rest of the night?" Auntie KiKi turned in her seat, facing us all. "So now that we're here and procrastinating, who's going to get out of this nice cozy comfy car and open that gate? Big Joey said he'd get it unlocked for us, so my guess is he did. We need a volunteer from the audience."

We all looked at Mercedes.

"Why me?"

"You're used to dead people," KiKi added.

"In the Peaceful Pasture room at the Slumber, not . . . here." Mercedes twirled one of her curls around her finger. "Fine. It's always the pretty sexy girl that gets eaten by the zombies first, so I guess I fit the bill."

Mercedes unclicked her seat belt and put one foot out the door as if stepping on eggs. She switched her phone to flashlight and crept to the gates, pulled on the lock, which gave way, then threaded the chain back through the grating, the scraping of metal on metal giving me the chills, Mamma and KiKi rubbing their arms as well. Mercedes swung the right gate open, the creaking loud against the eerie quiet. She waved us through. I started up, our tires crunching the gravel as we inched along. Mercedes closed the gate, then hopped back in the car and slammed the door shut. We all exhaled in one big whoosh, Mamma, KiKi, and I applauding.

"Sweet mother, this is one scary place," Mercedes said, her voice shaky. "We need to get Willie dumped right quick before something happens that we don't want to happen, and around here at this time of night anything can happen."

Headlights doused, I crept along under aged trees and low-hanging moss floating in the breeze. Moonlight slipped through here and there, reflecting off white marble tombstones, benches, and statues. Little rusted iron fences marked the perimeter of old family plots with mossy urns and benches.

"I believe that there's Miss Marguerite Laveau's grave," Mercedes whispered into the dark. A few bottles of top-shelf rum lay at the base beside baskets of fresh eggplant, candles flickering in the darkness, and a clay bowl no doubt filled with money. Without saying a word, we all bowed our heads and made the sign of the cross.

"My mamma once said," Mercedes went on in a hushed voice, "that her no-good great-uncle Louie stole five dollars from Marguerite's grave and dropped dead before he reached the gates."

"I heard his body was withered clear through to the bone right there on the spot," Mamma added. We all made the sign of the cross again. Everyone in Savannah knew that if you needed help with finances, love, or family matters, you went to Marguerite, and no one ever messed with the voodoo queen, alive or dead.

"Up ahead looks good enough." Auntie KiKi pointed to a crypt flanked by large columns and a weeping angel. I pulled to a stop, killed the engine, and we got out next to two purple rhododendrons in full bloom, the quiet seeping into our bones. "This is a fine place for a coffin to go missing. It's hidden, not too hidden, it comes with flowers, and I already said one prayer for Willie so he's good to go."

"We got to get permission," Mercedes said. "This time it's not for Willie but whoever this here spot belongs to 'cause it sure doesn't belong to us. Unless you all want to end up like great-uncle Louie, we need to keep the calm around here."

Using the flashlight, Mercedes located the name chiseled on the gravestone. She stepped back and we joined hands. "Monroe Raleigh," Mercedes said. "We ask you kindly to let Willie Fishbine park here for a spell till he gets claimed for his own resting spot. And we are mighty sorry indeed to burden you with this lousy scumbag, but with a little luck the police will be here tomorrow to claim his worthless hide and get the miscreant creep out of your way."

Auntie KiKi stared at Mercedes. "That didn't sound too calming to me."

"The truth is the truth, dead or alive, and lying to Monroe wouldn't be right. Now who's got twenty bucks on 'em?"

KiKi pulled bills from her skirt pocket. "I was putting another fifty on Dead-Eye to knock off Sharpshooter. It's a long story." She cut her eyes to Mercedes. "So now you're paying the dead?"

" 'Course not." Mercedes winked and slid the fifty into her cleavage. "You're paying me for saving you all since you didn't have enough good sense to do it yourselves. Now let's ditch Willie and skedaddle."

I crawled into the back of the Beemer, dropped the seat, brace against the front seat and put my feet to the coffin. Then I pushed.

"He's a comin'," Mercedes grunted. "We're pulling on this end best we can. Sure weighs a ton for such a little guy." The box slid forward, teetered on the edge of the trunk, then tipped onto the ground, still leaning against the Beemer.

"Willie's standing on his head." Auntie KiKi called to me. "Bet he hasn't done that in a while. We'll hold the feet end and you pull forward. If we scratch the back of the car, Putter will ask questions and I sure don't want to try and explain to the man how they got there."

I shimmied into the driver's seat, turned over the engine, moved ahead, and heard the coffin drop to the ground with a solid *thunk*.

"Rub off the fingerprints," I yelled back to my partners in crime. I raced around, took off my jacket, and helped rub, getting rid of any lingering evidence. We all stood back and KiKi pressed the button on the trunk to close it down. "Good enough."

"What are you doing here, and what's good enough?" came a voice behind us.

Auntie KiKi, Mercedes, Mamma, and I all screamed and spun around, staring into a blinding light.

"What are *you* doing here?" my unflappable mamma

demanded in her best judge voice, her hands planted firmly on her slender hips.

"I'm the night watchman." He lowered the beam. "What's your excuse?"

I needed another excuse? I should keep a list in my purse. "We're . . . checking out a final resting place for my auntie here." I patted Auntie KiKi on the shoulder.

"What!" KiKi yelped.

"Just look at her, all banged up like she is, the arm, the leg, the eye. We're looking for just the right spot and we brought her along to get her approval."

"Right spot!" KiKi screeched.

"At midnight?" The watchman added.

"She's fading fast, time is of the essence, and placement in the right moonlight is so important, don't you think?"

KiKi kicked my ankle and the watchman shrugged. "Actually, it's kind of nice you're all here doing this for your auntie. At least you're not here to dance on some rotten husband's grave or throw rocks at your cheating wife or grandfather who cut you out of the will. I get a lot of those. Then there's the flip side where we've had this open grave for days and no casket's shown up or even a family member wondering where the casket is."

The watchman tipped back his hat. "This might sound a little crazy, though you're the ones driving around looking at graves at night, so maybe not, but have you seen a casket out here? Not one that's in a grave, mind you, but all by itself out here in the open air? One's gone missing and the police have had me looking for it for hours. I tell you,

233

I've looked for a lot of things in this here cemetery over the years—lost earrings, dropped prayer book, cats, dogs, a yellow polka dot bikini top—but never a casket."

"Now that you mention it . . ." Mamma stepped aside. "This is why we stopped where we did. We spotted this casket in the bushes and wondered, *Dear me, whatever is a casket, of all things, doing out here all unattended?*"

The watchman stared bug-eyed and open-mouthed and I added, "But now you found what the police are looking for and they'll be mighty grateful, I'm sure. And if they need to talk to us, I'm Lou Ella Farnsworth and here's fifty dollars for your assistance." I held out my hand to Mercedes, who forked over the bills looking none too happy about the situation.

"I don't get much appreciation around here." The watchman stuffed the bills in his pocket and tipped his cap to Auntie KiKi. "Sorry about your . . . condition. Take some comfort in that you'll rest nice here; most do. Not all, of course. There are always a few who are a mite antsy and tend to roam."

He looked at Auntie KiKi hard. "Yep, you're a roamer, all right. You got that frisky look that's not about to end when you do."

"I'm going to get you for this," Auntie KiKi groused as we piled in the car.

"You already have." I started the car. "Tomorrow I have dance lessons with Bernard Thayer."

"And you are not allowed to cancel."

"Would I do that?"

I dropped Mercedes, Mamma, and Auntie KiKi off in

front of Cherry House, where they'd left their cars. I pulled the Beemer into KiKi's garage, now Willie-free, and crossed the dewy grass to Boone and BW sitting on the porch, man and dog silhouetted black against the light in the display window.

"It's nearly two," I said, sitting beside Boone. "You should be asleep."

"Hard to sleep with my fiancée cruising around a cemetery at midnight with that certain something in the trunk, especially with taking her mother and auntie along for the ride. Nice family outing?"

"All I needed were the keys to the Beemer, but Auntie KiKi and Mamma decided to fill in for Big Joey because he was tied up and they weren't about to take no for an answer. The thing is, as soon as a certain someone's body is claimed, it won't take long for Aldeen to realize he had help in the croaking department and a whole new set of problems are bound to spring up."

"Good to know you won't be bored." Boone held me a little tighter. "But tonight, what's left of it, there are other things to think about besides Aldeen and the croaking department . . . much more fun things." Boone planted a soft kiss on my lips. "Wanna play?"

* * *

"Don't get up; you can sleep in for another hour." Boone reached past me and BW to kill his phone alarm on the nightstand. "I have a breakfast meeting with a client or I'd be staying right here with you."

I rolled over, the heat of Boone's body keeping me warm against the morning chill. "My guess is you're meeting Uncle Putter, and whatever you guys are cooking up, Mamma and I can help, just saying."

Boone ruffled my hair. "Nothing to worry about, sweet stuff."

"Why do I feel like *yet* should be tacked onto the end of that statement? Uncle Putter's in town and not telling Auntie KiKi, KiKi's at the Pines and not telling Uncle Putter, and you're in the middle of it all. How can anything good come out of this?

"And you, soon-to-be-wife, are too smart for your own good."

Boone pulled jeans and a blue shirt from his half of the little stuffed closet, then headed for the shower. I got a white skirt and yellow top from my side, then invaded Boone's space to use the sink. I ran a comb through my hair, brushed my teeth, and washed my face to Boone singing a version of Adele that would bring tears to her eyes and not in a good way. I did a quick makeup routine and said a selfish prayer that we'd have a second bathroom sooner rather than later, and, please God, make it sooner. I went downstairs and got BW's veggie hot dog from the fridge.

"Sit. Hot dog." BW parked his butt, barked twice, got his treat, and I got a banana. I found a plastic bag to scoop with in case BW left a prize on someone's perfect lawn.

I yelled, "Love you; off to see KiKi," to Boone upstairs with him yelling the same back without the KiKi part. I hitched up BW rather than taking the scooter. "I need to return Auntie KiKi's Beemer keys," I explained to BW as we turned onto Drayton, rush hour traffic clogging the narrow streets. "And walking gets in our ten thousand steps for the day. The thing is, with you having four feet, does this mean you only have to do five thousand steps? We should look that up on Google."

"And where are you off to this morning?" Smiling, Earlene had stopped the bus in the middle of the block right next to BW, not giving a flying fig that horns were honking.

"The Pines, and let me get this straight. With BW here, you're all sweetness and sunshine and ask me if I need a ride? Without dog I have to chase you down the street and risk life and limb?"

"The pup's got better hair and he laughs at my jokes." Earlene hitched her chin. "Besides, I got important dirt to share, and here you are right in front of me."

Gossip or exercise? BW and I climbed on board. I tossed two fares in the box, Earlene gave BW a treat, and we took our usual seats across from Earlene as she started off. "Gone to any bar mitzvahs lately?" I asked.

"No, I have not." Earlene's eyes shot wide open. "What did I miss now?"

"Nothing. Nothing at all." When would I ever learn to keep my mouth shut and not meddle in people's love lives? I was a meddling queen and couldn't help myself. Maybe because I wanted everyone to be as happy as I was with Boone, though I doubted if anyone could be that happy.

"Is my man stepping out on me?" Earlene whimpered.

"That's it, isn't it?" Steering with one hand, she reached under her seat and pulled out *How to Get Your Man and Keep Him*. "This here is the bible on landing the guy of your dreams. Big Joey's mine, all mine, and I'm gonna catch him sooner or later, and right now it's looking later."

"Maybe you should just be yourself?"

"And how has that worked out for me so far? Pitiful, that's how. I need inspiration, and this book is it." Earlene stopped to let two riders on, then hit the gas. "But now it's down to the business at hand. A police dispatcher is on my route and she takes the early bus and we always get to talking. Guess who the cops found in the middle of Bonaventure Cemetery last night without benefit of grave? She said it was like the old boy just dropped right out of the sky, casket and all."

"More like dropped out of the back of a Beemer."

Earlene gave me the wide-eyed look. "Dang. You do get around, girlfriend. So now the police think Willie being toes-up had a little help getting that way and it's connected to my little blue hat lady found in that garden."

"Did your dispatcher friend mention the connection?"

"She said they were looking at some Spring Chicken vitamin rip-off over there at Sexy Pines." Earlene chuckled. "Those old codgers must be needing a little extra help in the spring department, if you know what I mean."

And I so wish I didn't. Earlene pulled to the curb. "Well, here you are. Let me know what's happening at Sexy. I'm the kudzu vine on wheels around here, doing my civic duty to keep everyone informed and up to date on current scandals."

Earlene gave BW a final pat, closed the doors, growled away, and BW and I turned for the Pines. If the police thought there was a connection between Willie and Bonnie Sue, there was. But how could the connection be Spring Chicken? Bonnie Sue might have bought some vitamins or stock certificates at best, but so what? And why were the Lincoln Continental and that red Mustang I'd seen before parked at the curb sporting license plates of BOOMER1 and BOOMER2? Was that music coming from the patio? Beach Boys? Surfing something?

Maybe Mamma and Auntie KiKi had slept in today? Maybe they weren't in the middle of whatever was going on? And maybe it would snow and pigs would soar overhead.

Chapter Eighteen

"Be there or be square," Auntie KiKi laughed, holding up a red drink with an umbrella and assorted fruits on a skewer sticking out the top. She had on a straw hat adorned with flowers and a stuffed parrot on her shoulder and a pink boa around her neck. What the heck was in that drink!

"Is that Mamma, my mother the judge, jitterbugging with Mr. Jim, and is that Clive *and* Crenshaw sitting over there by the hibiscus? How'd that happen? They look happy to be here." I shouted over the band.

"Everybody likes them both. Smart, funny, lots of connections around Savannah. Whichever one of the duo was missing moved in early this morning. Mrs. Dunwitty was visiting her daughter in Charleston and decided to stay. Anna and Bella didn't want to take any chances this spot would get snapped up and jumped on it, but let me tell you, moving C and C in here isn't what all the fuss is about." KiKi waved her drink over the crowd. "This here event is

Anna and Bella's little shindig. Those two are kicking the Boomers into high gear, and that's all of us here!"

I handed Auntie KiKi her keys, and she dropped them in her pocket. "I'm not going to be needing these as much as I used to. Driving's nice and all, but there're other ways of getting around town. Fact is, I'm headed to the spa at ten in that there red Mustang you see at the curb, and Anthony's going to take me. The rascal jumped ship from Uber to Boomer."

"Boomer?"

"Like in baby boomers." Auntie KiKi laughed and took a drink of red stuff. "There was a time back in sixty-five I wanted a Mustang convertible. I couldn't afford it, of course, with Putter in medical school and me teaching dancing to keep him there. Now the ride of my dreams is here waiting for me! I can let my hair fly in the wind and not fret about a parking space 'cause I got a driver taking me around. Not all the time, of course, but for a fancy lunch it's just the ticket."

Auntie KiKi handed me her drink, jumped up, and tossed her cane into the bushes. "They're playing 'Twist and Shout' and I gotta twist. I haven't twisted in years. Too bad your uncle isn't here; a little twisting would be darn good for him. He was the twisting king, you know. Had the best sideburns east of the Mississippi." KiKi snagged BW's leash and the two of them joined the others on the patio.

"Don't look so concerned." Anna came up beside me. "No alcohol in the drinks, but we want everyone to have a fun time and that's what Boomers is all about."

"Dancing on the patio?"

"There's no money in that, but there sure is in getting old people where they need to be in the style they like and appreciate. Bella and I got the idea from all that crappy community service we got stuck doing and running people here, running people there. Now we're going to make a fortune doing it! Talk about turning lemons into lemonade. We have a GTO, Thunderbird, and Jaguar XKE on order. If you're over sixty, we'll move you, get your pet to the vet, take you to your doctor's appointment or lunch, and you'll arrive in cars like the ones you made out in or drag-raced in or went to prom in. Isn't that the best idea ever?"

"Let me guess, you have young sexy drivers?"

"Too much like the grandkids carting you around, and who wants that? Sixty is the new thirty. Our drivers show up wearing a letter sweater or a poodle skirt and maybe put a big ole corsage on your wrist like they did back when. We interviewed the drivers and had them drive us around to see if they're a good fit for our Boomer image. If Bella and I are happy with the drivers, then our customers will be too. This here is a kick-off party, and we have four more today. Places like the Pines are pure gold. Fact is, Willie Fishbine knew an opportunity when he saw one and was going to invest with us, but he never got a chance to write the check."

Bella handed me a stack of cards. "That Bonnie Sue lady who lived here designed these for us and was doing a layout for AARP. She had a good eye and worked real cheap. I think she had money problems. That sucked for her but was great for us. Here, put the cards in your shop, not that any of your penny-pinching customers can afford us. We got a classy operation going on. We're tapping into retirees with money to spend."

Anna and Bella strutted off and I made my way over to Mamma sitting at one of the little patio tables, huffing and puffing and smiling. She had a drink in hand, cheeks pink and eyes bright. "Well, that's a fine way to start the day."

She leaned closer to be heard over the blaring music. "Sure beats the elliptical at the gym or that horrid spinning class I joined. Honey, you look beat; get in there and kick up you heels and get your blood moving."

I took the seat next to Mamma's as the band started in on "Wild Thing," the whole patio erupting in cheers and waving their hands in the air. I scooted my chair closer so we could talk. "You know how Anna and Bella looked like candidates for the offing-Willie campaign? Well, he was about to invest in Boomers and Bonnie Sue did the advertising layouts. If Anna and Bella wanted to make two more openings at the Pines, they wouldn't knock off the people they did business with. Tell me you and Auntie KiKi had some luck finding the gym shoe guys, because right now we're running out of murder suspects."

"Honey, take a look around here; everyone's wearing gym shoes. But you know, this Willie-investing-in-the-Boomers news sure puts Arnett in the spotlight. The last thing she'd want was for daddy to spend money. She wanted it all for herself. If she knew Willie was about to write a big check to Anna and Bella, she'd want to stop him, right?"

"Kill her own father?"

"Slipping a few peanuts into the chicken salad or whatever isn't like picking up a gun or knife, and if there's one thing I've learned from years on the bench, anyone is capable of anything with the right motivation."

"Plastic surgery and a hot guy on your arm?"

"Toss in years and years of a stingy daddy and it's got the makings of a perfect storm. Sometimes people just get fed up and snap."

"Willie wrote Bonnie Sue into his will, and Arnett was thrilled Bonnie Sue wasn't around to inherit. Maybe Arnett was glad to get rid of both of them?"

"Bonnie Sue's wake is tonight and you should come. Funerals are always a good place to pick up the latest gossip, and there's bound to be a good turnout with Foley and Emmitt fighting over who'll do the first eulogy to their lady-love. Emmitt's written 'Ode to My Southern Wench,' and there's talk that Foley's bringing his harmonica. How could you possibly say no to a harmonica at a wake?"

I dragged rock 'n' roll BW, now with sunglasses and a tie-dye bandana around his neck, off the dance patio. I needed to get back to the Fox by ten to open up, and I hoped I wouldn't run into the sisters once I got there. Maybe they'd be at another fan rave and I could avoid the things-are-looking-really-bleak conversation.

I heard a wolf whistle behind me, followed by, "Hey, hot stuff, wanna lift?" I turned around to find Boone in the Bugmobile pulling to the curb.

"Do you enjoy giving people a good laugh by riding around in this thing?" I asked him.

"And look who's walking a dog with sunglasses and tie-dye."

"You win." I jumped in, BW flopping down in the back seat, Boone staring down at him. "He's snoring? I think he's already asleep."

"He's had a good morning and that makes one of us. Anna and Bella are out as potential murderers. Arnett looks a little more promising, but mostly I'm running out of suspects. How was your morning meeting?"

"I say tonight we get pizza and drown our sorrows with a beer."

"As long as my beer includes root and diet and how about Screamin' MiMi's? The pizza's good and we can walk over to Bonnie Sue's wake. We can see if anyone sticks out. I'm not expecting an X on his or her back and a guilty sign around their neck, but maybe something will catch our attention."

"Dinner and a manhunt, my kind of date." Boone made a left onto Price and a right onto Gwinnett with red and blue strobing lights, everyone within a three-block radius standing in the street and two cruisers at the curb. Boone slowly pulled to a stop in front of Cherry House. "I've got a feeling our bad morning just got a whole lot worse."

Leaving BW in the back to recuperate, Boone and I got out of the Bug just as Annie Fritz and Elsie followed Aldeen and two police officers from the sisters' house.

"We didn't do it," Elsie blubbered, waving frantically at me.

"They got the sisters in handcuffs?" I said to Boone.

"Really? Did the cops think they'd get overpowered by rolling pins and pie plates?

"It's standard procedure." Boone offered.

"Screw procedure."

"We're innocent," Annie Fritz sobbed. "Though hats off to whoever did in Willie; he sure had it coming. Just look at all the trouble he's still causing."

Arleen had on her official detective garb of blue poly suit, white blouse, and cop face. "And you," she said to Boone as she came over. "Don't even think about getting those two out on bail this time around. We know for sure now that the sisters did in Willie and Bonnie Sue. We got 'em dead to rights. I'm not saying the sisters didn't have a good reason for doing what they did, but folks can't just go around offing the scum of this earth who do them wrong, or there'd be bodies piled high as the courthouse over on Bull Street."

"Wait a minute." I held up my hands, trying to get some control over the situation. "You have motive for the sisters killing Willie; that's all." I tried to be rational, reasonable, think clearly and not be hysterical, but hysterical was winning out fast. "You can't arrest the sisters just on motive. Granted, Bonnie Sue was planted in with the lettuce and tomatoes, but the sisters have no motive to kill her, meaning they were framed, pure and simple."

Aldeen folded her arms, looking smug, and that was so not a good thing. Aldeen never bluffed. If she looked smug, she had a reason. "We found Willie, casket and all, over at Bonaventure Cemetery. Some Lou Ella person and her family were looking at burial sites at Bonaventure for their sick auntie, of all things, and . . . and . . ." Aldeen's voice trailed off, her brows knitting together as she stared at me. "It was you with the casket? You . . . you hid it! This is what I get for going out to din . . ." Aldeen's brows furrowed more. "You did that too? You arranged the whole bloomin' thing. That's interfering with police business."

"Actually, that's a date."

"My guess is you already know Willie's untimely demise was an allergic reaction to peanuts, but what you probably don't know is the inhaler in Bonnie Sue's handbag that we found when we dug her out of the garden belonged to Willie and there were pulverized peanuts in the mouthpiece. One swig from it and Willie was a goner."

"Okay, so Bonnie Sue whacked Willie."

"Except Elsie's prints were on Bonnie Sue's handbag."

"She picked it up to toss in the garden plot with Bonnie Sue." I said.

"And Annie Fritz's fingerprints were on Willie's inhaler in Bonnie Sue's purse. We didn't bother to check the contents of the purse that closely until we realized Willie had some help getting dead. The sisters killed Willie because he scammed them, Bonnie Sue knew they did the deed, and the sisters killed her too. They thought burying Bonnie Sue along with the inhaler was the end of it all, and it would have been if it weren't for that dog of yours."

"BW?"

"He may be in line for a Savannah Super Citizen Award. He'll have a plaque down at the riverfront on the hero monument. The news outlets are going to eat this up with a spoon."

I held Boone's hand tight, probably cutting off circulation. "We don't want a spoon. We don't want a plaque. The sisters are our friends and they wouldn't kill anyone. They make red velvet cake, for Pete's sake, and great pies and cookies, and they may be the biggest leaves on the kudzu vine and they may have done a jig when Willie bit the dust, but they weren't the only ones jigging."

"They were the only ones who left their fingerprints behind, buried the body, and had the feather pillow in their car. They have motive, means, opportunity."

"You got this all wrong."

"I doubt it, and thanks for the date and be sure and let me know when we're going shopping for bridesmaid dresses. I think I lost another two pounds."

Sirens wailing, the cruisers headed off down Gwinnett. The crowd started to break up, and I sat down on the curb by the Bug because my legs refused to transport me up the sidewalk to the Fox. "What are we going to do now?" Boone sat down beside me and I choked back a snivel. "Got any great ideas? Even little ones would help."

"For openers, Aldeen's got it wrong about Bonnie Sue. Her death wasn't an afterthought or a reaction to Willie's murder; it was planned right from the beginning. The inhaler winding up in Bonnie Sue's purse was planned. First knock off Willie, then Bonnie Sue, then frame the sisters. Annie Fritz's prints on the purse come from dumping the body in the garden, but the big question is, how did the killer get Elsie's prints on the inhaler?"

"Because . . . because the sisters helped around the Pines. Willie saying 'Can you get me a martini, a glass of water, my inhaler' would be a natural request. The killer takes the inhaler, laces it with peanuts, and sets it on Willie's bedside table. He takes a swig and lights out."

"Here's the tricky part. The killer had to switch the laced inhaler with the fingerprints with the fresh one before the coroner came, meaning the killer had access to Bonnie Sue's things. The killer had to have put the fingerprinted inhaler into Bonnie Sue's purse after he smothered her."

Boone looked me dead in the eyes and we both said, "The killer lives at the Pines."

I jumped up. "And my mother and auntie are there right now, nosing around and asking even more questions that're bound to draw more attention! We got to get them out of there."

Boone pulled me back down. "Trying to tell the judge and your auntie what to do is not going to happen. They want to help, the sisters are their friends too, and your mother and KiKi are stubborn just like another lovable member of the family who shall remain nameless in the interest of pre-marital bliss."

"This time I'm laying done the law." I folded my arms and jutted my chin. "I'm giving Mamma and KiKi one more day, just twenty-four hours to find something at the Pines, and then they're moving back home and I'm not kidding."

"Do you want to inform them of this deadline, or should I?"

After depositing a still-zonked-out BW in the house, Boone headed for the police station to see if he could help the sisters. Bail again would be a long shot at best, but he knew people on the inside, and they could watch out for two little old ladies, especially if that looking-out included promises of cakes and pies.

Morning at the Fox was slammed, with clothes coming in, clothes going out, and Joy Herman's grandson playing hide-and-seek in the blouses and turning over the whole rack. At least all the extra hoopla took my mind off the sisters and their dire straits for a bit.

"You should have called me." Mamma looked at the pile of clothes on the counter and came around to my side and started hanging. "You're swamped here and need help. I'm still staying at the Pines but I can lend you a hand." She gave me a hug. "And I heard the police hauled off Annie Fritz and Elsie. What should we do?"

"And whatever it is, count me in." Arnett whooshed into the Fox, hair dyed to a soft copper, new dress clinging to her liposuctioned figure. "I want to contribute to their defense. I know I gave the proceeds from the sale of my clothes here for their cause, but I want to do more." She dropped a wad of bills on the counter. "This should help."

I stared at the money. "They haven't even been charged yet."

"Of course they'll be charged. They're guilty and who

could blame them. Not me." Arnett added a few more bills to the pile. "My daddy hoodwinked them out of money and that little harlot Bonnie Sue was part of it. The sisters were ticked and knocked them both off. It was all right there in my daddy's checkbook that I came across this morning. Money he made from Spring Chicken investors, the deposits, and the checks he wrote each week to Bonnie Sue 'for services rendered.'"

"*Services?*" Mamma and I exchanged knowing looks and I said, "Bonnie Sue was known at the Pines for her . . . unique skills. Maybe that was the service?"

"Skills schmills," Arnett scoffed. "My daddy was not the sort to pay for pleasure, especially that kind of pleasure. A good bottle of Kentucky bourbon now and then and that was it. Fooling around was not why he was giving Bonnie Sue money, I can promise you. The only reason my daddy paid money was to make more of it, period. My bet is on old Bonnie Sue being part of his sales force; that was the only way to get money out of the old geezer. The night he died I'd been at the Pines earlier to get a loan—just a loan, mind you—for a lip job and an eyelid tuck. He wouldn't cough up a dime; that's the way he's been all my life. I checked into the clinic anyway, and good thing I did. Now I look amazing, thirty again, the doctor even said so. Not only did I wind up getting the money to pay for the procedure; I got Dexter Thomas to boot. Best money I ever spent . . . or more to the point, Daddy ever spent. Life is good for me and I owe it all to Elsie and Annie Fritz."

Arnett took the bills and slapped them into my palm. "If they need another infusion, you just let me know. There's more where this came from."

Mamma and I watched Arnett wiggle her hips out the door. "All this time Bonnie Sue selling shares in Spring Chicken for Willie was the connection between the two of them? Why didn't I see that?"

"We were thinking Bonnie Sue super sexpot, not Bonnie Sue super swindler. Willie sweet-talked the women into parting with their money and Bonnie Sue sweet-talked the men, along with a few other things thrown in to make life interesting. Willie and Bonnie Sue stayed apart, so it didn't seem so much like a con game and more like 'I have this fantastic deal and because I'm your friend I'll let you in on it.' It's really kind of brilliant if you think about it."

"And maybe it *is* the reason why Mr. Jim's hurting for money now. Bonnie Sue could have persuaded him to invest like she did the others. Mr. Jim's a guy; he liked Bonnie Sue. Bonnie Sue liked anyone who could grow facial hair. Losing the money was bad enough, but Mr. Jim's pretty miserable that he can't give his one and only daughter the wedding she wants and that he's struggling to make ends meet on the Pines. So, what if he blamed Willie and Bonnie Sue for his situation? Except what doesn't fit is why he would frame Elsie and Annie Fritz. They're all friends and even business partners."

Mamma hung up a pink Gap T-shirt. "It was the easy way out for him and better than getting caught and going to jail for life or worse." Mamma reached for a yellow raincoat. "We can add Mr. Jim to the suspect list, but Arnett has to go. She was having a lip and eye plump the night her daddy died. KiKi and I are still working on the gym shoe guys and finding out who they are. We asked Emmitt and Foley, but they had no idea what we were talking about. All they can think about is Bonnie Sue and who loved her more. The problem with everyone else is that 'Did you own a gray pair of gym shoes and put them in the trash?' is a tough conversation starter, though it might come to that if we can't think of something else. And we can't look too eager or everyone will know we're up to no good."

I grabbed the hanger out of Mamma's hand. "That's it, you're done. All this nosing around and asking questions is bound to get the killer more suspicious than they are already. Boone and I think he lives at the Pines and we know the gym shoe guys live there. It's getting too dangerous for you and KiKi to be there. You both need to come home now and that's final."

"Oh, Reagan, honey," Mamma chuckled. "You are just too sweet to worry like that." She kissed my cheek. "All I can say is, fat chance."

*   *   *

"Pizza is not exactly diet food," I said to Boone as we crossed Hull Street after parking the Bug. "I should get a salad with oil and vinegar."

Boone reached for my hand. "A few minutes of peace and pizza sounds good to me, and woman does not live by lettuce and tomatoes alone."

"If she's getting married and needs to fit into a wedding dress, she does."

We ducked under the black-and-white awning of Screamin' MiMi's and claimed our preorder of double pepperoni pizzas, two salads, two beers—one root, one not—from Lou at the counter. The eating area at MiMi's was small, with mismatched chairs and jars of Parmesan and crushed red peppers at the tables. The place was way more hole-in-wall than cuisine and big on takeout to anyone who wanted good pizza or just a slice to eat al fresco over in Crawford Square.

Boone led the way past two girls in electric green biker shorts chowing down on calzones to a table by the chalkboard sporting the regular menu and daily specials. He cracked open the box, we took a moment to savor the deliciousness in front of us and I spotted Dexter Thomas at a table in the corner. Some babe with flashy jewelry including a gold bracelet and crystal heart sat with him, sharing a sausage-and-mushroom pizza.

"Yeah, I just saw them too," Boone said, keeping his eyes on the pizza. "And that's the gal Dexter was with over at Abe's on Lincoln. Any idea who she is?"

"None, but I'd say this is woman number three in Dexter's current list of female companionship. But what are they doing here? MiMi's is close to the Slumber, so it's convenient to his work, but it's not exactly the sort of place you'd expect to see Mr. Up-and-Comer plus honey."

"Unless Mr. Up-and-Comer plus honey doesn't want to be seen."

"Dexter?" came a voice from the front by the cash register. "Is that you?" Eugenia asked, all bubbly and coming his way. "What are you doing here?" She giggled. "You don't like Italian food."

"Neither do you. What are you doing here?" Dexter paled.

"Oh, Dex, now that was a tiny little old fib. I love Italian. I just said that to please you and I stopped in here to get a slice before the wake at the Slumber and . . . and . . ." Eugenia slowed. "And who is *this*, Dex?" Eugenia's smile froze and she nodded at the woman.

The flashy woman stood, an equally fake grin in place. "I'm Dexter's . . . sister from out of town."

Eugenia glared at Dexter. "You don't have a sister, only a brother; you told me so yourself. And you two were holding hands and not in a sister–brother sort of way, and is that lipstick on your face?"

"Pizza sauce."

"It is not pizza sauce! And I know you, Dexter Thomas, you would never bring family to a place like this to sit at these unseemly tables and eat, and ohmygod she's wearing my bracelet! She's wearing the bracelet you gave *me*," Eugenia screeched, holding up her own bracelet.

Eugenia pointed a stiff finger at the woman. "Who are you and what are you doing here with my boyfriend who's supposed to be at a Rotary Club dinner getting an award? Dexter, what is going on? I demand to know right this minute, you hear me?"

Chapter Nineteen

Everyone at MiMi's sat perfectly still except for iPhones snapping pics, videos, and Instagramming. Dexter slowly got to his feet. It was drama Savannah-style. The only thing missing was the popcorn.

"Now Eugenia, sugar."

"Don't you *Eugenia, sugar* me. Who is this woman, Dexter Thomas?"

"She's . . . well . . . a friend."

"Oh, for crying out loud, Dexter, man up," the woman said. "It's over. Even this stupid girl can figure out the truth by now."

"Stupid?"

The woman faced Eugenia. "I'm his wife." She held up her left hand, the wedding ring catching the light. "And the only reason Dexter is with you or at least pretending to be is that he wanted to buy Sleepy Pines cheap and needed you to get your daddy to sell it off for the price he wanted." She turned to Dexter. "And you bought us all the same jewelry? Dex, sometimes you are such a schmuck."

"You don't love me? You used me!" Eugenia growled.

"Just like he used that biddy, Arnett," Wife went on. "What a joke you both are, not that it matters. We don't want the Pines now, and we don't need Arnett's money." Wife tossed her auburn hair and hooked her arm through Dexter's. "We've decided to go into a partnership with Elder Planning and build a retirement village complete with all the amenities. We're selling Eternal Slumber to a big conglomerate and making a killing."

"I'll show you how to make a killing!" Eugenia picked up the half-eaten calzone from the biker's plate and flung it. Dexter ducked but Wife didn't, the glob hitting her square in the nose, cheese and sauce sliding off her chin.

"How dare you!"

"Oh, I dare, all right," Eugenia bellowed and sailed a meatball, catching Dex in the eye.

Wife snapped a slice of sausage-and-mushroom from her own plate, flinging it at Eugenia. The triangle did a complete flip midair and landed across her chest, sticking like glue.

"This is a new dress!"

"Well, now it's not, is it," the wife huffed. "And you need to cool off." She threw her glass at Eugenia, Coke flying everywhere as Eugenia fired off a breadstick dunked in pizza sauce.

"That's enough!" Lou barreled out from behind the counter, grabbing Eugenia, and Dexter snagged his wife before she unloaded a really yummy-looking Italian salad with black olives and anchovies.

Boone picked a piece of pepperoni from the pizza and popped it into his mouth. "I wonder what Lou has in store for the second act."

By the time we'd finished our pizza and fought our way through the crowd trying to get into MiMi's—thank you social media—it was nearly seven when we got to the Slumber.

"This place is packed too." Boone looked at the line snaking across the lit porch and onto the sidewalk. "Didn't anyone stay home?"

I counted on my fingers. "A murder victim's wake, a gigolo unmasked who happens to own this place, and the great pizza war? How could anything top that? Trust me, no one's staying in tonight."

"Did you hear what happened with Eugenia?" Auntie KiKi whispered as she and Mamma hurried up to Boone and me. Line cutting was a big no-no except in times of needing to use the bathroom right quick and urgent gossip that simply could not wait another minute.

"We were there." I nodded to Boone. "I wish I knew where Eugenia was now, and Arnett. They have to be devastated."

"If either of them has an ounce of Southern pride, they're spitting mad." Auntie KiKi added, "And if I know Eugenia, she's getting out her daddy's shotgun right this minute, polishing it up, and aiming for Dexter Thomas. I bet that's one man who won't dare show his face around here for a while."

The four of us signed the big blue guest book and headed for the Greener Pastures room. Emmitt and Foley stood on one side of the casket with a potted fern between them, and Mr. Jim greeted mourners on the other side. Not that there were many doing the meet-and-greet thing; most seemed interested in the latest talk about the great pizza smackdown, the sisters in jail, and Dexter Thomas playing Eugenia and Arnett and nearly getting away with it.

"You know Mr. Jim better than me, so I'll hold down the tea table and catch the talk there." Boone nodded in that direction. "Let me know what you find out on your end."

"I'm coming with you." Auntie KiKi said to Boone. She patted her big black funeral purse. "Getting through these things requires notable fortification, and I mean more than hymns and a few candles. I brought along some much-needed liquid refreshment. Tallyho."

"I think she's already refreshed," Boone whispered to me, then followed KiKi.

Mamma and I headed for Mr. Jim. "It's nice of you to do this," I said to him as Mamma took a small detour to chat with Mrs. Jones-Brown beside the casket. No doubt she was checking out more details for the philandering Mr. Jones-Brown. "Was the fern your idea?" I nodded to Emmitt and Foley.

"I'm thinking a brick wall to separate them would be better. Bonnie Sue didn't have family and the last place she lived was the Pines, so it's kind of my duty to see her off. Maybe there will be some peace and quiet at the Pines now."

"Now that she and Willie aren't peddling Spring Chicken vitamins and scamming everyone . . . like you maybe?"

"Me?" Mr. Jim's face reddened, his hands clenching. "The scam gave the Pines a really bad name, pretty much ruined my credit. The place is full of residents now, but what about later on? Who wants to stay where they're scamming old people?" He leaned close. "I'm mighty glad Bonnie Sue and Willie aren't around any longer, I can tell you that. They got what they had coming."

"What about Elsie and Annie Fritz? Easy patsies?"

Mr. Jim's face reddened. "Why are you asking all these questions? I have other people to talk to." Mr. Jim hurried away and I joined Mamma at the casket. Mrs. Jones-Brown was now checking out floral arrangements.

"What did Mr. Jim have to say? He looked pretty intense about something." Mamma asked.

"He has no love lost for Willie or Bonnie Sue. He thinks they ruined his business, and he might be right." I nodded at Bonnie Sue. "She sure looks peaceful enough for all the trouble she's caused."

"She looks plumb worn out, if you ask me."

Two more mourners walked toward the casket to pay their respects. Mamma started to leave, but I held her in place and whispered, "There's something next to Bonnie Sue."

"It's probably a man, honey; they just can't leave the woman alone."

Acting as if I were itching my nose, I pointed to the white satin pillow and the corner of a gold paper sticking out. "Right there. I need a distraction so I can get it. Maybe the killer left it?"

"Maybe it's a check for those services rendered we talked about before. And," Mamma added, "you can't go rooting around a dead person."

"Tell your sister that, but right now can you ask Foley when he's going to give his 'Ode to a Southern Wench' and tell him that you can't wait to hear it because you know it's going to be great."

"Emmitt's doing the ode."

"Exactly."

Muttering about me soon being Walker's problem and not hers and alleluia for that, Mamma walked over to Foley. She took Foley's hand and asked about the ode. Foley's eyes squinted, his face red. He stepped around the fern, yelling at Emmitt and waving his cane.

"You put her up to this, didn't you? You think my harmonica tribute to Bonnie Sue's not as good as your stupid ode. Well, let me tell you, if a harmonica's good enough for Springsteen, it's good enough for me and better than some stupid poem." Foley pulled a harmonica out of his suit pocket and started on "The River."

"Put that away, you old fool; you're ridiculous," Emmitt bellowed. "I'm going to deliver my ode now before you embarrass the love of my life even more than you already have, if that's possible."

Foley shoved Emmitt. He fell back, knocking over the fern, losing his balance, and Foley used his cane to snag the walker, keeping Emmitt upright. "You're ruining the entire wake. You're an embarrassment."

"You're the embarrassment."

Emmitt waved his walker over his head; Foley shook his cane. Everyone was staring at Emmitt and Foley and I snagged the paper from under the pillow. The funeral director grabbed Emmitt's walker and Mr. Jim grabbed Foley, saying, "You're both going to sit down and have some tea and behave. You're worse than two-year-olds."

"He's the two-year-old," Emmitt pointed at Foley.

"You are," Foley added.

I sallied up beside Mamma and said, "Got it." We inched our way to the side of the room and away from the mass confusion. I unfolded the paper.

"It's a chicken with a big black X through it?"

"It's a Spring Chicken stock certificate and someone's pissed." I got closer to Mamma and kept my voice low. "Mr. Jim was standing by the casket all evening. He could have easily slipped it in. I think leaving this certificate was telling Bonnie Sue just how he felt. Elsie's fingerprints were on the inhaler that killed Willie, and it was found in Bonnie Sue's purse. It would be so easy for Mr. Jim to do that and frame the sisters. Willie and Bonnie Sue ruined everything he's worked hard for; he's losing his family home and he can't pay for his daughter's wedding. He's had enough and knocked off Willie and Bonnie Sue, but we need more than speculation. Mr. Jim is here now and I'm going back to the Pines to look around and see if I can find anything that ties him to the murders, like stock certificates that made him lose even more money."

Boone joined the huddle, looking at the paper. "Chickens?"

"Spring Chicken stock certificate. It was in the casket. I think the killer was sending Bonnie Sue a message and Mr. Jim was right next to the casket all night. Willie and Bonnie Sue not only scammed Mr. Jim's customers, but he could have gotten scammed too. That's double motive. Even Aldeen would have to see that and how easy it would be for him to mess with the inhalers and frame the sisters. This is our one shot to look around the Pines with everyone from the Pines here for the wake."

"I'll come with you," Boone said.

Mamma shook her head. "We can't all leave; it'll be too obvious, especially with Reagan asking Mr. Jim some pointed questions. He'll know something's up." Mamma turned to Boone. "You watch things on this end. If Mr. Jim leaves or anything else we need to know about comes up, call and we can get out of the Pines."

"And leave KiKi out of it because . . . because she's too banged up already," I said to Boone and exchanged glances with Mamma.

Boone heaved a sigh. "I don't like you two going off on your own like this. If you get caught," he said to Mamma, "it could ruin your career."

"And if you get caught it'll ruin your career," Mamma shot back.

I kissed Boone. "You are now officially one of the Summerside girls plus dog. And just so you know, love and a lot of worry come with the territory."

Boone headed for the tea table and KiKi to tell her she'd been left behind. That was bound to go over really big, but the thing was I needed to do this more often. I still had no idea what was going on with Uncle Putter, but it definitely involved KiKi, and keeping her on the straight and narrow wouldn't hurt.

Mamma and I faded out the side door and aimed for the car. She took driver side, I slid into the passenger side, then we headed down Broad. "Park on the street next to the big fir tree," I said to Mamma when she got to Tattnall. "That way we just look like another car, we're kind of hidden, and if Mr. Jim does show up we can make a fast getaway."

Mamma pulled to the curb and killed the engine. We took the deserted sidewalk, then faded into shadows and cut through the back parking lot, avoiding the more direct route of the squeaky wrought iron gate. Using Mamma's iPhone flashlight, we made our way around bushes and flower gardens to Auntie KiKi's room and the French doors leading out onto her little patio. Since we didn't have KiKi's door key, I held the flashlight and Mamma wedged her American Express card between the doors where no American Express card had a right to be. "I thought I'd be better at this." Mamma finagled the card back and forth.

"You're a judge, not a thief; there's a learning curve."

The doors gave way and Mamma grinned and pushed one open. We crept through KiKi's room and opened the door to the hall, the small lamp in the living room casting the only light our way.

"You know what the Spring Chicken stock certificates look like," I said to Mamma. "Look for that and anything else suspicious in Mr. Jim's office and living quarters that ties him to Willie or Bonnie Sue. I'm going to look around for those dueling pistols that have gone missing."

"Don't you think Emmitt and Foley are just kidding about this dueling thing? It's more like two old men sounding off to feel young again and defend their lady? They may be enemies and do a lot of blustering and name calling, but a duel?"

"Tonight they got into a shoving match, nearly knocking each other over. Who knows how far they'll go, and the guns are missing. Love does crazy things to people—like make them buy a big fluffy dress and give it a name. I think Emmitt and Foley are still obsessed with Bonnie Sue. She must have been one heck of a lady."

"I don't think lady's the right word, honey."

I pulled Old Yeller onto my shoulder. "Call me if you need something."

Mamma shined her flashlight down the hall toward Mr. Jim's office. I pulled out my old-fashioned flashlight and took the back hall to Emmitt's room at the end. Since American Express and I were not acquainted, I used my library card to jimmy the lock. Mamma did it better. The room was larger than Auntie KiKi's but with the usual bedroom furnishings.

I opened the top drawer on the desk, the next drawer, then the bottom one and pulled out a stack of Spring Chicken stock certificates. Obviously the love of his life, Bonnie Sue, meant way more to Emmitt than the scam, since he was still going on and on about her. A picture of two little girls, probably grandkids, sat on top of the desk next to an assortment of Revolutionary War books. There was a picture of men in Revolutionary War garb on the wall and another of Emmitt by himself looking proud and distinguished in his blue uniform. He even had a mustache and sideburns. A silver cup with a blue ribbon sat on the nightstand, inscribed "Emmitt Gilroy, Siege of Savannah, Revolutionary War enactment." Four others read "Performing Excellence, Emmitt Gilroy."

I didn't find the pistols under the bed or in the nightstand or under his pillow. I opened the closet to find pants, shirts, new gym shoes, a blue wool colonial uniform, and boots on the floor. A sword lay propped against the back wall, a musket beside it. I pushed the clothes to the side, the musket sliding to the floor. I picked it up, the gun smelling of oil and gunpowder, then put it back.

Enactment was a big part of Emmitt's life and, from the looks of things, he was good at it. He was a good . . . actor. Really good. Too good? And he and Foley were in the reenactments together.

"Reagan," Mamma huffed, running into the room and over to the closet, a flashlight in her hand. "My phone died. That flashlight app thing just eats the battery, so I got this light out of Mr. Jim's desk and I wanted to make sure your phone was working in case—"

"What are you doing in here?" came Emmitt's voice from behind us. Mamma and I turned around to see Emmitt, but instead of holding a walker, he reached into his dresser drawer and pulled out a dueling pistol and aimed it right at Mamma.

I stepped in front of Mamma.

"Reagan! For God's sake, don't move!" Mamma screeched. "He has a gun. Old guns can still kill people and I don't want it to be you."

"Except . . . except guns have to be loaded first," I said to Mamma standing behind me and Emmitt in the doorway. "And my guess is the one Mr. Emmitt is holding isn't loaded at all."

"You guess!" Mamma shrieked. "Guess!"

"Powder maybe, no ammunition. Emmitt and Foley are not enemies; they're friends. The best of friends."

"Honey, Reagan, did you dip into your auntie's fortification? All those two do is argue. Just do what the man says."

"They're pretending to be enemies," I said, trying to put the pieces together. "So no one would suspect they were in cahoots to knock off Willie and Bonnie Sue. Those two swindled Emmitt and Foley with the vitamin scam. One of them left the Spring Chicken certificate in Bonnie Sue's casket; they were there the whole night too. And Emmitt and Foley know about guns, old ones from doing the reenactments, and they would never point loaded guns at each other and they'd never let a friend fall over if he tripped, like at the wake tonight."

"I was afraid you'd catch that," Emmitt said in a shaky voice. "You catch a lot of things; you kind of got a reputation. With KiKi asking so many questions when she got here, we knew you'd figure out what we were up to sooner or later, and when she ordered that snazzy iPhone case that matched the luggage we saw, we were afraid she knew what we did, or at least what we planned to do. We're leaving tonight; it's a good time with everyone at the wake. Load our stuff into this old car we got and—"

"Emmitt," Foley called down the hall. "Hurry it up, will you? We have to . . ." Foley came up behind Emmitt and looked from Mamma to me. "Sweet mother, why did you have to be here? Look, just let us go, okay? What's the harm? We've lost all our money and we can't afford to stay here anyway."

"The harm!" I stammered. "You killed two people! You framed Elsie and Annie Fritz."

Foley stood beside Emmitt. "That's just it; we didn't kill anyone. We wanted to, even had a plan—not near as good as the one that worked, I can tell you that. Somebody beat us to knocking those two off, somebody really smart."

"If you're so innocent, why are you running away?" I asked.

"Because everything looks like we're not innocent because we're supposed to be not innocent. Does that make any sense? We even toasted ourselves with Mr. Jim's best bourbon when Willie and Bonnie Sue got killed because we did everything but pull the trigger, so to speak."

"This is the police!" Aldeen's voice boomed down the hall. "Put your hands above your heads so I can see them and turn around slow."

"We didn't do it, I swear," Foley said to me very matter-of-factly. "We really didn't, I swear." He dropped the pistol and he and Foley faced the police.

"Reagan!" Boone bellowed, pushing past the cops. "I called you and called you when Foley and Emmitt left the wake and then I called your mother, then the police. With Emmitt and Foley both gone, I got a bad feeling." Boone snagged Old Yeller off my arm, pulled out the flip, and pried it open. He closed his eyes, leaned against the wall, and draped his arm around me. "Sweet thing, the phone only works if you keep it charged."

Chapter Twenty

"Just look at this," Arnett wailed, slapping a letter down on the counter as soon as I opened the door to the Fox the next morning. "This just came in the mail. Some old farts, Clive and Crenshaw something-or-other, are threatening me with a class action suit over that Spring Chicken vitamin thing. They're representing the investors, and since I inherited Willie's estate, they want my money."

I picked up the paper. "I thought the vitamin thing wasn't against the law."

"It wasn't, but there are some gray areas. If I fight it, the bloodsucking lawyers will get everything and it will be tied up in court forever."

"So you're here to get a job?"

"I'm here to see if any of my clothes sold so I can get some cash and buy a cup of coffee. My accounts are frozen, my credit cards don't work, I have no money even for Starbucks."

Boone came down the steps behind me smelling like musky lime and all things wonderfully male. He picked up the paper, gave it a quick read, then handed it back to Arnett. "Settle."

"Excuse me," Arnett gasped. "Mind your own business, you have no idea what this is all about."

Boone look pained. "Oh, trust me, I know more about Spring Chicken than I ever wanted to. Settle out of court. The money's not really yours, but if you get a good negotiator you'll probably get to keep some of it; the investors don't want their money tied up in court forever either. They're old; time is of the essence. They'll agree to so much on the dollar and you can all get back to your lives."

Arnett glared at Boone. "Who are you?"

"An innocent bystander." Boone kissed me on the cheek. "I've got a meeting with Mr. Jim. I'll catch up with you later."

"I charged my phone last night," I yelled after Boone as he headed out the door.

"Thank you, kindly," he yelled back.

"Wow, now that's a guy." Arnett parked her hand on her hip and salivated.

"And how are you getting along without . . . are you doing okay?"

"Dexter was a flash in the pan. I knew what I was getting into. This isn't my first stroll around the block, honey. I had a good time, he had an agenda; I won, he lost. I feel sorry for that Eugenia girl. She wanted to marry the jerk, poor little thing. Besides, last night I was at the Olde Pink House and got a bit tipsy, didn't want to drive home, and called Boomers."

"Let me guess, Anthony?"

"He sang Rigoletto all the way home. I think I'm in love."

I gave Arnett the money she'd forked over for the sisters' defense since they were home free . . . literally, after getting released from jail. I was expecting a red velvet cake on my doorstep anytime now.

Arnett headed out the door, and with no break at all, KiKi stormed in. I had been expecting her on my doorstep anytime as well.

"I shouldn't be talking to you," she huffed while storming around the hallway. "I'm still ticked about last night. How could you leave me out of the action like you did? You and Gloria just pranced off into the night and all the fun, and you left me with the windmill cookies and Mrs. Jones-Brown rattling on about her rotten husband. I wonder if he has any idea what she's up to?"

"Boone was with you." I started pricing clothes that had come in yesterday and getting them ready to put out on the sale racks.

"He ran off like a shot when he couldn't get you on the phone and Emmitt and Foley were nowhere to be found. I think he loves you."

I stopped hanging for a minute and blushed like a schoolgirl. "I think he does too."

"Since we got the Willie/Bonnie Sue mess straightened out, your mamma helped me move out of the Pines this morning and I want to get the house in order before Putter comes home tonight from golfing. The thing is, I forgot my favorite robe; it's hanging on the back of the closet door. Bernard Thayer is headed this way for a dance lesson because someone standing in this very room canceled his lesson yesterday. Let's make a deal, if you get my robe, I'll give the lesson and we'll call it even."

"I'll close the Fox for lunch and get it." I stopped pricing and put down my pen. "I was thinking you . . . *we* should try and tone things down a bit. No more caskets in the Beemer, no more midnight runs to Bonaventure. Let Savannah take care of itself for a while."

"Walker's making a fuss?"

"Walker puts up with a lot, and maybe Uncle Putter is tired of putting up with a lot. He's been doing it for while now, you know."

KiKi grabbed my hand, her face serious. "Something's going on with Putter. You're flipping your hair and your eye's twitching."

"I know nothing." At least that part was true. "I'm just saying let's concentrate on the wedding. Weddings are safe. We have cake and flowers and dancing and we'll wear pretty dresses. I have mine; we need to get yours."

"You're not leveling with me and I'm finding out why."

"All's level, like Kansas-prairie level. I'm just trying to enjoy the wedding plans." I made a cross over my heart. "Promise."

At noon I taped an "Out to lunch, be back at 1" sign on the door. I never closed for lunch, but this time I felt like I owed Auntie KiKi. I had canceled on Bernard and she'd been left out of the Emmitt/Foley take down last night.

The Bernard part was for my good, the left-out part for her good.

I hitched up BW and headed for the Pines. "Its ten-thousand-steps time," I singsonged to my walking companion. He didn't look overjoyed.

It felt good to have the sisters back in their house on one side and Auntie KiKi back home on the other side. The Willie/Bonnie Sue mess was another matter. They hadn't deserved to die for swindling people, but I understood where Emmitt and Foley were coming from. They'd lost their money and their home. But instead of saying they were glad they'd done what they did, they'd insisted they were innocent. Why not take credit for what they did?"

I opened the squeaky gate to the Pines, and BW and I cut around the fountain and across the deserted patio. I opened one of the patio doors, a bad smell washing over me. I kept the door open and stepped inside to quiet. Usually there was a TV blaring, the clanking of dishes, people talking, Mr. Jim hurrying around. "Hello." I called out. "My aunt moved back home and she forgot her robe, and what is that smell?"

"Bug spray. They're spraying for . . . bugs. Get the robe and then you getter leave."

"I'm sorry about Dexter."

"Not as sorry as he's going to be." She laughed, kind of a creepy laugh. "Just go, will you?"

"Eugenia, that smell isn't insecticide, it's . . . gasoline? Your shoes are covered in it."

"No, they're not."

I pushed my way past Eugenia, BW following me into the kitchen, to see Dexter Thomas, dazed, his forehead bloody, gagged and tied to a chair. He was soaking wet with . . . gasoline? There were puddles of it all around the kitchen.

I stopped dead, terror shooting up my spine. "Eugenia, this is a really bad idea."

I turned around to a dueling pistol aimed at my chest. "Why didn't you just leave?" Eugenia yelled. "I told you to go. You had your chance and now it's too late. And before you get any wise ideas to leave now, this gun is loaded, not like Emmitt's last night. My daddy used to fire this thing every New Year's Eve—tradition, he said. I paid attention. Sit over there."

"Why burn down the Pines? I don't get it."

She waved the pistol. "Insurance money." She glared at Dexter. "And because some people got it coming, even you. You got Walker Boone and I got nothing. No wedding, no dress, no Sugar Bell. You get it all. I hate you!"

"I get that you hate me but . . . but let my dog go. He's never hurt anyone; he doesn't even bark at people. Don't take this out on BW. Besides, if he gets away, it'll look like I just got trapped in the flames. Please." I bent down, snuggled next to BW, and slid off my ring. Petting him, I twisted the dental floss I had around the back of the ring into BW's collar, holding the ring in place. At least I hoped it would.

"All right, fine. Just get him out of here before I change my mind."

I stood. I looked BW in the eyes, trying to be stern. BW

275

and I didn't do stern; we did "How about we split this cookie and watch Gilmore Girls?" I pointed out the kitchen door and yelled, "Go."

BW looked at me, confused and hurt.

"Get out!"

He didn't budge. I picked an apple off the counter and threw it at BW, hitting him in the side. He yelped, breaking my heart, then took off. I bit back a sob thinking that the last time I would see BW I was mean to him. This sucked but the only thing I could do right now was play for time.

"Where is everyone?" I asked as I sat down to keep Eugenia calm. "You got them locked up in the basement?"

"Your fiancé's got them all up at the bank—sent a bus for them and everything. He wants to turn Sleepy Pines into a co-op where the residents buy into the house. Then the place would have money for repairs and everything that needs to be done around this dump."

Keeping the pistol aimed at me, Eugenia picked a pink plastic lighter off the table where Auntie KiKi had had brownies and me an apple the night of the storm. Eugenia flicked the lighter, the orange light dancing in her hands, Dexter white as the cabinets behind him. "It sure is gonna be one big old repair job," Eugenia giggled, "once I get done with the place."

"Your dad's okay with the co-op idea?"

"Better than having to sell it like a lot of big old homes in Savannah do. These places are money pits, nothing but big outdated money-sucking money pits for years and years and years. Daddy could still be manager with the co-op and live here, and that's what he wants, but I don't. I have to burn this place down before it goes co-op. The money's mine, I'm done being poor, this way I get the insurance money and I get rid of Dex all at one time. It's one of those win-win situations."

Eugenia sat on the edge of the table facing Dex and me, the window behind her. She swung her legs back and forth, flicking the lighter, pistol still pointing my way. "Why couldn't Daddy just sell to Dex like I wanted him to?" she said to herself more than to me. "Dex would have left his wife and married me. Wouldn't you?" She glared at Dex and he nodded in agreement. "I had the dress picked out, a date at Sugar Bell; I even picked out the flowers, pink hydrangeas and white gardenias. Doesn't that sound lovely?"

Eugenia looked at me. "Guess how I got old Dex here today? I texted him that Elder Planning was making the Pines part of their investments and Daddy wanted to show him around the place to see how much it was worth. He fell for it. Dexter Thomas will do anything that makes money for Dexter Thomas. He's just like Willie and Bonnie Sue and going to wind up just like they did."

"Willie and Bonnie Sue?"

"They deserved it, with their scam. I planned those two murders down to the finest detail. They deserved what they got for scamming everyone out of money, including my dad. We were just making ends meet and then Daddy invested, trying to make a quick buck, and things got worse. You gotta love the ground peanuts in the inhaler. I never dreamed those sisters would bury Bonnie Sue's body. I thought the police would find the inhaler, then Bonnie Sue in their Caddy, and just charge Elsie and Annie Fritz. It was so easy to get Bonnie Sue in the car. I told her the sisters wanted to buy more shares in Spring Chicken. She showed up and I smothered her. I wanted the scandal to ruin the Pines, make Daddy sell the place; then I would get Dexter. So easy. But did any of my ideas work out? Nothing worked out like it was supposed to, but now it will. This is another good idea. This idea is foolproof."

Something moved in the window behind Eugenia. *Oh please, God, let it be Boone and not the cops.* The cops had a habit of storming into places and yelling, like they had last night, and in that case it was fine. Today, Eugenia was upset enough to drop the blasted lighter and set the whole place on fire and herself right along with it. The trick was to get to Eugenia before she dropped the lighter, and then there was the little problem of the pistol. The pistol had only one shot to worry about. Just one.

"Eugenia," I said, trying for distraction and maybe a little trust. "The best revenge is living well. Just let Dexter go and get on with your life." I stood up very slowly.

"Easy for you to say. You have a life; you have a guy."

"I didn't always have the guy."

Eugenia did a little shrug, then added a demented smile. "But after I get the insurance money, I'll be living pretty good too."

She flicked the lighter again. "It's showtime. I was waiting till the schools let out, and today happens to be an early dismissal. I volunteer at the school libraries, so I know about these things. The fire department will have a much harder time getting here with school traffic clogging the roads. The fire can really catch hold and we've had issues with the plumbing around here, so the sprinkler system isn't working all what well, especially with a little help from yours truly."

I heard tapping in the hallway, nails against hardwood. I'd heard it a million times before and it always made me feel happy. Today was no different. I turned to the door, BW suddenly standing there wagging his tail.

"Hot dog," I yelled. BW barked twice, the sound echoing in the big tiled kitchen, making Eugenia jump. She fired the pistol into the air as I lunged for the lighter. Boone raced into the kitchen and grabbed Eugenia. The lighter slid from my fingers, Eugenia slipped out of Boone's grip, I got Eugenia and Boone got the lighter, his string of swear words filling the room as the lit end landed in his palm.

"Police!" Aldeen yelled from the doorway, two uniforms behind her rushing for Eugenia. Boone handed Aldeen the lighter. "Are you okay?" she asked.

"Better than him." Boone nodded at Dexter.

I headed to the fridge to get ice for Boone's hand and he pulled me toward him, BW trotting over. "I now have new respect for dog tricks."

"I had to throw an apple at our dog to get him out of here."

"He's a hero." Boone held up the ring. "Earlene saw a very sad BW with leash trotting across Barnard. She got him on the bus with a treat, found the ring and called Big Joey, who called me. The three of us figured that was SOS Reagan-style and that meant the Pines."

"That's pretty fast work, mister."

"Hey, in case you didn't notice I'm a fast operator." Boone kissed me hard. "And you should know, sweet stuff, that this is just the beginning."

Auntie KiKi's Very Best Martinis

Hi, Everyone,

Reagan and I and Bruce Willis spend a lot of time together talking about the latest murder here in Savannah and who in the world could have done such a thing. Usually Reagan and I are sitting on the front porch of Cherry House, and more often than not, thanks to yours truly, martinis are involved. Many of you have wanted to know just want kind of martinis I have in that silver shaker I bring along, so here I am to share my favorite recipes. Some have vodka, some no alcohol, but all are mighty tasty. Next time I'll share my gin martini treasures.

Love from Savannah,
Auntie KiKi

Both Worlds Martini

Chocolate martini for when you need both chocolate and a martini

1½ ounces chocolate liqueur
1½ ounces crème de cacao
½ ounce vanilla vodka
2½ ounces half-and-half
chocolate syrup, for rim
ice

Mix all ingredients in a cocktail shaker filled with ice and shake. Pour into a chilled cocktail glass rimmed with chocolate syrup. Add cherry skewered on toothpick. Does that sound delicious or what?

Espresso Martini

Just what you need to wake up those brain cells

2 parts vodka
1 part Galliano Ristretto
½ part fresh coffee
gomme syrup (optional)
ice

Shake all ingredients in a shaker with ice and double strain into a chilled martini glass.

Lemon Drop Martini

When you need a little zing in your life

2 ounces vodka
½ ounce triple sec
½ ounce lemon juice
ice

In a shaker with ice, add vodka, triple sec, and lemon juice. Shake well. Strain into chilled martini glass rimmed with sugar.

Apple Martini

May not keep the doctor away, but it sure tastes good

2 ounces Smirnoff Green Apple
½ ounce apple schnapps
splash sour mix
slice green apple
ice

Add Smirnoff Green Apple, sour mix, and apple schnapps. Shake with ice and strain into chilled martini glass. Garnish with the apple slice.

Beach Bum Martini

Perfect for lazy summer days

2 ounces vodka
juice of ½ lemon
2 teaspoons Baker's (extra-fine) sugar for rimming glass
lemon slice
ice

Mix vodka and lemon juice; pour over ice. Shake well. Pour into a glass and stick a lemon slice on the rim.

Hot Southern Nights Martini

To share with that certain hot person in your life

2 ounces mandarin vodka
2 tablespoons orange juice
8 feathers fresh rosemary
orange slice
ice

Muddle rosemary; add to vodka and orange juice. Pour over ice. Shake, strain, and pour into a martini glass with an orange slice on the rim.

Sweaters and Scarves Martini

For getting rid of the chill in your bones

2 ounces Grey Goose vodka
1 pinch fresh ginger
1 fresh green apple
1 tablespoon lime juice
dash ginger ale
ice

Muddle ginger and two apple slices. Add to vodka and lime juice. Pour over ice, shake, strain, and pour into a glass. Top with ginger ale and add an apple slice to the rim.

Summer on the Veranda
Watermelon Martini

For summer sippin'

sugar
kosher salt
6 ounces watermelon juice (mash or use food processor
    and strain)
2½ ounces vodka **or** S.Pellegrino sparkling water
2½ ounces limoncello **or** orange liqueur **or** orange juice
1 ounce fresh lime juice
ice
watermelon wedges for garnish

Chill glass in freezer. Combine sugar and salt; dip damp-
ened glass rim in sugar/salt mixture. Fill cocktail shaker with
the watermelon juice, vodka or sparkling water, liqueur,
and lime juice. Fill shaker with ice and shake six to eight
times. Strain and pour into the glasses and garnish each
with a watermelon wedge.

Savannah Martini

When you visit Savannah, have one of these at Jen's and Friends and think of your Auntie KiKi. ☺

1 tablespoon finely grated orange chocolate
1 teaspoon sugar
2 orange slices
½ cup premium chocolate ice cream, at room temperature
    for 5 minutes
1 ounce orange vodka **or** fresh-squeezed orange juice
ice

Gently stir together the chocolate and sugar and put it on a plate. Run an orange slice around the rim of a chilled martini glass and dip the rim in the chocolate/sugar mixture to coat. Add the ice cream and vodka to a cocktail shaker with ice and shake well. Strain into the prepared glass and garnish with the remaining orange slice.

Pussy Foot Martini

No alcohol and so yummy

1 ounce orange juice
1 ounce lemon juice
1 ounce lime juice
2 tablespoons grenadine syrup
1 teaspoon sugar syrup
1 egg yolk
cold sparkling water (optional) or a shot of vodka
orange slice
ice

Pour all the juices and syrups into a cocktail shaker with ice and add the yolk. Shake well, then strain into a large tumbler half filled with ice cubes. Top off with fizzy water if preferred. Garnish with an orange slice.

The Prissy Fox Martini

No alcohol so you can keep a clear head for shopping

juice of a ripe pink grapefruit
juice of half a lemon
2 ounces sugar syrup (made with equal parts sugar and
    water, heated until sugar is dissolved, then cooled)
cold sparkling or soda water
2 mint sprigs
crushed ice

Pour sugar syrup into a tumbler, then add one mint sprig,
stirring and bruising it lightly. Add citrus juices and stir.
Top off with crushed ice and the sparkling or soda water.
Garnish with the second mint sprig.

Non-Alcoholic Cherry House Party Martini

A party fave and no one gets zonked

2 ounces pineapple juice
1 ounce freshly squeezed lime juice
2 tablespoons grenadine syrup
cold ginger ale to top off
lime slice
loads of ice cubes

Shake the juices and grenadine in a cocktail shaker over ice and strain into an ice-filled glass. Top off with ginger ale, the right amount to your taste; stir and garnish with lime slice.

Christmas in Savannah Martini

Perfect with those Christmas Carols
Vodka added or no thanks

3 ounces cranberry juice
3 ounces red grape juice
half a star anise
half a cinnamon stick, plus one to serve
2 cloves
slice of peeled fresh ginger root
1 teaspoon brown sugar
1 ounce vodka (optional)

Simply put all the ingredients except the extra cinnamon stick in a pan and warm up very gently, stirring, and keep hot (not boiling) for several minutes until the spices infuse. Strain into a thick glass tumbler or mug and serve with the cinnamon stick for stirring to release the steam. Drink while hot. Add vodka if you like.